WE LIVED IN DRUMFYVIE

Margaret Lyford-Pike and Rosemary Sutcliff combine their talents to recreate seven hundred years in the life of an imaginary Scottish burgh. The folk of Drumfyvie tell their own stories—of castle and alehouse, of battlefield and workshop, of merchants waxing rich and beggers clapped in the stocks, of witch-hunts and Covenanters, of death at Flodden Field and devastation by the Plague.

The great folk in the high castle play out their power struggles and private tragedies. The traders carry Drumfyvie's wares to the world outside, and bring back wines, spices, new fashions and ideas. And the common people go on as they always have, working their trades and fighting the wars, like Jamie, the herd-boy who saved Drumfyvie from the English, or Old Nannie, who knew more about herbs and healing than was good for her, or Daft Geordie Breck, hero of the day at Queen Victoria's jubilee.

Drumfyvie history is Scottish history seen in microcosm through the day-to-day lives of ordinary people, shaped and transformed by the great events outside.

Margaret Lyford-Pike
and Rosemary Sutcliff

WE LIVED IN
DRUMFYVIE

Blackie: Glasgow and London

ISBN 0 216 89972 9

Blackie and Son Limited
Bishopsbriggs, Glasgow G64 2NZ
5 Fitzhardinge Street, London W1H 0DL

Printed in Great Britain by The Anchor Press Ltd,
and bound by Wm Brendon & Son Ltd,
both of Tiptree, Essex

CONTENTS

Foreword

It is I that will tell you a tale, and a grim one. I, Robert Armstrong, one-time steward to Duncan the Red, him that was first Sheriff of Drumfyvie.

But first, there are things that you should know, for the better understanding of the time and the place.

So then : In the year of Our Lord eleven hundred and twenty-four, David I came to the throne of Scotland, him that was youngest son to King Malcolm Canmore and Queen Margaret of blessed memory. Scotland had been torn by the threat of wars, and by troubles within herself, and David had been sent as a bairn to be brought up in the safety of the English Court—his own sister being Queen to Henry I.

All his growing time and his young manhood, he was in England, and he was forty years old before, his elder brothers being dead, he came back to rule his own land. And him married to an English wife and grown long-used to English ways.

Along with all the rest, he had grown used to Norman–English ways of government, and when he came north, he brought with him English friends to help him set these up in Scotland. Aye, and all kinds of other English ways as well.

A thing very near to his heart was the making of Burghs—towns, you might call them—but towns of a very special kind; for they are towns that live altogether by trade, and they belong to the King himself, in a manner of speaking.

Of course we in Scotland had had our villages and townships of a sort, for many a long day—wee settlements with maybe twenty or so households, growing each their own barley and grazing each their own few sheep, producing just enough for their own needs; in a bad year not even that; and very seldom anything to spare.

I was reared myself on a farm just outside one such township, by the name of Drumfyvie. Set midway between the Highlands and the Lowlands it is, at the place where an ancient trading

route comes down to cross a branch of the Forth. It has open country round about it, and near at hand a dark fleece of forest that makes good acorn-feeding for pigs in the autumn. The sheep grazed on the Common lands;' and the Drumfyvie sheep have always given good thick fleeces, so that it sometimes happened even in those days that Drumfyvie folk had something of wool or woven cloth beyond their own needs. And when that happened, a merchant travelling down from the north would be glad enough to take it, for selling at some English fair.

Well, so there were a good few other such townships on river fords on old trade routes, and to some of these, Kind David was minded to give royal charters, and the new title of "Burgh" as had long been the custom in England.

In England, trade had long since become a way of life. The English traded all over Europe, exchanging their own merchandise for wine and spices, silks and iron, from places across the Narrow Seas. King David had seen the prosperity that this brought to the country, and it was in his mind that Scotland should prosper likewise. So he set about making his Burghs, his trading towns, and giving each into the safe keeping of a man of his own choosing. Often 'twas one of his English friends—which did not best please the Scots—but sometimes 'twould be a Scottish Lord who was of the King's way of thinking. Each Burgh must have its castle, new-built if there was not one there already, where the King's man, the Sheriff, would live, and his household and his men-at-arms with him, for the protection of the town and its trade—aye, and for tending to the King's interests there also. And each Burgh must have its own officers—Provost and Bailies and the like—and laws to suit its needs.

Now one of the chief differences is this, that throughout the rest of the land a man must work for his Lord in peace and follow him in war, as his Lord serves and follows the King. But a Burgh lives by trade, and how can a tradesman carry on if he is forever being called up for service in peace or war? So the Burgh folk just pay their rent, their dues to the King for his protection, and go on with their own affairs. But they're the King's men, for all that.

Och well, I'm thinking that's all you need to know. So I'll start telling you the story of Duncan the Red.

8

Duncan the Red
A.D. 1137

I mind fine, how it all began, on a wild evening a while before Michaelmas, some twelve years after King David came to his throne.

It was in the Hall of the King's Castle, high on its grey rock above Edinburgh town. A chill wind from the Forth was whining in at the narrow windows, setting the torches flickering in the wall sconces, so that the light of them fleered up and down, sending long fingers of shadow over walls and floor. And the hangings stirred on the walls, and the smoke billowed sideways in stinging clouds from the central hearth.

My master, Duncan the Red—Strathardle, to give him his proper title—had sent for me on a wee matter of business that could as well have waited until he came home after Michaelmas. That's to say, it could if it had been anyone's business but Red Duncan's. His had always to be settled on the instant, and as his steward I was forever on the run. But be that as it may, 'tis so, I came to be in the King's Hall that evening, with a long wet ride behind me.

My, but the place was full of folk! Ladies gay as flowers in their bright silks; lords in tunics just as many-coloured, with their cloaks drawn about them, 'gainst the whistling draughts. Squires and pages scurrying hither and yon to keep the drinking cups filled with the good red wine; great deerhounds lying stretched out under the trestle tables. And I mind a priest or so, with long black gowns, dusty hemmed, and a harper playing to himself, for 'tis sure that no one else was listening to him amongst all the talk and chatter!

And through it all, I went seeking my master. Not that I had much difficulty in finding him, for he was the tallest man in the place, and the one with the reddest hair and beard. Indeed, why else would he be called Duncan the Red?—unless 'twas for his temper, of course!

Well, so I found him, and cleared up the wee matter of business.

9

And when 'twas done I left him, but I didn't leave the Hall at once, for one of the pages offered me a jack of ale, and I settled down on a bench nearby, for a wee bit of rest and refreshment. And while I sat there, my master and young Sir Robert Maitland, one of the King's Norman friends, came to the end of the table, and fell in an idle sort of way to casting the dice. I was a wee thing surprised to see them playing together, for my master was bitter set against the Norman in-comers. But like enough, Sir Robert, who was a friendly and peaceable soul, had suggested the game; and Red Duncan was never one to refuse a challenge. And indeed, it came to me after a while that my master was not above trying to pick a quarrel even while they played, just by way of adding spice to the game.

"Your throw," he said, and flung himself back against the wall. "Your luck's in, tonight, as far as mine's out. But that's the way of it in all things, these days, is it no'?"

"Meaning?" Sir Robert raised his brows as he took up the dice cup. But he was quite pleasant about it.

"Och away!" said my master. " 'Tis well enough for you, with your clipped Norman voice and your fine Norman ways. It's you and your kind are the lordly ones now at Court—and us that must bend our necks to our own King as though he were some foreign conqueror!"

Sir Robert shook the dice in the leather cup. "I do not see much bend to your neck, my bonnie Red Duncan . . . Ah-ha!—a six!"

My master looked at him down his great beak of a nose. "I would have you mind, Sir Robert, that I am the Thane of Strath-ardle, not used to easy bowing and scraping."

"I'll mind it," said Sir Robert. "Your throw, Thane of Strath-ardle."

"I have more things on my mind than the casting of dice."

"Such as?"

"Too many changes in too few years. It takes a man all his time to get used to them."

"And you are one for the old ways. Still your throw."

My master shook the cup and sent the dice rolling, but never looked at them. "The old ways did well enough till our David came into his own. Now all things must be new—a whole new way of life, a whole new way of rule. And how is it better than

our own familiar way that fitted as easy as an old coat?"

"For one thing," said Sir Robert, suddenly serious, "it means a settled government, which is a thing Scotland has never had before."

My master smiled in a way he had that showed his dog-teeth. "Myself, I've done well enough without a settled government."

"I don't doubt it. But has Scotland? Oh come man, others of your kind have taken to the King's new ways, why not you?"

"They take some stomaching, these new ways."

"But why? It's all simple and sensible enough, once you understand it."

"I didn't say 'twas not simple," Red Duncan said. "I said it took some stomaching! As to understanding—listen how well I can recite my lesson." He leaned forward, smiling still, and thrust his red jut of beard almost into Sir Robert's face. "The barons and the great lords hold their lands from the King himself. For these lands they pay homage, swearing to serve him in war or peace, and bringing with them an agreed train of knights and men-at-arms. Right?"

Sir Robert nodded.

"The knights and lesser nobles hold their manors and estates from the barons in their turn; and in the same way, the ordinary folk hold from the knights of their manor their barley strips and the roof over their heads, and their grazing for a wee cow. There! Have I not learned the lesson well, Sir Robert Maitland?"

Sir Robert laughed outright. "None better, my Lord Duncan, though somewhat grudgingly . . . Nay now, it's an unbroken chain of government, reaching from the King to the least of his subjects. And it works!"

"Maybe, Sir Robert, maybe," my master said, very clear and deliberate. "But one thing I know fine: I know that all land is become the King's, and every man bound down to it some way or another. And I know something else—I know that freedom is a bonnie thing!"

I heard him speaking, and I saw who was coming through the press of folk nearby—and my heart fair fell over itself into my belly!

"So is law and order," said the King, close at Sir Robert's shoulder.

Sir Robert sprang a'foot. "Your pardon, my Lord King. I did not see you—"

"No," said the King, quiet-like. "But Red Duncan saw me."

My master got up more slowly, and the two stood and looked at each other—not just like King and subject, either.

"Aye," the King said at last. "You're a brave man, Strathardle, and I like you the better for it. But for all your dislike of the new ways, I am thinking that if I were to offer you one of my new Burghs, with its castle to build and hold, you'd not refuse it."

Red Duncan looked the King straight in the eye, and, said he, "If I were a Highland Chief, with the hills safe between you and me, my Lord King, I would be refusing gladly. But Strathardle lies close under your hand. So give me this new Burgh, and I'll be your man, and build your castle, and hold it for you as well as any Fitzalan or Montgomerie or other of your Norman friends."

The King smiled, a small smile. "Not so fast, friend. I said 'if', remember."

"So you did, my Lord King, so you did. But let you remember 'twas I that took a boar's tusk in the shoulder for you, that time at the hunting, when the beast charged and your horse threw you. I am thinking that but for the scar on my shoulder, that aches yet when the wind is in the east, Scotland would likely have another King this day."

"Truly I remember," the King said. "I owe you something for that, and 'twould be an ill thing if the King of Scotland left his debts unpaid." He made a wee gesture towards the dice on the table. "But that can wait. Finish the game." And he moved on, turning to speak to some other friend in the crowd.

I slipped away too, in search of somewhere to lay my head, for I'd a deal to think about, suddenly, and a long ride home in the morn.

We did not expect Strathardle home until after Michaelmas, but only two days later, there he was at the gate, his men behind him and his favourite goshawk on his fist. And within the hour, he sent for me, to the private chamber behind the Hall. He was standing over the fire, still carrying the goshawk. Awful like each other, they were : the same hooked beak, the same fierce bright

stare. I've often thought but for the feathers 'twould be hard to tell one from the other.

"Ah, Robbie," said he, not bothering to look round. "You were born in Drumfyvie, were you not?"

"I was that," I said.

"When were you there last?"

"I've not been back since I was a laddie."

"So it's not much you'll be able to tell me about the place," he was scratching up the goshawk's neck feathers, the creature bobbing its head and hunching its wings in pleasure. "But you have kinsfolk there? Someone you could visit, no man thinking it strange?"

"I've my Cousin Jock that's saddler there," I said. "But what's Drumfyvie to you, Strathardle?"

"What am I to Drumfyvie, rather," said he. "I am to be their Sheriff."

I stared at him, and 'twas a moment before I could get the words out. "But Drumfyvie's not a Burgh!"

"Not yet. But the King is minded to make it one."

Aye well, I gathered my wits together somehow to listen to the rest of what my master had to say ...

King David, it seemed, was to visit one of his Priories at Michaelmas (he was a'most as great for Priories as for Burghs) and him taking a roundabout way to pass through Drumfyvie, and Red Duncan was to ride with him, to get a first sight of the place.

"But it's little enough I'll see, just riding through at the King's heels. So I'm thinking I'll do well to have someone I can trust, and who knows the folk and the lay of the land, to take a longer look, and give me the bit of information and advice from time to time. So away with you to your Cousin Jock—and keep all this under your bonnet, meanwhile."

Fine I knew that my master had never taken a bit of advice in all his life; it was the information he was after. Still, he might make the better Sheriff for knowing something of his Burgh, and I made a wee promise to myself that I'd not be passing on anything that 'twould be better for Drumfyvie he should not know.

Well, so when Red Duncan was away back to Court, and I'd

set things in order at Strathardle, I took horse for Drumfyvie.

The place didn't seem to have changed much, and Jock was fine and pleased to see me. 'Deed, I think he was glad of company, for he'd neither wife nor bairns of his own. We were sitting in the wee place behind the shop on the first evening, talking over old times with a pot of ale between us, when a laddie came in with a leather belt of his master's that needed stitching, and a great dog padding at his heels—a black dog, with white paws on him, I mind. Jock took the belt, and bade the laddie come back for it next day, and sent him away home to his master.

"And who might that be?" said I, for the bairn caught my interest.

"That's Donal," says Jock, setting the belt aside. "Ian the Swineherd found him under a hawthorn bush—four, five years ago, 'twould be, after a band of wandering-folk had passed by."

"D'you tell me?" said I. "Well, it seems he's found a place for himself here."

"Aye. Ian kept him, to help wi' the pigs. He lets the laddie sleep in the byre, unless he has a sow farrowing there; when that happens, Donal has just to sleep in the shelter of the peat stack, with Whitefoot beside him to keep him warm."

"Whitefoot?"

"The dog. Did ye not see? He followed Donal back from the outfield one evening at hay harvesting. Just a half-starved pup, and no one ever knew where he came from, but he's followed at Donal's heels ever since."

The days passed, and I helped Jock at the saddler's trade, and got to know the folks that came and went. Some I minded from my young days, and some, but not many, minded me.

Then 'twas the day before Michaelmas, and on a sudden a great crowd of knights and men-at-arms came riding through Drumfyvie! The whole town came running to see, myself with the rest, not letting on that I knew any more than they did, what it might mean; for I'd kept all things under my bonnet, as Strathardle bade me.

So they rode through, the King and the companions of his household, and the men-at-arms clattering on behind. 'Twas the kind of thing I'd seen often enough before; the smother of horsemen flashing blue and gold and crimson, and the dust-cloud swirl-

ing up from the horses' hooves; and then all past and gone, and the dust-cloud sinking. But long after the last sound of hoofbeats had died away into the distance, the folk of Drumfyvie stood in the trackway staring after them, aye, and staring at each other, too.

"Yon was the King!" somebody said.

"The King? Och away!"

"'Twas the King, I'm telling you! Him at the head of them, on the black horse. Did you not see the bonnie goldwork on him, and the lions that the men-at-arms had for badges on their sleeves?"

"But what would the King be doing in Drumfyvie?"

"Riding through to some place else, I wouldn't wonder."

But old Effie, the herb-woman who had her bothy at the other end of the town, spoke up strangely, "They were not just riding through, neither the King nor the red-headed one beside him. They were not just riding through at all."

Folks turned to look at her, for 'twas well known that old Effie had the second sight. And I mind there was a moment's silence, and the autumn wind seemed to have taken a chill edge to it that it had not had before.

Then Jock said, "For why else, would they be coming, Effie?"

Effie didn't look at him, nor at any of us. She seemed to be looking away into some distance of her own. "Changes," she said. "They came to bring changes. The wind changed as they rode by, and all the air flickered . . . Many and great changes, and whether for good or ill, I cannot see. There's a cloud, a stormcloud, and I cannot see . . ." Her voice rose to a wail, "But I'm fear'd, fear'd for Drumfyvie, fear'd for us all."

Aye well, there was a deal of talk for days afterwards of course; and some said that Effie was but an old woman gone in her wits, and some said she'd never yet foretold anything that hadn't come to pass. But only myself knew how close she was to the truth, and even I didn't know the whole of it, and the good cause she had to be afraid.

It was the edge of winter when at last the news came, and that evening when the men got home from the fields, there were little

groups, eager and excited, all up and down the straggle of the town street in the dusk.

"A Burgh!" said Ian the Swineherd, cocking his head as though he couldn't just believe what he heard. "Drumfyvie to be a Burgh! It's not true?"

"Aye, 'tis true enough! We'll be seeing some life now!" Isa, the Webster's lassie, stood with her hands on her hips, her eyes dancing in her head. "There'll be merchants and craftsmen knocking at our gates from all over the world!"

"Rogues and vagabonds, more like!" said my Cousin Jock, who is given to looking on the dark side.

And old Dougal sighed to himself. "Aye, and the price of bread will rise."

"Why would that be, then?"

"The price of bread always rises."

"There'll be more folks to feed, for sure."

"Eh, weary me," Old Effie joined in. "What did I tell you? Changes—great changes. Life will never be the same again." But the "sight" was not on her, as it had been that other time. She was just an old body who liked things to bide as they always had been, and no one paid her any special heed.

"Maybe we'll have a fair!" said Isa, making her skirts swing.

And Ian gave a kind of croak—he'd an awful cold on his chest and shouldn't have been outdoors. "Here! That means we'll be having a castle—a castle and a Sheriff! 'Tis so with all Burghs, so I've heard. And who'll be Sheriff of Drumfyvie?"

"Have ye not heard that?" Tam the Blacksmith had re-shod the horse of the man who brought the news. " 'Tis a Scot turned Norman, some kind of friend to the King. Duncan the Red, they call him."

"There was yon great red-headed man with the King when he rode through—" Isa began.

But someone cut her short, "Red-headed, or red-handed, would that be?"

A few days later, my master sent for me, and I was away back to Strathardle, to tell him whatever I had learned that it seemed to me good that he should know—good both for himself *and* for the folk of Drumfyvie, that is. Also I had to break in the man

that was to follow me as steward on the old estates, for I was to go with Red Duncan when the time came for him to take his place as Sheriff of the new Burgh.

That winter, as I heard tell, there was a great tree-felling in Drumfyvie Forest, and with the first uncertain days of spring, men were sent from the Strathardle lands to begin work on the castle that was to stand at the western end of the town. And before March was out, I was back with my Cousin Jock, to keep an eye on how all things went. It was not easy, that second going back. The folk looked at me with different eyes. They'd known all along that I was servant on some great estate, but even Jock had not known that I was Strathardle's man. But I was glad that the thing was out in the open, for I'd not liked the part of spy. Folk accepted, though grudgingly, that I had had to keep my master's secret until the King made all things known; and given time, I thought I could show them that I was but a man doing his job, and had not broken faith with them.

As time passed, Red Duncan himself came more and more often, to see that his castle grew as he would have it. He was not a man who liked rest himself, and not a man who liked to see others resting. He drove himself, and he drove the workmen, and he drove me, and when he was there, I'd be so weary each night that I'd like enough fall asleep at Jock's fireside with my supper bannock half eaten—and then be called out at midnight to the great tent that he'd had pitched for himself within the raw new stockade, to have my ears filled with a fresh batch of orders that could as well have waited till morning.

The castle, you must understand, was not built in stone, like those that are beginning to rise nowadays. 'Twas a motte and bailey stronghold built in turf and timber, the outer bailey for the stables and storehouses and workshops, and the keep rising above, on its mound. At Drumfyvie at least we didn't have to build the mound, for a round hillock that had always been there served the purpose as well as though it had been made for it. Queer tales there were about that hillock . . . Aye . . .

Well, most of the able-bodied men of the town soon found themselves, whether they would or no', labouring alongside the Sheriff's own workmen at the castle-building. Even Ian from the swineherding. Not that I'd call him able-bodied, that spring;

for he hadn't shaken off the cold that he'd caught back at the start of winter—if it was a cold. Settled on his chest, it had; and he'd a cough that fair shook him to pieces. He was not fit for the heavy work, but fit or no', off he had to go with the rest, leaving just Donal and Whitefoot to look after the pigs.

So the strong turf and timber walls went up, and the keep began to rise on its hillock—the keep that would be the Sheriff's Hall and the strong-point of the castle all in one. Quarters for Red Duncan's men-at-arms, stabling for his horses, kennels for his hunting dogs, mews for his falcons. Brewhouse and bake-house, workshops and armoury, great kitchens and store-sheds. And all the while, there was my master coming and going, with his red hair and his harsh mouth, and most times his big goshawk on his fist, till folks began to dread the sight of him.

Still, things went well enough at the start—until the day Old Effie went up there to bring her son, Daft Fergie, his noonday bannock and cheese that he'd forgotten to take with him. Daft Fergie's real skills lay in the forest, but he was good for odd jobs, even if he did wander a mite in his wits, and so he'd been called in to the building work with the rest. Well, up Old Effie came, the first time she'd ever been inside the walls, the first time in months, as I believe, that she'd been up that end of the town, for she kept as far as might be from all that had to do with the changes in Drumfyvie. And she took one look towards the beginnings of the keep, and she let out a screech to raise the hair on the back of your neck.

I came running from where I'd been speaking with the over-seer, and others gathered from all over, and in the midst of us, Effie, with the bannock and cheese fallen at her feet, was rocking herself to and fro and keening as women keen for their dead.

"Sorrow and grief! Sorrow and grief! They are building on the fairy mound!"

And I mind I felt cold down my back in the sunlight.

One of the Drumfyvie men said quickly, "Och, there's the old stories. But I've not seen nor heard aught that wasn't canny, while I've been at work up yonder."

But I noticed that two or three of those standing nearest made the sign of the Horns with their fingers against ill luck, and Old Effie was no way comforted.

"Laddie, Laddie, there's some that never hear nor see, so there are. But many's the time I've seen the Good Folk on the hill, I'm telling ye! Many and many's the time, and they will be taking payment from them that build on their land. Payment in the lives of men, as they always take it!"

Unseen by any of us, Master Gilliechrist, the parish priest, had come into our midst. A very gentle man, but he spoke up fine and stern at that. "Effie! Be quiet, woman, this is heathen talk! Think shame on it, and put such fancies from you as a good Christian should!"

But Effie did not seem to hear. She just stood there wailing. "Death! Aye, there'll be more deaths than one, before the People of the Hills are satisfied! Fairy Folk, Wee Folk, call them what you will, they aye take their payment."

Ian tried to comfort her, but he was taken with a fit of coughing till he couldn't speak. And I mind Master Gilliechrist gave him a keen look. "You'd best take care with that cough, my son. Ask Effie here to brew some herbs for it. She's wise in such things, if she's not wise in all others."

"'Tis a cold," said Ian, getting his breath back a bit. "Just a cold that I got back in the winter-time. It's left me a mite sore in my chest; but 'twill mend when I get back with the pigs. There's naught better for soothing a sore chest than the smell of pigs."

I was looking at him, thinking 'twould maybe take more than the smell of pigs or a dose of herbs and bee's-bread to set him right, if he stayed much longer here at the heaving and hauling; and when I looked round again, Effie had crept away. Only she'd left a kind of chill behind her.

'Twas after that, things began to go wrong—there were accidents, and the work went slower. And Red Duncan didn't fail to notice, so that I had a hard time of it trying to save the backs of Strathardle and Drumfyvie men alike. But time went its way and the work got done, and spring drew on to summer, and the cuckoo was calling.

Yet still there seemed a chill, a shadow over all Drumfyvie. Partly, in a kind of way, it was the shadow of the Castle itself. Folks watched it spread and grow, and it seemed strange to them, even if there was no harm in it, like stiff new clothes that sat

uneasy on their shoulders. But partly it was Old Effie's "seeing" that they couldn't quite forget.

Then came the black day when my master, on one of his visits, gave the folk of Drumfyvie their first taste of what he could be like when the wicked mood took him.

He was standing with me and the overseer, watching the men at work on the keep. And as he watched, something made me glance aside at him, and I saw the stormclouds gathering in his face. "It seems to me that every time I come, the work goes more slowly," said he, and then in a roar, "Horns of St. Luke! Are you all asleep?"

The overseer seemed to shrink. "All—all should be finished by Lammas, Strathardle—my Lord."

Duncan gave that odd smile that showed his dog-teeth. "It had better be, it had indeed, my friend. The roof was almost as near to being thatched over, the last time I saw it, as it is now. This does not please me. And when Strathardle is not pleased, lesser men stand clear! Listen to me, and listen well, for I shall not trouble myself to speak twice : Tomorrow I ride hawking. I am tired of tents and have a mind to sleep beneath my own roof when I return at sundown. *And* with never a gap in that same roof, save only the smoke-hole, to see the stars through. Do I make all clear?"

The overseer began to stutter like a July cuckoo. "Aye, Sir— my Lord—I—I—We'll do the b-best we can. It's been none so easy to get the reeds, the spring b-being that dry this year, ye see . . ."

But my master was looking away over the wretched man's head, at something else that did not please him. "It's none so easy to keep the men working, either, seemingly. Who's that basking like a cat in the sun, sleeping away the day with his head on his knees?"

And I looked, and—dear God!—'twas Ian!

The overseer did his best, poor man, "He's a good workman, my Lord—one of the b-best I have, but he's sick. He should be home in his bed, but you gave orders—"

"I gave orders that this castle was to be built," said Red Duncan, speaking every word separately, "and no man at the building of it sits idle unless he be dead!"

"My Lord—'twill not happen again—"

"No," Red Duncan agreed. "I do not think that it will happen again. But just to mark the matter on your memory, and his, I am having the man flogged. My men-at-arms will see to it."

The overseer started one more plea, "Sir—I beg you—"

But my master cut him short. "Have a care, Master Overseer. If you try my patience too far, your back shall be as bloody as his, by sundown."

Well, so all was done according to Red Duncan's orders. And the next day he rode hawking; and at sundown he returned, as he had said he would, to sleep in his own Hall.

As he rode through the Burgh in the dusk, folks had gathered along the way, to watch him come, for there was nobody in all Drumfyvie hadn't heard of yesterday's on-goings at the Castle. And Ian was one of their own—our own—harm one, harm all . . .

I was up at the Castle, but I heard what happened, later, from Jock. My Lord took no heed of the folk, but just rode through their silence, looking neither to right nor left, his great goshawk on his fist, and his falconers, and the dogs following behind. But when he came near to the Castle gate, there at the edge of the crowd stood Master Gilliechrist, barring the way, so Red Duncan must needs rein in his horse. He and the priest looked at each other long and hard, then my master tipped up his head and asked, seemingly of the air about him, "Is the roof yet on my Hall?"

And Master Gilliechrist said, "The roof is on your Hall. And the sick man ye had flogged yesterday is dead."

The folks in the street made a kind of murmuring; and then there was just the silence again, until Red Duncan broke it.

"If he were so near to death, then 'twas a charity to help him on his way! Out of my path, all of you!"

The goshawk gave a harsh cry, as though it were adding its voice to its master's. But then Old Effie stepped out from the crowd, almost under the horse's nose.

"Out of my path, hag!" said Red Duncan. "Away, off with you!"

But Old Effie stood her ground, and 'twas plain to all that

once again the "sight" was on her, and her with a face like a sleep-walker's.

"I will out of your path, my Lord, when I have told you that which I have to tell. This castle of yours is built where never mortal man should raise his walls. And for that, the People of the Hills call for payment . . . The life of one man they have already, and maybe there'll be others, afore all is done. But this I know, before themselves count the price paid, the first Lord of Drumfyvie shall die an ugly death, slain by his own familiar companion, with never a woman to weep for him, nor a son to wear his sword!"

Duncan sat on his great roan horse and looked down at her; and then he laughed, and his laughter was not a good sound to hear, so Jock told me, and I can well believe it.

"Why you—you crazy old harridan! D'you think to frighten *me* with such bogey-tales! Out of my way before I ride you down!"

And with that, he set spurs to his horse, and would have ridden her down, in truth, if Master Gilliechrist had not snatched her aside, and was away through the Castle gates, his following behind him, and the goshawk on his fist beating its wings and screaming like a tormented soul.

There's more, aye there's more, but I'll need to tell you the rest another time, for there's Jock shouting for my help in the workshop.

The Red Sheriff
A.D. 1139

Well now, I'm back to tell you the rest of the story.

Upward of two months later, when the workmen were all finished and away, Duncan the Red—he was a baron now, no less—paid his homage to King David, in the Great Hall of his new castle. ,

And being steward of his household. I was there with the rest, to see and hear him swear his fealty, his hands between the King's hands, his red head bowed low. I'd never thought to see the day Red Duncan of Strathardle would bend his knee and his neck before a King he looked on as little more than a Norman in-comer. But he was a man to see where his interests lay, after all.

"Here, my Lord, I become liege man of yours for life and limb and earthly regard; and I will keep faith and loyalty to you for life or death, God helping me."

Listening to the words as they sounded clear down the long timber Hall, I wondered, was it in him to make a good Sheriff? Despite his wicked temper and the bad start he'd made? Oh, it all looked fair enough now, the harvest-time sunshine striking down through the small high windows on the reds and blues and golds of the King and his nobles, and my master's own bright head. But how would it go on? I was Strathardle's steward, the Sheriff's steward; but I was Drumfyvie born and bred, and I was afraid for my own folk, so I was ...

But down below in the new Burgh, there was ale for all, and three oxen of my Lord's providing, roasting whole on spits in the open space where soon the Market Cross would stand. Oh aye, Red Duncan could be open-handed when he chose. So the new burgesses and their families drank the Sheriff's ale and filled their bellies with his roast beef, and even old Dougal ceased his doubts and grumblings, and was heard to say that Red Duncan had started off ill enough, but maybe he was learning.

Certain it was, the new Burgh was already prospering more than the old township had ever done, with new houses going up

almost by the day, and fresh merchants and craftsmen coming in all the time—men such as the Flemish weaver whom folks called "Peter the Fleming", or just "Peter Fleming" because nobody could get their tongue round his outlandish foreign name. And to let you see how well the Burgh was doing, there was plenty of work for him without taking it away from Tam the Webster. Soon, other websters followed on his heels, and the tanner took on more apprentices to help him, and so did my Cousin Jock. Then a leather-merchant's factor came, and so it went on.

Within the next couple of years, we'd a kirk named for St. Ninian, the Burgh's patron saint, and a Market Cross where we held the new Midsummer Wool Fair. And an alehouse where the lads would go cock-fighting in the evenings when the day's work was done. And we'd a Provost and Bailies to run the Burgh's affairs. Aye, and a new mill with a red-faced miller as pot-bellied as a toad to keep it working. Old Dougal had a word to say about that!

"Drumfyvie's mill—'tis no' Drumfyvie's mill at all! 'Tis the Sheriff's. And here's us has to take our corn there for the grinding, whether we will or no'. And who gets the most of the money we pay yon crafty-looking miller? Why, Duncan the Red, of course. Did I not tell you, right at the start, that the price of bread would rise?"

But apart from the mill, my master had little enough to do with the Burgh folk, except, of course, when he sat in state, presiding over the Sheriff's Court four times in the year, to hand out justice without mercy to them that broke the law. King's Law, that is, not Burgh Law. Burgh Law was for the Provost and Bailies.

For a while, then, things went well enough, till towards the end of the second summer, there began to be trouble from the Forest Laws—King's Law, that is, for 'tis the King's forest now.

In the old days, you see, any man with the skill to get a deer had free run of the forest for his hunting, save only when the King or the Nobles wanted it to themselves for a day or so. But now on a sudden, the forest wasn't for poor men, any more. 'Twas just for Red Duncan and his like. Folks took it ill, though most of them obeyed the new laws. But Daft Fergie . . . He'd hunted the red deer all his days, that one, and Old Effie, his mother,

looked like having trouble, with him not being one to understand new things easy.

And then one day, word came down from the Castle that all the dogs of hound size in the Burgh must have the two middle toes of their forepaws clipped short, so they could not chase the deer—leastwise, not to run them down. I'd heard that was the way of things in England, but 'twas strange to us Scots, very strange.

Donal—he worked now for James, the new swineherd, as once he had worked for Ian—Donal must have been sick with worry for Whitefoot, when he heard the order, because, for all Whitefoot looked like a sheepdog more than aught else, and had never been known to hunt more than a mouse, still he was as big as any of Duncan's feather-heeled deerhounds, so there wasn't much chance that he'd escape this particular bit of forest law.

And he didn't. An evening or so later, taking a bit stroll down by the burn that fed the mill-stream, I came on the pair of them, Donal bathing the dog's bleeding forepaws in the cold quick-running water, half-crying the while, "Oh Whitefoot, I'm sorry! I'm that sorry. But if we'd run away we'd just have got to being outlaws—because nobody'd give us work, not the two of us together—because you *are* something big, and folks wouldn't know how clever you are at herding the pigs . . ."

He was so set on his task that he did not see nor hear me until I spoke to him. "You've had Whitefoot up to the Sheriff's officers, I see."

He looked up then, with a start, but when he saw who 'twas, I saw the relief in his face, and it warmed my heart. By that time most of my own folk, Drumfyvie folk, had forgiven me that I was Red Duncan's steward, and come to know that they could trust me well enough, but I had not got past being grateful.

"I didn't think they'd do it to him. It's not as if he was a proper hound. But my master said he wasn't looking for trouble, and if I didn't take Whitefoot up to the foresters with the rest, out we could go, the pair of us, and he'd find another laddie to help him with the pigs. But now I cannot stop the bleeding, and —and—"

Whitefoot licked his hand.

And something twisted inside me. "If he was mine," I said,

"I'd take him along to Old Effie. She'll know what to do, and have the herbs to do it with."

He looked at me, not answering for a moment, and I knew that he was scared. Most folks were scared of Effie, these days. She seldom went about the town any more, but kept herself and Fergie close in their wee turf bothy, and working in the kale plot or tending the healing herbs that were her stock in trade. And I've noticed that when folks keep overmuch to themselves, it most often scares other folks away from them too, let alone when they have the "sight". So I didn't blame the laddie for hesitating. But 'twas only for an instant. Then he nodded, and got to his feet. "I'll do that, Master Armstrong, so I will." And he whistled to Whitefoot and set off, the big dog limping painfully after him.

And watching them go, and seeing here and there the smear of blood left on the burnside grass, eh but my heart was sore for the pair of them.

But when next I saw Whitefoot, some two or three weeks later, he was off to the pig herding with Donal, as gay as a lintie, trotting along as though he had never had nor needed more toes on his forepaws than he had now.

"Old Effie put a kind of salve made with St. John's-wort on his paws," the laddie told me. " 'Grace-of-God' she called it. Awful wise, Old Effie is."

But we'd not heard the last of the Forest Laws—for soon after, a fearful thing came about. For at the Sheriff's Court that Michaelmas, Daft Fergie was sentenced to hang, for shooting one of my Lord's deer!

I told you, did I not, that Fergie's chief skill lay in the forest, and being daft, he couldn't understand that the forest was not his to hunt in any more. And so, 'spite of all Effie's trying to keep him safe home on the kale plot, the thing happened, he was caught pulling his arrow from the carcass of a new-killed fallow doe. He didn't even deny that 'twas his arrow, for he saw no reason to. He was proud of the clean kill, and not feared at all.

Well, so Daft Fergie was tried, and flung into the prison below the Castle guardroom, to bide for his hanging. You see, judgement had been given late in the day, and the morrow was the

Sabbath, which is an ill day for a hanging, so 'twould have to wait till the Monday.

But on the Sabbath evening, after Vespers was said and the Kirk was out, Master Gilliechrist, good parish priest that he was, came up to the Castle along with Peter the Fleming and Andrew Brec, him that had the largest grazing rights in all the Burgh, asking for word with the Sheriff. I went myself and told my master, for I thought it better that way than to leave the telling to one of his heedless squires. But he just said, "They can cool their heels. I go to see my hawks." And off he went to the mews.

The three men waited, stubborn as oxen. Oh aye, they waited till the last of the sun went off the Bailie Court. Then Red Duncan came back, carrying his favourite goshawk on his fist. 'Twas now close on supper time, so giving the three of them scarce a glance, he bade them wait on, while he went up to his Hall, and took his leisure over the roast sucking-pig with dried plums. 'Twas the edge of dusk when he sent for them at last, but the torches had been lit in the Hall, and I saw their faces well enough from where I stood a little behind my master's chair, and "There's three brave men," I said to myself. "If there are no more in all Drumfyvie."

"Ye wish to speak with me on some matter?" said the Sheriff, leaning back like a man who has supped well, and still gentling the neck feathers of his hawk.

Master Gilliechrist answered for the rest, facing Red Duncan across the high table. "Aye, my Lord Sheriff, we do. On the matter of Daft Fergus, son to Effie the Herb-woman, whom you now hold captive and waiting to hang for the crime of shooting one of your deer."

"I spoke the last word on that matter yesterday, in Court. Do you grow hard of hearing, then?"

"Nay, my Lord. We heard you clear enough," said Peter the Fleming. "But—let you forgive us my Lord, it seemed to us and to our fellow burgesses of Drumfyvie, that maybe your last word was spoken in anger, and you not taking time to think. We hope indeed it may be so."

My master stared at them as though he didn't rightly understand what he'd heard. "You question my judgement, then— which eould be a worse misfortune than to grow hard of hearing."

But Peter the Fleming was not yet done. "Your rule is a hard one, my Lord, yet we have never before questioned your authority. But this time——"

"*This time?*" Red Duncan's voice rose suddenly, and Master Gilliechrist put in his word quiet and quick, trying to turn aside the coming storm.

"We hope, we believe, that you do not know just what you do on this occasion, my Lord. Daft Fergie is somewhat of a special case . . . These Forest Laws are old and well understood in England. But here, in your own Scotland, they are new. Some of the simple folk do not yet understand them, and they are slow to learn."

"Then all I can suggest is that you should help them to learn more quickly, Master Priest."

But Master Gilliechrist was not held back by the menace in his tone.

"This young man, Fergie, cannot learn, my Lord. He is foolish in his head. He did not understand that he was doing aught wrong. Surely, then, he cannot be held responsible."

Red Duncan ceased for the first time his gentling of the goshawk's feathers, and leaned slowly forward across the table. "Can it be, my friend, that I am to bend the laws of this land for the idiot son of a witch?"

"My Lord Baron, laws are left loose in the hands of your kind, to enforce or not, as you think fit. You have the choice and we beg you to show mercy to this man, for the sake of Him that died upon the cross to redeem us all from our misdoings."

Red Duncan looked at them all, one after the other, taking his time about it, and then he laughed, like a dog-fox barking on a frosty night. "Mercy? I? Sir Priest you have chosen the wrong man to come to with such mealy mouthings, you have indeed."

"You refuse, my Lord?" said Master Gilliechrist.

"The man hangs tomorrow."

"Then God give him peace," said the little priest, and crossed himself. But there was more he had to say, and he said it, standing before the Sheriff like a hero. "Yet if we cannot save Fergie we can, maybe, save others after him. The Provost thought it best that he should stand aside from this matter, if 'twere possible. It seems that it is not. And so it is, I must tell you, my Lord, that

since there seems no other way, we intend to appeal against you, *as is our right*, to the King himself."

My master let out such a roar of fury as even I had never heard from him before. And at the sound the great goshawk bated wildly on his gloved fist, and with a scream of rage and terror and a savage beating of wings, tore its jesses from his hold, and was away down the Hall, through the smoke of the fire and out by the open door into the autumn dusk.

Red Duncan was on his feet and bellowing, "Splendour of God! You fools! Do you think to threaten *me* with the King and the King's justice? Jehan—you there, get back my hawk. De Vitre, help Jehan . . . Guards! Take these men and put them in the guard-house—and keep them close. I may hang them too, if I am so minded!" And with that, he began to laugh, not as he'd laughed before, but like a madman or a devil, going on and on . . .

Master Gilliechrist and the other two were marched away, and I crept off to my own quarters, thankful he neither saw me go nor called for me again that night—though it's but little sleep I got, with that wicked laughter sounding in my head.

Next morning the Burgh folk saw the body of Daft Fergie hanging crow-black against the sky above the bailey wall.

They gathered in stunned, whispering knots below the castle and at street corners and about the Market Cross. It was as though they waited for something, they did not know what, and there were some that doffed their bonnets and said a prayer. And a wee while after noon, the Castle gates opened, and Master Gilliechrist came out. I was on my way back from some business of my master's and so I saw him come—he looked years older than the night before. And I heard what he had to say to the folk who gathered round him.

"As my Lord Sheriff's messenger, I am sent to tell you, in case you have not chanced to look above his Castle walls this morning, that he has carried out his sentence on Daft Fergie, and that if you raise any further trouble, he will hang beside him also Peter Fleming and Andrew Brec, for having caused his favourite goshawk to escape. Go to your homes now, and pray for the soul of Fergus. I go to Old Effie, it may be that she will need me." And with that, looking neither to right nor left, the priest went his way.

The next part of the story I heard later, at different times and from different folk, and pieced together for myself. But at the time, I knew nothing of it, me being the Sheriff's steward . . .

This is the way it went.

That evening, as soon as 'twas dusk, the Provost himself, with a small company of men, Jock amongst them, gathered in Old Effie's cottage, with Donal and Whitefoot keeping watch before the door. They'd no need of long talking. They all knew that by law, in case of desperate need, any Burgh might appeal direct to the King himself for justice against their own Sheriff. All that needed to be decided was who should take Drumfyvie's plea to the King's Grace—take it quickly, under cover of the dark, and risking Red Duncan's rage if he were caught! By rights, it should have been the Provost, but all were agreed that at such a time his place was in Drumfyvie.

Who then?

Old Effie said, "I will go. There's not one among ye has my right—for 'twas my Fergie they hanged up this day for the hungry crows."

But the others said 'twas work for a man, and failing the Provost, the best man to send was Master Gilliechrist, him being the parish priest. The King would surely listen to the likes of him!

So in the end, the Provost's own horse was brought—he being the best beast outside the Castle stables— and his hooves muffled in bits of old felt, so as to make no sound, and led down to the narrow footgate at the end of Fighting Cocks Lane, where Master Gilliechrist was already waiting. Everybody had a hand in thrusting him up into the saddle—he was not what ye might call a horseman—and he gave his helpers his thanks and blessing. And "Go home and pray, good folk," said he. "Pray as ye've never prayed before."

And then he was away into the autumn night.

It so happened that King David held court in Dunfermline that Michaelmas, and Master Gilliechrist, by the grace of God, and him knowing the road, reached the place by noon of the next day. Aye, and got his word with the King, speaking for all the burgesses of Drumfyvie. And by nightfall, on a fresh horse from the stables of Dunfermline Palace, he was on his way back. And with him young Sir Robert Maitland, at the head of a

company of men-at-arms. The night was warm for the time of year, but never a star shone, and there was a muttering of thunder away among the hills, that they heard with anxious ears, not wanting a storm just then, to slow them down.

Luck was with them at the first, for the storm broke far up in the high moors, and all night long, as they pushed on with desperate speed, they saw never a drop of rain. But when they came to the river ford, the storm in the hills had sent the water down in spate, and there was nothing they could do but wait for the swirling brown torrents to go down, or ride many miles upstream seeking the nearest bridge. Either would take time, and time was a thing they could ill spare. In the end they pushed upriver for the bridge.

But of all this, of course, the people of Drumfyvie—and of the Castle—knew nothing in the world until afterwards. The towns-folk knew that Master Gilliechrist and the Provost's horse were missing, and had a fair idea why, but they took care not to speak of it; and save for myself, no one in the Castle knew even that.

And then 'twas the second morning after Master Gilliechrist had gone, and the thunder that we'd heard overnight beginning to grumble again along the northern hills. And I mind, folk began to stand about in the street, even close under the Castle walls, looking for the priest and the help that he should bring with him. The help that surely he should have brought by now. I knew well enough the doubts and fears gathering in their hearts. Was the King maybe angry at their complaint? Was he going to uphold his Sheriff, against his Burgh? "The high head ones'll likely hold together," somebody said uneasily. And was he maybe holding Master Gilliechrist captive meanwhile?

Aye well, something of the same doubts were in myself, and troubling me sore.

"There's something brewing down there," said my master. "Well, I gave them fair warning as to what would happen if they made trouble." And he gave the orders to the Captain of his men-at-arms. And soon, above the nearing mutter of the thunder, both town and Castle heard the sound of hammering, and knew that another gallows was being raised—a gibbet big enough for the hanging of two men.

'Twas then that the Burgh left its waiting, and from all parts

of the town folks began to move in towards the Castle gates. Some
had their bows that they'd fetched from hiding places in the
thatch; others carried reaping hooks and skinning knives; and
the smith out in front of them with his great hammer in his hands.
Yet none of them seeming just sure what to do next. But I mind
the day was darkening and the thunder rolling closer, and watching from the high Hall window, it seemed to me that there was
something kin between the angry, frightened, waiting crowd, and
the storm that didn't break—but would break by and by . . .

Then Old Effie pushed out to the forefront of the crowd. I
saw her plain, in her old faded poppy-coloured cloak, and she
crying to the folks about her, "Are ye for letting two more of ye
hang alongside my Fergie?"

"Master Gilliechrist's not back yet," someone said.

"Ye cannot wait for Master Gilliechrist!" she skirled back.
"If we're for saving Andrew Brec and the Fleming, we'll need to
get them out ourselves!"

There was a confused murmuring from the crowd, uncertain
still, but beginning to take on an awful threatening note to it.
She was stirring them. Aye, she was that! There began to be
shouts of "Red Duncan!" and "Murderer".

"Shouting's no good," cried Effie. "Stones and arrows! Come
on now, I'll loose the first stone, for my Fergie hanging there!"

And she tore up a stone from the wayside rubble at her feet,
and flung it straight at the timber rampart. It caught one of the
men-at-arms full in the face, and he yelled for the pain of it.
The crowd roared back, and a few more stones came whistling
over the rampart. But the crowd down in the street couldn't see,
and Red Duncan on the roof of the gatehouse couldn't see, what
I could see from the highest window of the Keep—a band of
horsemen swinging in through the East Gate, drumming up the
street, and one in a black priest's gown riding beside the knight
at their head!

They couldn't see, and above the uproar that they were making
they couldn't hear the distant drum of hooves. I saw my master
turn his head and give an order to the archer beside him, pointing
to Old Effie in her scarlet cloak. 'Twas all like a kind of evil
dream, and there was naught I could do in this world but see
it happen, as the man nocked an arrow to the string, and bent

his bow and loosed, and Old Effie dropped in a crumpled heap at the blacksmith's feet. And him with his hammer still in one hand, and a stone in the other raised to throw.

But before ever he threw it, the horsemen were into the hinder part of the crowd, forcing their way through, and scattering the folks right and left as they came. And I knew their leader for Sir Robert Maitland, by the device on his shield—and Master Gilliechrist riding as grim as any weaponed knight beside him.

And at that moment, above the frightened and angry uproar of the crowd, above the drum of hooves and Sir Robert's shouted orders, the storm broke at last, with a booming crash of thunder to drown all else. And with the thunder, a strange thing happened, so strange I'd not have believed it if I hadn't seen it for myself.

Out of the very heart of the storm, as though maybe 'twas frightened by it, Red Duncan's lost goshawk came back. It darted out of the lightning-jagged sky, just as its master turned to hurry down the narrow gatehouse stair. Duncan failed to see it, and the hawk, missing the gloved fist that should have been held up for it, dived at his shoulder and clung there, its great wings clattering and beating about his head. Aye, the man missed his footing, and with a yell, crashed headlong down into the courtyard more than twenty feet below.

And as he fell, there was a second crash of thunder, almost a'top the first, and the heavens opened and the rain came hissing down. But by then I was out from the Hall and heading full tilt down the stairway into the outer bailey and across it toward the gate.

In the grey downpour at the foot of the gatehouse stair, the first Lord of Drumfyvie lay dead with his neck broken, the goshawk crouched on his body, glaring at the world out of mad marigold eyes.

I didn't check there, but as I passed him by, Old Effie's words were in my head as clear as though she'd but that moment spoken them. "The first Lord of Drumfyvie shall die an ugly death, slain by his familiar companion, with no woman to weep for him and never a son to wear his sword."

His men-at-arms were bearing him away as I hurried out through the now open gate. The crowd had already begun to melt away. Sir Robert stood there in the rain, looking down at Old

Effie, and her lying in her sodden red cloak, with Donal kneeling beside her—Whitefoot too, I mind, whimpering and pressed against his master's leg. Just as I got there, Master Gilliechrist was signing her with the cross. "Rest eternal give to her, O Lord, and let light perpetual shine upon her . . . Amen."

"She's dead," Donal said.

"Aye," the little priest said, "she's dead, Donal."

Sir Robert looked from the old emptied face to the laddie's bent over it. "She was your mother? Your grandmother?"

Donal looked up then and shook his head, wretchedly. "No. She was Daft Fergie's mother—him that Red Duncan hanged three days since. But she was awful kind to me and Whitefoot."

A few days after, when all things had been taken care of, and Drumfyvie was quiet again, Sir Robert was away back to Dunfermline, the Provost with him, and myself also—me that had seen all that passed and been Strathardle's steward—to make his report to the King. Well, he told the whole ugly story, the two of us standing by to bear him out in it. And the King listened, his eyes on each of our faces in turn. I reckon he was a man 'twould be hard to lie to.

"And so you found these two, Brec and the Fleming, in the guard-house with their hands already bound for their hanging," he said at last.

Sir Robert gave him back look for look. "Duncan the Red seems to have been a notably ungentle overlord."

"Even so we cannot encourage our burgesses to revolt against their Sheriff."

"There was but little trouble, my Lord King," said Sir Robert. "I'd not say they revolted, or anything like it. An old woman threw a stone and was shot down, on Duncan's orders, by one of his archers. Duncan's own death had nothing to do with the Drumfyvie folk at all."

The King didn't answer at once, but just sat looking at Sir Robert and pulling at the lobe of his left ear, which was a trick of his when he was thoughtful. "Maitland," he said at last, "you are very quick to defend these Drumfyvie folk. Almost 'tis as though you felt them to be already your own. Can it be that you have the ambition to be the Burgh's second Sheriff?"

Sir Robert smiled, and despite the careful courtesy of his

speech, I mind that it was no courtier's smile. "I have no ambition, my Lord King, but to serve you in whatever way you will have me. But I've a sympathy with the Drumfyvie folk. I think they have suffered much, these past two years, and it is in my mind that they deserve a better Sheriff than Strathardle."

"And it is in your mind that you'd make a better Sheriff than Strathardle?"

"Aye," said Sir Robert, and looked him straight in the eye. "It is in my mind that I would."

I'd not, myself, be sure of how it all came about. But certain sure it was, that a few weeks later, here in the Hall of his own Castle, Sir Robert Maitland, second Sheriff of Drumfyvie, swore his allegiance to the King. All the Castle folk, myself among them, had crowded in to see and hear, and just within the doorway stood Donal, with Whitefoot on the end of a bit of rope. The laddie was as proud as the new Baron himself. Now, he had a place of his own in the world—the Castle Kennels, for he was the new Sheriff's new dogboy. And like enough, he was taking much the same kind of oath to Sir Robert within himself, as Sir Robert was taking to the King.

And me? Ah well, Sir Robert brought his own steward with him, of course. And to tell you the truth, I was beginning to feel myself a wee thing getting on in years. So I just settled myself in with Jock behind the saddler's shop. I look after the accounts and that, and we get on together fine, Jock and me.

Midsummer Fair
A.D. 1160 3

There now—that's the shutters up and barred.

Midsummer Fair safe over for another year, and but three heads broken in all the town, as I hear! Times are not what they were!

My, but I'm weary! 'Tis me feet, ye'll understand. I've scarce been off them these past three days.

Ah well, 'tis done with now, so just sit down at the fireside, Wattie, and take a wee rest to yourself. Who's Wattie, did you say? Why, me, of course. Me that's been potboy at The Fighting Cocks tavern these twenty years and more.

With three yearly fairs in the Burgh—Blackthorn Fair, St. Ninian's in the autumn for the Burgh's patron saint, and Midsummer Fair—that makes more Fair Days than I care to count, and not many of them as peaceable as this. But there's one Midsummer Fair I mind above all the rest—'way back when I was little more than a laddie.

It began just in the usual way, with the wine and ale tasters coming round the day before, to make sure the drink was proper strength and the pewter pots not dinted to give short measure. I'd like fine to be an ale taster myself! And then first thing next morning, with the Town Drummer beating away for dear life before and after, the Provost proclaimed the Fair from the steps of the Market Cross: "Hear ye! Hear ye! I now proclaim the conditions of the Midsummer Fair. All shops within the Burgh shall be closed, and no merchant shall sell or show for sale any goods within the town, excepting within the bounds of the Fair. All merchants shall give proper value of wool, cloth, ironware, leather and whatsoever other goods shall be bought and sold within the bounds of the Fair ..."

Drumfyvie Midsummer Fair lasts three days, ye'll understand, and 'tis a wool fair above all else, the country round about being grand for sheep. And the open space around the tolbooth and the Market Cross is all taken up by the dealers in raw wool,

and after them the weavers and cloth merchants. But the lanes of booths where the smiths and leather workers and bonnet makers carry on their trades reach way up and down the one long street from Castle Port at one end of the town to East Port at the other, and into the wynds and side alleys; and there's stalls with bright crocks, and ribbons, and gingerbread, and linnets singing their hearts out in wee wicker cages. And everywhere the merchants go, crying their wares and haggling over prices, and pedlars call their sweetmeats and cheap-jack jewellery. And there's tumblers in their spangled hose; and most years there'll be a dancing bear, shambling on his hind legs, poor beastie, to the tune his master pipes for him. And the sights and the smells and the noise fair set your head spinning.

'Tis usual for the Sheriff to come down from the Castle on the first day—unofficial, as ye might say—to take a look around the booths and make first choice among the goods that's for sale. Sir Robert Maitland was Sheriff in those days—only the second we'd had, for we were a young Burgh then.

Aye well, down he came, and his youngest son, Richard, with him and his daughter, Margaret, that was a mite older than the laddie—thirteen to his twelve, maybe.

By that age, young Richard should have been off serving as a page in some other household, that being the outlandish custom of the great folk. But as I heard the story, his mother was awful sick at his birth, and ailed from that time on, and begged so hard to keep him when the time came for him to go as a page— he coming so long after all his brothers—that Sir Robert let her have her way. And by the time she died, maybe he'd got over-used to having the bairn in his own household. Howsoever, there he still was, till the time came for him to go for a squire . . .

Well now, down Fighting Cocks Lane that passes our tavern, the dealers in furs and fine leather goods had their stalls, as in-deed they still do. And I'd just gone out with a pot of ale that one of them had called for to seal a bargain, when into the lane comes Sir Robert and the two young ones, with the lassie's old nurse huffing along behind. He stopped right before our door, where a merchant from Norway, a yellow-haired, blue-eyed giant called Thorkel Thorkelsson, had set up his trestle tables and spread his wares. Skins, for the most part, wee soft skins for

stitching into a hood or maybe to line a pair of gloves, and big rough fox pelts, not like any fox I'd seen in these parts. He'd a few trinkets, brooches and the like made from amber or a kind of ivory—walrus ivory he called it—but mostly 'twas just the skins; and above all others one great bearskin—och, twice the size of any I'd seen before, long and shaggy, and a queer kind of yellow-white colour, like snow on a trackway where folks and animals pass to and fro. Ye could tell 'twas the finest of all his wares, and the pride of his heart, by the way he stroked and spread it, to make sure 'twas always showing at its best.

Aye, there was a kind of magic about that skin, so there was! And I wasn't the only one to feel it—the lassie Margaret had her eyes on it the instant her father halted at Thorkel's stall. Sir Robert himself paid no heed to the bear's skin, but chose out a piece of tawny red fur and held it up to the light.

"This fox pelt, master merchant, have you three more like it? Well-matching, such as would serve for the shoulders of a cloak?"

Thorkel looked well at the skin. "Surely, my Lord, we should find such a match. Boy, bring forward the pile of fox pelts yonder, That is right—lay them here before the Sheriff. So—now, if my Lord will look through these . . ."

But before the Sheriff could lay a hand on the pelts, there was the lassie Margaret tugging at his sleeve. "Father! Father, look! Do look!"

"Whatever it is," said Sir Robert, not paying much heed at that stage, "I will look presently. Just now I am trying to find four matching foxskins . . ."

But she was too full of longing to be set aside like that, and she tried again. "My Lord Father—Sir! The beautiful white skin! *Now*, not presently—will you not look at it? Oh Father, *please*!"

Thorkel answered her: "Ah, little mistress, you have eyes in your head. You pick out the most fine and beautiful thing I have for sale. It is the skin of a great snow bear, from a land far to the north, where for half the year the sun never rises and for half the year never sets. And all the winter long, strange lights like—like streaming banners of cold fire play across the sky, and make patterns not of this world!"

The lad Richard joined in. "A *bear*! But it's more than twice as big as the one we saw dancing by the tolbooth yonder!"

Sir Robert finished his seeking through the fox pelts, and turned to Thorkel Thorkelsson. "These four will do well enough, master merchant. How much do you ask for them?"

But before Thorkel could answer, the lassie was at it again, and she scarcely able to get the words out, for the eagerness that was in her. "Father—you'll mind 'tis my birthday next week? And you did promise—Father you *did* promise I should choose a gift at the Fair! Anything I pleased, you said!"

Sir Robert looked round at her at last, quirking up his eyebrows. "And you have found something that pleases you? But may I not finish my business first, sweeting?"

"Yes, Father," says she, quenched for the moment, then bursting out again. "Oh, but I have! The white bearskin—the beautiful snow bear's skin. Look, Father—may I have that? Oh may I? It is in my heart that I shall never see anything else I want so much, in all my life!"

"I devoutly hope you will, one day," said Sir Robert, half smiling, and he looked from the lassie to the great yellow-white skin and back again. And I could see he didn't rightly understand the way she felt. I did, but that was not much help to anybody. "Well now," said he, speaking reasonable like, "such a skin would be the worth of at least five birthdays. Can you not think again, child?"

But Mistress Margaret was not in the mood for reason. "No, Father, this is the only gift I want. I'll not ask for another gift until I have had five more birthdays, if only you will give me this! Oh can you not *see* how beautiful it is?"

At that, the old nurse thought fit to take a hand. "Whisht now, my lamb," said she, "ye can't be wanting the like of that great hairy thing. Sir Robert, 'tis not fit for a girl bairn, and me trying to bring her up a lady! Ye might as well buy her a warhorse and a pair of breeks and be done with it!"

Sir Robert nodded. "Aye, Old Nurse, you are in the right of it. Take her and find her something more fitting for a birthday gift. Something bonnie. There are booths in plenty to choose from, surely." And he turned back to Thorkel Thorkelsson and the price of the fox pelts.

The nurse took firm hold of Mistress Margaret by the hand, and turned her to the next stall.

"See now, here's a pair of green leather shoes," said she. "Look at them, my lamb—all sewn with fine gold thread . . . What would you do with yon great shaggy pelt, now?"

The lassie stood her ground and said she, "I do not want the shoes, Nurse dear. And what would I do with the white bearskin? I'll tell you— I'd be putting it on my bed. And in the cold nights of winter I'd be rolling myself up in it, and I'd be looking at the stars through the little high window, and I'd be as warm as if 'twere my own fur growing on me—and I'd dream!—strange, wonderful dreams, with magic in them! That's what I'd do!"

"The Lord save us!" cried the nurse, fair astounded. "The bairn's bewitched, surely! And in front of these good folk too! Do you want all Drumfyvie to think you're out of your wits? Come away with ye, back to the Castle now!"

I never saw just how it ended, for my master was bellowing for me, and I had to scuttle back into The Fighting Cocks, and when next I looked out of the door, Sir Robert and the two young ones and the nurse were all gone; and the great snow bear's skin still lying there. So the lassie hadn't got her way, and I mind my heart was sore for her, till in the hurry-scurry of the day, I forgot all about it.

So the first Fair Day passed, and the second, and by nightfall, with the day's business over, The Fighting Cocks, like every other tavern in Drumfyvie—and there was a good few, by that time— was brim full and running over into the street. Folks were sitting on the bench before the door, and sprawled all over the roadway, propped against the booths and each other. And my master and me the both of us had our hands full, keeping the ale jacks from running dry. Thorkel Thorkelsson was there inside the tavern, and Tam with the dancing bear, the bear enjoying his sup of ale along with the rest. And in the sudden flare of a torch, I caught a glimpse of young Richard Maitland that should have been asleep up at the Castle long since, and him in his oldest clothes and the dirtiest face ever I saw on a laddie. I wasn't altogether surprised to see him—there's ways out of most castles, for them that knows them and has the head for heights—and I'd seen his face while Mistress Margaret was trying for the snow bear's skin, and

40

reckoned there was a kind of magic on him, too; though with him it wasn't the skin, but Thorkel Thorkelsson himself, and the tales he might have to tell. Anyhow there he was, half-hidden among the rushes at Thorkel's feet, listening like one of the shepherds on the first Christmas Eve, to the tale that the Northman was telling him—and anybody else who cared to listen above the uproar, for he'd the fine carrying voice, so he had.

"And there are, you must know, young Master, in my land, ghost bears that can be killed only with spears that have certain magical runes carved on their blades. Such ghost bears I have myself hunted, together with the so-small, slit-eyed people who live in those parts. Ah yes, all that I tell you is true! Three times as tall as a man, these ghost bears are standing, and all other spears pass through them as through a cloud, leaving no mark behind. Yes, and other strange creatures I have hunted and fought with in my land—"

At first the folks around him listened open-mouthed, then as the tales grew wilder and wilder, one or two laughed, quiet-like among themselves. Thorkel glanced at them, and far back in his eyes there were bright sparks of anger. Not many folk had bought his furs that day, and he'd drunk a deal of ale, and what with the one thing and the other, he was ready to turn quarrelsome.

Suddenly he broke off in his story, and shouted, "My land is a better land than this land, and it breeds better men! Much better!"

Some folks were still inclined to laugh, but others took it amiss, and there was an angry muttering. Drumfyvie lads don't like to be told there's better men than theirselves, and in some outlandish place they've never heard of. I could see Jamie the Town Herd, and Willie the Smith, and Duncan the Saddler away in the corner, their faces stiffening, and them just about to start trouble, like a threesome of barnyard roosters with their hackles rising. Thorkel saw them too, and started up his tale again—not shouting, now but pitching his voice good and loud—"When the fighting fury comes upon a man of my people, sometimes I have shut him in a place to keep him quiet a little. But he—he does not need to batter down the door; he walks out through the nearest wall! And I, Thorkel, have fought also with the Troll women who ride the roof ridges in the black of the winter nights! Once, one such came to

my house. I climbed up to her—she was big as a snow bear, but black and squat—her wild hair streamed in the shouting wind. She had the strength of ten men, but still I fought with her—so —and so—I seized her by the hair and we struggled to and fro, to and fro along the iced ridges of the roof—"

He was afoot by now, and acting out his battle, staggering this way and that as he wrestled with empty air.

"Here! Keep your fists to yourself!" roared Sandy the Weaver.

One of the prentice lads doubled up with laughter. "My Grannie used to fright me with better tales than that! You've no more fought a Troll woman than Tam's bear has! That's for sure!"

"My bear dances better, too," observed Tam, and so saying, he put his wee pipe to his lips and began to play. The poor beast grunted, angry like. Maybe he'd had enough dancing for one day, and maybe a wee thing too much ale—but for all that, he reared himself up on his hind legs and began to shamble about to the pipe tune. All the folks began laughing, then—and Thorkel let out a great roar of rage.

"You make a mock of me! Me—Thorkel Thorkelsson!"

"Stand clear!" cried Jamie the Herd, laughing fit to burst apart. "Stand clear! Master Thorkelsson's going to walk through the wall for us!"

Thorkel let out a bellow fit to bring the roof about our ears, and snatched a torch from the wall and whirled it flaring round his head. Tam dropped his pipe and cried out, "Would ye now! Setting the place alight, and all for a parcel of senseless tales, you madman!"

But 'twas young Richard saw first what was going to happen, and he shouted, "Thorkel! No! Leave the poor beast be!"

I doubt if Thorkel even heard him. Fair demented with rage, he was, and before there was a thing anyone could do, he pushed the torch straight into the bear's face! Man! 'Twas all hell let loose! What with the screams of the bear, poor creature, and the folks shouting, some trying to keep the bear off Thorkel and some trying to keep Thorkel off the bear, and some going for Thorkel themselves, and a few fighting each other by way of a change, the thing had the makings of as bonnie a riot as ever I saw!

And then, just as it was bursting into full flower, as ye might say, who should come in at the door but the Sheriff's Margaret with a plaid flung round her, and she shouting through all the din: "Richard! *Richard!*"

The laddie looked round, "What—why—*Margaret*! What in the name of Heaven are you doing here?"

"Seeking you! *And* I knew this is where I'd find you! Richard, come away—quick now! Father's men-at-arms are on their way, and if they catch you—"

Fine I knew what that would mean! Trouble for us all for breaking the Peace of the Fair; trouble for my master—and me too, as like as not—for having a riot in The Fighting Cocks; and as for Richard Maitland . . .

"Round the back, both of you," said I. "Quick now!" And I grabbed the pair of them and hauled them round the back of the tavern and out into the yard. And if you'll believe me, what did they do, once outside, but turn on each other like a pair of young fighting cocks themselves!

"Why couldn't you mind your own business?" Richard shouted. "It was just getting to be good sport in there!"

"Good sport, is it?" flared his sister. "And what kind of sport would it have been if Father's men had found you in there, all mixed up in it? You'd be thrashed till you could neither sit nor lie!"

"Oh *you*! You're always following me and prying after me, and—and being a year *older* than me—"

"I'm not, then! Prying after you, I mean! Even though I *do* know the way you get out of the Castle and never take me with you! You're the mean one, Richie Maitland, so you are!"

"Just because I'm not wanting a lassie always on my heels—"

But I'd had enough of both of them; and there was work waiting for me back inside the tavern. So I told him roundly, "She's risked a whipping herself, following on your heels this night, my young Lord, and you owe her something for that. But I dare say it can wait, and so can your quarrelling. Now, out with you both —see, through the kale plot." And I bundled them both through the hedge—not a moment too soon, either, for the men-at-arms were just pushing in at the tavern door.

Inside, when I got back, there was fine hot work going on;

aye, and plenty of broken heads before all was done. It took a dozen men to quench Thorkel Thorkelsson, never mind the rest. But 'twas done at last, and the man hauled off to the lock up and The Fighting Cocks cleared for the night. Things seemed a bit flat, after that, I mind . . .

Well, so next morning, Thorkel was brought up before the Bailies, and them sitting as the "Court of Dusty Feet", which is the special court for trying Fair cases, and got sentenced to eight hours in the stocks for being drunk and bloodthirsty and breaking the Peace of the Fair. I went along to take a look, as soon as I could get a few moments to myself. And there he sat, with his legs out in front of him, and the leg-board clamped down on his ankles, looking uncommon sorry for himself! Of course, you'll understand, the stocks are set just before the tolbooth, and so right in the midst of the Fair, and a good crowd had gathered, with rotten eggs and cabbage stalks and suchlike. A man in the stocks always makes for cheerful rubbish-throwing. But before the fun had got well started, who should come strolling along, calm as you please, but young Richard Maitland, wearing a clean tunic, and never a wrinkle in his hose, and looking as if he'd spent all night where he should have spent it.

He sat himself down on the bench close alongside Thorkel and began chatting to him in a voice loud enough for all to hear.

"Good day to you, Thorkel Thorkelsson. Plenty of room for two—I'll bear you company for a while, if you're not objecting," and he eyed the crowd, daring them to throw another cabbage stalk. But of course nobody did. 'Tis one thing to throw garbage at an evildoer in the stocks, that's just honest fun; quite another to plaster the Sheriff's son with rotten egg! Even the jeering died away. Still, the crowd didn't melt away—it grew bigger, in the way crowds have when they can, as you might say, "smell" something going to happen.

And meanwhile, Thorkel and young Richard sat chatting together in the stocks like a pair of boon companions.

"Ah yes, you are the good friend," said Thorkel, "the good friend when I have need of one, for it is I that am cast down this day! It is not the cabbage stalks that break my heart; no, it is that while I sit here, I lose the last day of the Fair, and there is much, so much, that I have still to sell lying useless in my bales.

My boy, he can only fetch and carry—he will be no good at the selling, without me to tell him everything. There is winter in my heart, and it is the poor man I shall be!"

"That's bad," agreed young Richard, wagging his head like a grandfather. "That's very bad . . . But—now wait you a moment, I'm thinking—" Suddenly he was fair hugging himself. "Yes! What a ploy it will be! Oh *what* a ploy!"

I pushed a mite nearer, so as not to miss anything, Master Richard being a young limb of Satan if ever I saw one.

"Thorkel Thorkelsson," said he, "you're a law-breaker and a head-breaker, and see where it's got you! But so far as I know there's no law says a man cannot carry on his business while sitting in the stocks! Wattie—Wattie Potboy, have you ever heard of such a law?"

"I have not, then," said I, loud and clear.

"And certain it is that no one can say we're not within the bounds of the Fair, us sitting right in front of the tolbooth." He was up off the bench. "Wattie, get a few fine lads together! We're off to The Fighting Cocks!"

And off we went, me rounding up a few friends in the bye-going. There was Davey the Fletcher's son, and Alan from the Mill, and a couple of prentice lads that had the day free, all of us heading through the crowds, for Fighting Cocks Lane. By the time we got to the tavern door I was in mortal fear lest my master should see me, and set me to rubbing up the ale jacks or some such. But in the crowd we got safe through to where Thorkel's bales were stacked against the wall.

His boy was sitting on them, looking fair bewildered, and he didn't properly seem to understand what we would be at, at first. But we pulled him to his feet and shook a bit of sense into him; and we heaved up the bales; and in the end he came along with us, hanging on to the tail of the great snow bear's skin that I carried myself.

And young Richard had the right of it. It was a great ploy, sure enough, and many's the good laugh I've had over the years, just remembering it. At first, when we got back to the tolbooth, the folks just stood round gawping. Then Richard got on to the bench and started to shout Thorkel's wares, as though he'd been a merchant or a showman all his days.

"Furs from the far north, where the sun never sets for half the year nor rises for the other half! Furs fit for the King himself in his grand Castle of Edinburgh! Come up, good folks, and take a look! Come closer, man—and you, good wife! You'll get no better furs than these anywhere, I promise you!"

And on he went. I suppose it tickled folks' fancy, the Sheriff's son turning merchant that way. At all events, they began to gather closer, and soon we were doing a fine trade. At first, 'twas just the cheaper bits and pieces that went; not the furs at all, just bone combs and wee brooches and the like. But after a while some of the richer folk stopped in passing, to listen and have a bit of a laugh to themselves, and next thing, they were turning over the skins, and some began to buy. One merchant, all clad in fine green cloth, with a great silver buckle to the belt that held up his paunch, called out, "Here, Master Thorkelsson, how much for these three beaverskins? Or do I ask your crier here?"

So Thorkel set himself to deal with the matter, and sold the skins for a good price. But before he'd finished with that piece of business, up stepped the wife of one of the bailies, asking the price of a brindled fox pelt. So Master Richard turned salesman as gay as you please. "Eight silver pence the pelt, fair mistress. 'Tis very rare to find them with hair as long as this one, very rare indeed—a bargain, Lady, at so low a price."

So it went on till noon. And then all at once there was a kind of hurried shifting and falling back in the crowd. And through the clearing they made came the Sheriff himself, and the Fairground officials following after!

He looked at Richard, while everyone waited to see what would happen; and Richard looked back; and neither of them batted an eyelid. And Thorkel Thorkelsson just went on sitting in the stocks, there being not much else that he could do, with a slow, friendly smile spreading over his face. "The fox pelts pleased my Lord Sheriff? Yes? He comes, maybe, to buy other skins?"

Sir Robert said gravely, "The fox pelts please me well, Master Merchant, but I come rather to see for myself the truth of a strange tale I was hearing, concerning your choice of a new trading pitch."

"Ah yes!" Thorkel beamed at him. "Allow me that I explain. My present position, it has been somewhat forced upon me. It

46

is also, as you will see, the reason that I cannot rise to greet your Lordship. I am indeed so sorry, for I am a courteous man."

Richard cut across his blethering. "Father, my Lord Sheriff, there's no law against a man carrying on his business while sitting in the stocks."

"You are a lawyer as well as a merchant?" enquired the Sheriff. But I saw his lip twitch.

One of the officials said quickly, "He's in the right of it, my Lord. Very awkward it is, my Lord, but 'tis true there's no law that even mentions such a thing."

"I am not surprised," said the Sheriff. "I imagine nobody has thought of such a possibility in times past, and I can guess who thought of it now."

Richard swallowed hard. "Well—it's the last day of the Fair, you see, Sir, and Thorkel Thorkelsson had a deal of skins left to sell— He had a bad day's trading yesterday. And there's no denying this *is* a good position. Fine and central and—Father, it seemed a sore waste not to use it!"

"I am sure it did," said the Sheriff.

"And indeed, we've done so well here, that if you *were* to want any more skins, it's little enough we'd have left to show you. Oh, except—Wattie, bring the snow bear's skin."

"You'd never dare!" I whispered.

"Would I not?" he whispered back. "It's you that said I owed Margaret something!"

"Not that accursed skin again, Richard?" said the Sheriff, sounding like a man sore tried. "Not *again*?"

But the laddie wasn't lacking in courage, nor in cool impudence, though to be sure his voice did shake a little. "There was nothing else in all the Fair that Margaret wanted, and it wouldn't come so expensive over five birthdays, Sir. And—" There was a sudden kind of gleam in his face. "Would it not be a fine thing for old Nurse, if someone were to do a thing she'd told them not to do—just once?"

The Sheriff looked at Richard, and Richard looked back, and I'll swear the same gleam was in the eye of both of them. Then Sir Robert said slowly, "You may be right. Boy, you may indeed be right."

He reached out, and brushed the long harsh fur this way and

47

that. "So be it, then, Margaret shall have her heart's desire, and maybe we will not make it serve for five birthdays . . . And now, your merchant days are done. Away with you, back to the Castle, and wait for me there. You and I will have a small reckoning when I have finished my business with our friend here in the stocks."

But as young Richard departed, maybe swaggering just a wee bit, up the street, and the Sheriff turned to his bargaining with Thorkel Thorkelsson, 'twas in my mind that the reckoning would be small indeed.

Aye, that's one Midsummer Fair I'll not be forgetting, if I live to be potboy at The Fighting Cocks another twenty years!

The Man Who Liked a Peaceful Life
A.D. 1314

There was a war going on when I was a laddie. Our King Robert —him that was surnamed The Bruce—was fighting it out with Edward the Second of England. Edward was wanting to add Scotland to his own kingdom, but the Scots wouldn't have any such thing. Independent, that's the Scots for you, and we've always been ready for a fight to keep that way.

Well, so I've a tale to tell about those fighting days, though I've never been what you might call the fighting kind. Jamie, the town herd of Drumfyvie, that's me. Herding's a peaceful life, taking it all in all, and suits me just fine, for I'm a man that likes a peaceful life. I'm not saying it hasn't its drawbacks—there's times it's cold and times it's wet—but there's space to sit and think, and look about you and listen to the whaups crying.

Not that I had much time for such things in the days I'm telling you of. Old Rob was the town herd then, and I was but the herd laddie, close on twelve years old when I went to work for him; and he kept me hard at it, seeing that the beasts didn't stray—for any that did were like to end up as an Englishman's dinner.

King Robert was not so long back from his months of hiding in the heather, and him with just a small band of friends and followers—enough for a few hit-and-run raids against the English. But Scotland was full of English men-at-arms stravaigling up and down the countryside, and just about all our Scottish castles, Drumfyvie among them, were still full of English soldiers, and all of them cattle thieves to a man! They took what they wanted, and there was nought that we could do to stop them. But at the least, they didn't take more than they needed, for the good and simple reason that, anyway since King Robert was back from the heather, they had no knowing when their next supply train would be ambushed, nor how long they might be needing our cattle to last them. So we bore with their thieving, there being no help for it; and we kept the herd safe as best we could from raiders.

Every morning, Rob and I'd be up at first light, with Bobtail and Jaunty, the dogs, collecting the cattle that folks drove out to us as we went down the High Street. Most of the townsfolk kept, as they still do, a cow or so in the byres at the back of their houses; and 'tis the herd's job to collect them together, take care of them all day long on the common grazing land beyond the East Port, and drive them home at cow-stalling time. It sounds easy enough, but there was always the chance of raiders. And more than once, in those days, we got the cattle back within the Port with the English close on our heels. And, of course, there's always the chance of a beast straying. When that happened Rob and the dogs and me would be out seeking her, after the rest were safely stalled, all night, maybe, till she was found. Some creatures seem to have the gift for straying—there was Spottie, I mind. A nice wee cow she was, but if you took your eyes off her for a moment, there she'd be, clean gone! Even the dogs couldn't keep track of that one. There was times I thought she had fairy blood in her.

Aye well, one February evening at cow-stalling time, Spottie wasn't to be seen, neither hide nor hair of her. So we drove in the rest of the herd, and then went back to look for the beastie.

"Take you the river woods, and Jaunty with you," said Rob. "Me and Bobtail, we'll head up along the ridge."

It wasn't the pleasantest of nights to be out after a stray cow. Not awful cold for the time of year, but with a thin mizzle rain, and a mean blustery wind that blew straight in your face whichever way you turned. I mind thinking it might turn to sleet before dawn, and thinking why couldn't the daft beast be glad to settle in her warm byre on such a night? If it had been any cow but Spottie, I swear I'd have found what shelter I could along the woodshore, and pulled my plaid over my head and slept the night out that way. But I'd a liking for the cow, and a liking for Nick Fletcher, her master. And come to think of it, I'd best tell you about Nick Fletcher now, for he comes into my tale later on, and I shan't have so much space to talk about him then.

In his young days, Nick was one of the Sheriff's men-at-arms up at the Castle. That was before the trouble with the English, when we still had our own rightful Scots garrison up there. But when the English came along and the Scots were driven out, Nick

got a spear through his knee in the fighting. His leg mended well enough, but he had a stiff knee to the end of his days. The town's arrowsmith hid and sheltered him at the time, and later he wed with the smith's lassie, and took over the business when the old man died. Made a good job of it, too. I reckon he was always as interested in the fashioning of weapons as he was in the using of them. Sometimes he'd tell me tales of the Castle in Sir Rolf Maitland's time, him that was rotting in an English gaol since the Castle fell. And the last St. Ninian's Day he'd given me a whole penny to myself, for doing well with the quarter-staff against lads that were bigger ar d older than me. So I kept on looking for his lost cow; and it wasn't till near dawn that we found her, Jaunty and me, and I slipped the halter round her silly neck, and we turned back towards the town.

We'd got almost to the edge of the Burgh lands, when Jaunty turned fidgety and started scratching in the long grass under a hawthorn bush. I went to see what she was after, and she began whimpering, and there was a kind of stirring and scrabbling in the grass tangle, and a hand came up and grabbed at my wrist! I dropped Spottie's halter and gave my mind to shaking it off, seeing I'd no knowing who's it was! "Let go of me!" I shouted, and I wasn't far from panic, but whoever it was, hung on—and began struggling to his knees among the hawthorn branches.

He said, kind of thick and blurred, "Why you're nought but a laddie . . . But if I let you go, you'll like as not run off and bring the hunt on my trail."

I stopped struggling, and I looked at him well in the grey dawn light. He was young, and he was someone I'd never seen before, and there was the darkness of dried blood clotted in his hair and on his forehead.

"Are you one of King Robert's men?" I asked him.

He gave the kind of ghost of a laugh. "I'll have the guts out of the first grown man who doubts it!"

I was a wee thing put out, that he should not consider me a grown man, for I was over fourteen by then, though 'twas an odd time to be bothering about such a thing. "I'm not doubting you," I said, "and you can trust me, even if I *am* nought but a laddie."

"Aye, I think I can," he said, and loosed his hold on my wrist.

I rubbed it, for he'd gripped me sore. "You ran into the English then?"

"Three of us. In the scrimmage I got parted from the others, and dear knows what's become of them. I'm thinking I've come a good way since then, but I'm none too clear in my head . . . Where would I be now?"

"On the edge of Drumfyvie Burgh lands," I told him.

"The Devil take it! And Drumfyvie still in English hands! The sooner I'm away from here the better!—Give me a hand up—"

But his legs buckled under him and he fell back with a groan. "I'm as weak as a half-drowned kitten!"

"When did you last eat?" said I.

"Two days back, I think, maybe three . . . Curse! My head's bleeding again . . ."

I thought a moment, what was best to be done. "Bide here. Bide while I take home the wee cow, and I'll bring you some food, and a rag to bind that gash. Don't let anyone see you before I get back."

So I caught Spottie again—mercifully she had only wandered a few yards, with her halter trailing—Jaunty had seen to that—and again we set off back towards the town. I tethered her where Rob would surely find her when he came that way, which would be any time now, and left Jaunty to guard her. Then I headed for the end of Fighting Cocks Lane.

Even in wartime, the folks down that way never see properly to their own stretch of the town fencing, so there's always a few weak places in it. I soon found one, and got myself through, and headed across the town to Rob's house, where I lodged with him and his goodwife.

Folks were scarce beginning to stir as yet, but the goodwife heard me and called out from the back room. I called back that we'd found Spottie, and I was to fetch a piece of bannock for Rob's breakfast, for 'twas too close on herding time for him to get home.

I got the whole crockful of oatcake, and a knuckle of braxy ham. Then I found a wee broken crock, and scooped up some of the stuff Rob put on the cows' backs if they got sore. And when I'd all I needed, I bundled the lot in my plaid, together

with my spare shirt, which was all I could think of for bandage linen. Then I set off as though the Devil himself were after me, back the way I'd come.

'Twas almost daylight when I got back to my young callant under his hawthorn bush. And I crawled into the long grass beside him. "Here," said I. "Oatcake and ham, enough to last you through a couple of days—three, if you go canny with it." And while he ate, I got busy on his broken head, with the cattle salve, and strips torn from my spare shirt.

The food seemed to put fresh life into him, and after a while he managed to get to his feet—not too steadily. "I'll need to be on my way," he said. "But I'll not forget this morning, and I'm not ungrateful."

"You'll not get far on your own, that's for sure," said I, watching him swaying about. "You're as doddery as an hour-old calf."

"Needs must—" said he.

And then I heard my own voice—not sounding quite like mine, saying, as it seemed, of its own accord, "I'm coming with you."

He looked at me as though he'd not set eyes on me till that moment. "Coming with me? You don't even know which way I'm heading."

"It makes no odds," said I, "I'm coming with you. Wherever it is, you'll not get there else."

He went on looking at me, in a silence I thought he'd never break—and with the full daylight come, it was time we were away! Then he said, sudden, as though making up his mind, "I'm away down to the Borders, to my kinsman, Sir James Douglas."

That fair knocked the breath out of me, for Sir James Douglas was the greatest of the King's Captains, his right-hand man, you might say. "The Black Douglas?" I stuttered. "The *Black* Douglas? You're *his* kinsman?"

"A distant one. Men call me Johnnie Douglas. What do they call you?"

"Jamie," I said. "Just Jamie."

He gave a weak sort of crack of laughter. "So—you have his Christian name and I his surname. 'Tis a sign from Heaven that we should go after him together." And then he checked, "But I

53

was forgetting. What will your father say, young Jamie?"

"I've no father," I told him. We were on the move, down towards the river and the way south, by that time. "Only a master, him that's the town herd. He'll give me a good skelping when I get back, but 'twill be worth it."

"*If* we get back," Johnnie said. 'It's no bairn's play we're heading for—you understand that?"

"Aye," I said, and kept on walking. I knew we might well be going to be killed, either or both of us, before all was done; but I knew also—and I still don't know why—that Johnnie Douglas's way was my way. Him and his laughter and his broken head and the long knight's sword at his side.

We went down to the Border Country, Roxburgh way, and we were a week and more on the road, what with having to keep clear of the English, and Johnnie being a slow traveller the first few days. 'Twas cold going, with a north wind at our backs and a flurry of rain from time to time, but we got no snow. And after the oatcakes and the ham gave out, we left a trail of robbed hens' nests and the like, all the way to the Borders. And on the evening before the start of Lent, we came up with the Douglas and his men, lying-up in some rough wooded country a couple of miles outside the town of Roxburgh.

There were sentries posted, but they knew Johnnie fine—Sir John, they called him—and they passed us through. And there we were at last, standing before a tall, very dark man with a mouth like a wolf-trap and a pair of blue eyes like a bonnie lassie's. He spoke quick and soft—he was famous for that soft voice, and the wee lisp that he had—"Johnnie! Man, it's good to see you! But you've run into trouble by the looks of it—and where are the other two?"

"We ran into trouble, aye," said Johnnie. "And we got separated. If the others are not here before this, I'm thinking they must be dead."

The Black Douglas said, "God rest their souls," and he crossed himself. Then he looked from Johnnie to me and back again. "And who's this you bring with you?"

"Jamie that works for the Drumfyvie town herd, and stood my good friend when I needed one."

"Good man, Jamie," said the Black Douglas. "And welcome

to you—another dirk hand is worth the having; and you're just in time, the pair of you."

Johnnie's head went up with a wee jerk, "It's tonight? Shrovetide?"

"What better night, Johnnie?" I mind the Douglas had a bit of a gleam in his eye. "The English garrison will be making merry before the Lenten Fast sets in—too much eating and drinking to keep a proper look-out. And there's a mist coming up from the Tweed, for good measure."

So, later that night, with a square meal in my belly, wearing an old leather jerkin much too big for me, and with a borrowed dirk in my belt, *me* that was Drumfyvie's herd laddie, I went in with the Black Douglas and his men, to storm Roxburgh Castle.

And never before did men go into a fight the way we did, that Fastern Eve; and but once since, to my knowledge . . .

Every one of us had a big dark cloak, and some of the lads looked a wee thing overfed, as well they might, seeing they had long rope ladders bound round them under those same cloaks. We'd a dozen or so black cattle with us, too, and as the beasts moved across the open grazing land below the Castle, so did we, aye, on all fours! And what with the dark and the river mist, a sentry taking a chance look down from the Castle walls would never have seen the difference between man and beast.

Since I was well used to the herding, I helped the farmer who owned them to keep them drifting in the right direction, and as we drew nearer, my, but Roxburgh Castle looked an awful size, looming out of the mist, mountain high, and black as sin against the dark of the night!

And then at last we were close beneath the walls! And one of the bullocks chose that moment to let forth a wee bit bellow! Two sentries leaned out over the ramparts and laughed, and I mind their laughter sound uncomfortably close and loud in the stillness of the night.

"Someone's keeping his Shrove feast so well he's forgot to fold his cattle," said one.

And the other, "Aye, and likely he'll spend his Ash Wednesday rounding them up again—that's if the Douglas hasn't got them by dawn!"

And away went the pair of them in opposite directions, still laughing.

Down below among us, there was never a word spoken. We'd had our orders before we started, and every man knew what he had to do. There was just a kind of shifting in the shadows, as the men with the rope ladders unwound them. I'd had a good look at one of those ladders earlier on, and they had grappling hooks on one end, and a kind of socket, so you could lift them up on the point of a lance and hook them over the coping-stones of the Castle walls . . .

Just the faintest rasping sound they made as they were fixed in place, and that was all. Sim Ledehouse, him that had made them, was the first up, with the Douglas hard at his heels. I was none so far behind Johnnie on the next ladder. We dealt with the first sentries we met, quick and quiet, before they could let out a cheep; and with the rest of the lads streaming up behind us, we headed along the rampart-walk towards the gatehouse, We could hear faint sounds of laughter and feasting coming up from some place below us, as we took to the gatehouse stair, and, I mind, in a wee chamber over the guardroom a lassie was sitting by the hearth, rocking a bairn in its cradle and crooning to it, a lullaby that went this way—

Hush ye, hush ye, dinna' fret ye,
The Black Douglas shallna' get ye.

The Black Douglas checked an instant in the stairway arch, and "I'd not be so sure of that, Mistress," said he. She whirled round, and saw him, and began to scream, but he was already on his way again, and the rest of us pounding after him, down the winding stair. In the guardroom they were just snatching up their weapons as we burst in on them, and 'twas hot work for a while. The English put up a stubborn fight, but we'd surprise on our side, and the Black Douglas to lead us! I mind his war-cry rising clear above the shouts and weapon-clash of the fighting. "A Douglas! A Douglas!" I took it up with the rest, shouting at full pitch as I dived in with my borrowed dirk.

We cleared the guardroom and we cleared the Hall, cutting the English down in the remains of their feasting. And long before first light, Roxburgh Castle was safe for King Robert once more.

We only lost a handful of men ourselves. But one of them was Johnnie.

I'd seen him at first in the fighting, and then not any more. But afterwards, when I knew that he was dead, I couldn't rightly believe it. There was such a lot of life in Johnnie, you couldn't think of it all coming out through one red hole in his neck, where the point of a sword went in . . .

Next day, I took my leave of the band. The Black Douglas would have had me stay. "You'll make a bonnie fighting man with just a trifle of practice," he said. "And there'll be fighting in plenty yet, to give you all the practice you need."

I was the proud one, at that! And if Johnnie had still been there—well, who knows? But as it was . . . "I've my own work waiting for me back at Drumfyvie," I said, "and I'd best be away home."

He looked at me with a little frown between his eyebrows. Then it cleared, and he nodded. "Well, you'll have a bonnie tale to carry home with you."

"Aye," I said. "The bonniest tale ever—but there's one more thing I'd like fine to carry home with me."

"And what thing is that?"

"Just a thing in my head—the way Sim Ledehouse makes the hooks on the ends of his rope ladders. Would he be letting me take another look, think you?"

"Go and ask him," said the Black Douglas, "and tell him I sent you."

So I got my look—a good long one. And then I set out on my way back to Drumfyvie. I travelled quicker on the homeward way, without Johnnie to hold me back, and yet the road seemed longer, and awful lonely.

When I came to the edge of Drumfyvie Burgh lands again, with my brogues walked clean off my feet, it was close on cow-stalling time, and Rob was busy rounding up the cattle at the grey start of the dusk, with no one but the dogs to help him. I took a quick look at the herd, to see was Spottie with them, and she was, safe enough; even at a distance and in the fading light, there was no mistaking her, with the odd markings she had.

It seemed as if I'd never been away, and I should just take my usual place with the dogs and Rob. But I'd other business to

attend to before I took the skelping I knew I'd got coming to me. So I waited for full dusk, and then slipped in again through the weak place at the end of Fighting Cocks Lane, it being not yet mended.

I made my way to the house of Nick Fletcher—him I told you about, earlier on. He was the one to go to, being a weaponsmith and once a man-at-arms, and knowing the inside of the Castle and all. I got into his yard by the back way, just as Nick himself came out with a lantern, heading for the byre.

"Nick!" I called, quiet-like. "Nick Fletcher!"

He stopped, and raised his lantern. "Why, Jamie! Is it yourself, then? We were thinking—och, I don't know what!"

"Ye got Spottie safe back, then? I saw her just a while since, with the rest of the herd."

"Did ye so? Rob's so late these nights, being single-handed, I never know if she's lost again. You'll not try telling me you've been away seeking her these past three weeks?"

"I've been away down the Border Country," I said, and took a good deep breath. "You'll have heard, maybe, the Black Douglas was taking Roxburgh Castle from the English on Fastens-eve."

"Aye!" said Nick, and you could tell he was an old fighting man. "I heard—'twas news worth the hearing!"

"Well then—you'll have heard how 'twas done?"

"Not yet," he looked at me with his face puzzled in the lantern light. "What's all this about, man Jamie? Here, come into the house and tell me."

"Better we go into the byre for a wee while," I said. " 'Twill be more quiet-like there, and we'll not need to trouble the good-wife or the bairns."

"So-o! Like that, is it," said he.

And we went into the byre, and I told him the whole story, among the hay bales in the soft light of the lantern. And when 'twas all told, I came to the part that mattered most, the idea that had been in my mind since before I had my second look at Sim Ledehouse's rope ladders. "Nick," I said, "we could do the same here in Drumfyvie! There's bonnie fighters in plenty in the town, and most of them with a spear or an old sword hidden in their house-thatch. You have your own sword hidden yourself, you

told me once. The ladders wouldn't take long to make, and I could show you how the hooks go—"

Nick seemed fair dumbfounded. "Laddie! Laddie! You've taken leave of your senses!"

"I've not, then!" said I, near desperate with trying to make him see the simple sense of it. "Listen! Please, Nick, just *listen*! We can do it—but we'll have to do it quick, before the Castle folks hear just *how* Roxburgh fell. Nick, will you not even *think* of it?"

He stood leaning against the stacked hay, and he was thinking, I could see he was, and I held my breath until I knew where his thinking would take him. "But, Jamie," he said at last, "we'd not have a feast night to help us, and—"

"We'd not need one. Drumfyvie Castle's not a great place the like of Roxburgh—and you know every corner of it, you being man-at-arms there before the English came, and—oh Nick, I know your knee is not just what it was, but you could climb a rope ladder, could you not?"

He nodded, "Aye, I could do that, though I'm thinking I'd be a bit slow. But once up, I know my way fine round Drumfyvie Castle, and that's a fact."

He was speaking slow, thinking the thing out as he went; and I knew he wasn't thinking it impossible any more, though he'd not just made up his mind to it yet.

And then, just at that moment, Rob arrived with Spottie. In they came, Rob calling out all of a grumble, "Fine and late I am this night, but here's me with just the dogs to help me, since that young devil ran off!"

But Jaunty had sniffed me out, and was giving me all the welcome that was in her, her tail like a flag behind her, and her paws on my chest, and she licking my face from ear to ear. Rob pulled up short, and just stood glowering at me. And then, slowly, he began to take off his belt, the one with the metal studs all over it.

"So you're back, are you," said he. "Just wait till I've my belt off . . ."

"Leave that," Nick said, quick. "Leave it, I say! The lad's not been wasting the time he was away, as he'll tell you himself, once your head's cool enough to listen."

Rob stood with his belt in his hand, swinging it a little, "My head's cool now," said he, "and I'll hear him. But whatever 'tis he has to tell, he'd best tell quick, before my head maybe grows hotter."

And he propped himself against Spottie's flank, long-suffering beast that she was, and settled to listen. So I gathered my wits and told him the whole tale, much as I'd told it to Nick. And me with my heart hammering away up in my throat! And I'd barely finished, and Rob hadn't had the time to say a word, though his mouth was open wide enough, when Nick put in his bit.

"And it seems to me that *you're* the man we want, Rob, for I'm thinking we'll need the loan of a few of the herd in, say, three nights from now, and your help in handling them."

Aye, he'd done his thinking, had Nick, and made up his mind! So I never got my skelping, and I'm thinking you can maybe guess the rest!

It seemed Roxburgh was the start of something, for soon after Drumfyvie, other castles were falling, thick and fast, back into Scottish hands. Edinburgh fell midway through Lent, and Stirling at Midsummer, after yon great battle at the Bannock Burn.

'Tis all long past, now, and there's been a Maitland back in the Castle as Sheriff of Drumfyvie these many years. He'd have taken me for a man-at-arms, for he said, just as the Black Douglas did, that I'd the makings of a bonnie fighting man, and one that could use his head as well as his dirk hand. But I'm a man that likes a peaceful life. I told you, didn't I? The herding suits me just fine.

A Burgess Builds His House
A.D. 1360   5

Andrew Meikle, that's me. A burgess of Drumfyvie, as well res-
pected as any other, and a Master Glover, with a workshop at
the end of Castle Wynd, and a journeyman under me and a pair
of apprentices. But I'm not a Drumfyvie man by birth, and I've
had to work hard to get where I am now.

The wars with England were long over when I was born; and
the Bruce's heart lying quiet under the sod at Melrose Abbey.
But I mind how my Grannie used to tell of the fighting days,
and she sitting in the chimney corner. Rare tales they were, too,
and there were eight of us bairns to listen to them.

But eight bairns are over many for any farm tenant's cottage,
and so, me being the eldest, I left home as soon as I was old
enough, and walked the twelve miles into the Burgh, to make my
fortune.

It's not as daft as it sounds. Drumfyvie was growing fast, growing out of its turf-and-timber walls as a bairn grows out of its
clothes, so that they'd had to be let out more than once already,
to make room for all the new and in-coming burgesses to make
their homes and carry on their trades. There were weavers and
dyers, lorimers making horse-gear and fletchers making arrows,
glovers and carpenters, and cordwainers fashioning shoes. And
there were the merchants who bought all these things (and who,
even then, thought themselves grander than the folks who did
the making) and sold, or traded them, for gold and wines and
eastern spices, and all kinds of strange and wonderful things
from foreign parts. And as always in such busy and growing
places, there were plenty of chances for lads that had heads on
their shoulders and hands to their elbows and didn't mind hard
work.

Well, so I walked in to Drumfyvie that first day, with no shoes
to my feet, and my eyes as round as cartwheels with the size
and noise of it all. It was market day, and there were merchants
chaffering over prices, and traders crying their wares, and

country-folk with cheese and poultry to sell, and housewives turning over the woollen stuffs in the weavers' booths, and bairns running hither and yon, all among the legs of the market folk. Never in all my few years of life had I seen anything like it, even in my dreams!

But to cut a long story short, I got work before nightfall as jobbing boy to a Master Glover, to run errands and sweep up and the like. And after a few weeks, seeing I was interested, and liked the feel of the leather, and the scraps of gay silk over from lining the gloves, Master Donaldson let me try my hand at the stitching—just on the scraps, you'll understand. I was always good with my fingers, and after a while longer, my Master asked me would I like to be a real apprentice and learn the craft—and if I did well, maybe get to be a glover myself one day, and even a burgess, if I saved my wages to build me a house, according to the Burgh Laws, when my training was done.

So, I got to be a Master Glover, and I wedded a lassie and loved her well, but she went out of the world on the day that our son came into it. I brought the laddie up myself, and had him making gloves alongside of me; and then he wedded in his turn, and time went on a bit more, and I'd a wee granddaughter to spoil. It doesn't take long in the telling, and indeed, there's times when, looking back, none of it seems so long ago . . .

But within three years both my son and his wife were dead of the fever that comes sometimes in a wet spring. And there was I, left with the bairn, Grizel, to be cared for, and none but myself to do it—which was maybe the saving of me, after all.

"You've brought up a laddie to manhood," said I to myself, "and made none so bad a job of it. Surely you can do the same for a lassie!"

I kept her with me in the workshop, most of the time; and she took some minding, I can tell you, for she was forever into mischief of one kind or another. Indeed, I'm none so sure how I'd have got on but for my good friend Rabbie Bell—a glover like myself—and his wife Mirren. They'd never had a bairn of their own, but Mistress Bell saw to Grizel's clothes and that, and later, taught her the skills a lassie should have, so that by the time she was twelve, she could cook and wash and mend just fine, and it was my turn to be looked after. Aye, but she'd a mind of her

own, under her pretty sunshiny ways, and when 'twas once made up to a thing, even then, she'd not change it.

I was to find that out, soon enough!

I'd a decent, steady young journeyman by the name of Thomas, that I'd thought to bring into the business with me, seeing that I'd no son of my own to take it over when I'd done with it. Thomas, it seemed, was greatly taken with Grizel. He'd known her most of her life, and I was well enough pleased when he came to me one day when she was rising sixteen, and asked my leave to wed with her. He wasn't perfect, he didn't much care to be crossed, for one thing, but there's many like that—myself, I dare say amongst them. Yet he was a good steady workman, and it seemed to me 'twould be all very suitable.

When it was time to close the workshop for the night, I went through into the living-room, all set to tell the lassie the news I had for her. But I didn't speak to her at once. I waited till I'd supped the bowl of broth she had ready for me, and eaten my bannock and a bit of goat's milk cheese. I even waited till the dishes were scoured and put away, for I'd found long since that it doesn't do to surprise a housewife while she's busy with a meal.

Then, when she had finished, and came and sat down to her spinning by the fire, I told her what had passed between Thomas and me. She laid down her spindle and distaff, and sat listening, her hands folded in her lap and her eyes never leaving my face. And when I'd done, she said, quiet and gentle, "I'll not have him."

I couldn't believe I'd heard aright! And I tried again, speaking very clearly, in case she had not understood. " 'Tis but usual, when a man has no son of his own, that he should take his journeyman into his business, *and* into his family. It's done all the time, lassie."

"Not in this family, Grandfather," said she.

"But why not? I was that pleased, when Thomas spoke to me."

She gentled a bit. "But Grandfather, does it not matter that I should be pleased, too?"

"Of course it does," said I, reasonable. "But why should you not be? You've known him since you were a bairn, and he's a steady, well-set-up laddie."

"Aye, but that's not to say I'm wanting to marry him."

But I was not going to give in that easy, just to a lassie's whim. "He loves you well," said I, "for he told me so. He's a good steady workman, and he'll be a free craftsman next Michaelmas. What more do you want?"

Grizel lifted her chin. "Willie Anderson that's journeyman to James Scott will be a free craftsman *this* Michaelmas, a whole year ahead of Thomas. And his work is better finished than Thomas's will ever be."

I stared at her, feeling as if the wind had been clean knocked out of me. "Willie Anderson!—Willie Ander—So that's the way of it!"

"Yes, Grandfather, that's the way of it," she said. "And now, if you don't need me for anything, I'll away to my bed . . . Good-night to you."

And she was gone before I could fetch the breath for another word.

Now there's not much that I don't understand about gloves, but a lassie's different . . . After half an hour or so of thinking, my mind wasn't much clearer than it had been at the start, and I went to the shop door for a breath of fresh air, to see if that would clear it. It was a bonnie night, the sky shadowy blue behind the housetops, and a star or two, and a wisp of a new moon. A good night for a walk—just across to Rabbie Bell's, maybe. Mostly I head that way when I've a problem needs talking out. So over I went, and soon enough I was sitting with a cup of Mirren's elderberry wine, and telling the pair of them the whole story. I mind Mirren was knitting a stocking, and I didn't know if she was listening or just counting her stitches, for she never said a word.

Well, it was Rabbie that I'd mostly come to talk to. "It isn't as if I was asking her to do anything out of the ordinary," I wound up. "And here's me given Thomas permission to marry her, and thinking everything settled and just fine."

Rabbie grunted, "H-huh. But maybe if you were a lassie and had set your heart on a laddie of your own choosing, it might not seem so fine at all."

"I can see that in a way," I admitted, "but this Willie Anderson—he's a lad without a future. No prospects. You'll mind James Scott has a son of his own to follow him in the business, and

there's no place for Willie there when he's served his time. He'll have to make his way in the world; and the Dear Lord knows how he'll do it."

"Maybe the same way as you did," said Mirren, into her knitting.

But Rabbie was scratching about in his beard, which always means that he's a thought coming. "Well, seems to me that I would be for making things easier," he said at last.

I knew what he meant, for I'd had the same thought coming through the town, but I wasn't easy in my mind about it.

"You mean, I should take this Willie in with me instead of Thomas? But Thomas has always been a good enough apprentice, and a good enough journeyman, and 'twould be a hard thing to set him aside for a lassie's whim."

Mirren put down her sock at last. "Listen to me, Andrew Meikle, Grizel's not a lassie that's given to whims. She has her own mind, and when it's made up, she'll not change it lightly . . . Well, if she was my lassie I'd sooner see her married to Willie who has her heart, than Thomas who hasn't; for she'll not change that either. Aye, and if you want my opinion, Thomas has his eyes set too near together. I'd not put my trust in him, not for the lassie, nor for the business!"

So there was me, winded for the second time in one evening. "He's awful fond of Grizel," said I, hanging on to that. "He told me so."

But Mirren came back at me in a flash. " 'Course he told you so. I dare say he is, in his way. Grizel and what comes with her! Think now, if he was to wed with the lassie, you couldn't pass him over when it comes to passing on the shop—not your own grandson-in-law—so his fortune's made, as sure as the sun'll rise tomorrow!"

"You think that's in his mind?"

Mirren sniffed, and went back to her knitting. But it was what you might call a speaking sniff!

I just sat looking into the fire for a while, and thinking. Aye, thinking hard. "Well," said I at last—and I was still thinking the thing out as I went along—"You maybe have the right of it, you and Rabbie. But I know this—if she'll not be like other lassies, and marry a husband of my choosing, she shall marry

one that can make his own way in the world as I made mine."
I glanced at Mirren, but it doesn't do to let a woman think you're
setting too much store by a chance word of theirs. "What happens in the end, when I must be handing over the business—
that can bide for a while; but 'tis a year and a bit before Thomas
is through with his journeyman's time, while this Willie is through
at Michaelmas. If he can get himself accepted as a burgess by
the Burgh Court, and have his house built in the year's start that
it gives him, he can have Grizel. She'll likely plague the life out
of him, anyway, as she has me, these sixteen years past. If he
can't, then she shall take Thomas, and no more of this daft nonsense."

Mirren nodded. "That makes good enough sense. Mind and
tell Grizel in the morning, and bid her bring young Willie home
for a bite of supper. Then you can see the two of them together,
and size up the laddie for yourself."

So I told Grizel the whole, next morning. She flushed up a bit,
and her eyes turned very bright, and she gave me the best kiss I'd
had in a long while, before I went through into the shop to start
the day's work.

Come supper time, young Willie was there, and I watched
him like a hawk. He looked a good enough lad, and certain it was
that he and Grizel thought the world of each other. So after
supper, I sat myself down by the fire, and closed my eyes and
nodded a bit, just to let them feel they were as good as alone. They
stayed by the table, talking quiet-like—but there's nothing wrong
with my hearing!

"What'll we do, Willie?" Grizel said.

"We'll manage."

"Aye, but how?"

("A right practical lass, takes after me!" I thought.)

"I'll need time to think things out," Willie told her. "But if
the Provost and Bailies accept me as a burgess, we'll manage
someway. There's still tofts of land waiting to be spoken for down
the end of Fighting Cocks Lane, where they're pushing out the
town walls again."

"It's not the Provost nor the Bailies I'm afraid of," said Grizel.
"They'll know a good workman when they see one, and it's not
the bit of land either, Willie. It's the house. 'Toft and Tenement',

you have to own, all within the year of being made a burgess. That's Burgh Law. It costs money to build a house, and there'll be the leather for your Journeyman's Piece, and the cost of the tools, and ... How much money have you, Willie?"

"Seven years' savings in an old boot," Willie said proudly. " 'Twill buy us the roof-tree and the uprights—just about—and the rest we can get off the Burgh lands for the cutting and carrying home."

"Aye, but it's you that'll do the cutting and carrying home. Are you going to do the building, too?"

"Who else?"

"When?" said Grizel.

"In my spare time."

"Willie, Willie, how much spare time do you ever get out of that old skinflint, James Scott?"

"Not much, I'll admit ... But, lassie, we'll have a year to do it in. And I'll not have to pay the King a penny of rent on the land, all that first year."

And that made sense, I thought. Aye, a good practical laddie. And I gave a snore to let them think I'd dropped off sound.

It's true in every Burgh, that burgesses must pay rent to the King for the land their houses stand on; it's the King's land, after all. In Drumfyvie we pay five pence, and that's a tidy sum. But a new burgess is always allowed a year's "Peaceful Sitting", to build his house and start his business before he pays any rent at all.

But before any of that, Willie must make his Journeyman's Piece—a good pair of gloves, to prove his skill, before he'd be accepted for a Master Glover, let alone a burgess, at all. I hoped he'd have the sense to start early, and allow himself plenty of time for that.

I needn't have worried. He set to work next day!

He took the time he needed, and he had all the craft-skill he needed, too. He made a pair of doeskin riding-gloves with green silk tassles on the gauntlets, as fine as anything I could have made myself. And when Grizel brought them to show me, on the evening the last stitch was in, I couldn't fault them.

"Are they not fine and bonnie!" said Grizel, and her eyes

were shining. "Thomas couldn't make a pair of gloves as good as that if he tried for a hundred years!"

"Maybe yes and maybe no," said I, for I didn't mean to make it too easy for them. "He's not tried yet, has he?"

So the time went by to Michaelmas, and Willie brought his gloves to the Burgh Court, where all the burgesses of Drumfyvie were gathered to elect next year's Provost and Bailies, and attend to all other kinds of Burgh business, including the accepting or refusing of new burgesses.

There were a good few, that year, and it seemed a long while before it came to Willie's turn. But at last the Provost came to him.

"James Scott, this young man standing before us, William Anderson by name, asking to be accepted as a member of our community—this young man has been your apprentice and your journeyman for the required number of years?"

"He has that," answered James Scott.

"We are all satisfied, seeing this pair of gloves, that he has well and truly learned his craft. For the rest, have you found him honest and sober, a steady workman, and one who will likely make a worthy burgess of this free Burgh of Drumfyvie?"

"Aye," said James Scott.

"So then we come to the matter of pledges. As you are aware, a man seeking admission as a burgess, and having no house of his own, must find two worthy men to stand pledge or surety for him, that he will have one built and furnished, with bed and bedding, a trestle table, and all needful goods and gear, within the twelvemonth following. James Scott, will you stand pledge for your journeyman, William Anderson?"

James scratched his nose doubtfully. "Well—er—as to that, I'm none so sure. I've a family of my own to look to, you'll mind . . . A man must provide for his own before outsiders, surely."

"Mean old devil!" said I to myself. "So what's to be done now?"

But before I could open my mouth, there was Rabbie Bell on his feet. "Master Provost," said he, "I've no family of my own to look to, as well you know. I will stand pledge for the new burgess, and that gladly."

"Good, good, and who else?" The Provost looked us over.

And, well, what could I do? I found myself on my feet without quite knowing how I'd got there, and "I'll stand pledge for the lad," said I.

There was a bit of a stir in the Court, folks looking at each other and whispering, "Andrew Meikle!" and "Did ye hear that, now?" And when Dougal Begg that's as deaf as a bedpost finally got hold of it, he let out at the top of his voice, "Andrew Meikle, did ye say, *Well* I never! Young Thomas will be not best pleased, and him having to look for another job now, I'm thinking!"

I reckon that's what everyone was thinking, for all Drumfyvie knew by that time that Grizel and Willie were courting!

So Willie Anderson took his solemn oath to be loyal and faithful to the King and to the Burgh, and went off to get an armful of withes to mark out his land-holding at the end of Fighting Cocks Lane.

Thomas had had little enough to say to me since the day I'd had to tell him he couldn't take it as settled between him and Grizel after all. But from the time of the Michaelmas Burgh Court, he said never a word, except in the way of business. Oh he did his work well enough, but he'd a black face on him that seemed to darken the shop. I suppose you couldn't blame him overmuch. But if he didn't talk to me, he talked to others. I heard him airing his grievance to a fellow journeyman in The Fighting Cocks, one evening when I'd dropped in for a jack of ale. He didn't see me, for I was sitting in the shadow just behind the door.

" 'Tis the custom, after all," he was saying, "it's *always* been the custom. Wed the daughter, and you'll get the business when the old man dies. And it's not as if I wasn't fond of the lassie. Fond enough, anyway. Oh, one lassie's much like another, I know that fine, but 'twas my *right*, him having no son! Now 'twill be 'Good day to you, Thomas! You can take yourself elsewhere!' 'Tis a sin and a shame, Ritchie! That's what 'tis!"

So Mirren had been right about that one.

Ah well, by that time Willie Anderson had taken his seven years' savings out of the old boot, and gone down to the woodwright's for the timber to make the framework of his house. Just the usual—ten long stout poles, and the roof-tree that runs the

whole length of the place to hold up the thatch. Since the forest belongs to the King and his nobles, you can't just go and fell a tree for yourself, so big timber costs a deal of money, and I reckon Willie hadn't much left out of his savings after it was bought and paid for.

All that winter, every minute of free time that Master Scott gave him, he worked at his building, and now and again his friends would give him a hand. They seemed to be enjoying themselves, for there was always a good deal of laughing and joking mixed in with the hammering every time I passed that way.

Oh, aye, I'd a bit of business that took me—quite by chance —fairly often of an evening, down Fighting Cocks Lane, all through that winter and early spring.

Well before Blackthorn Fair, the framework was up. Four posts at the corners, each gable-pair leaning in to meet at the top, and the other three pairs doing the same in between; and the roof-tree right along the top, where the posts criss-crossed to make a kind of trough for it to lie in. Then there were withies to be cut from the marshy patch where the burn runs through the Burgh Lands, and woven into hurdles and fixed between the poles, and all to be daubed inside and out with mud bound together with chopped straw, to make the walls. After that there were the roof poles and rafters to fix. And one evening when I went past, Willie had begun to put on the heather thatch—making a good job of it, too.

I'm thinking he took no time off for supper, those evenings, and would have gone without, if it hadn't been for Grizel. I never saw her there, but she was away out of the house with something wrapped in a napkin, most evenings, as soon as *my* supper was on the table—and I pretending not to notice.

On the eve of Midsummer Fair, the last bunch of heather was tied in place, and Willie stuck up a wee fir-tree on the gable end, to tell all Drumfyvie the roof was on his house. I went down with Grizel to see it done, for 'twas something of an occasion.

"Oh Willie!" says the lassie, " 'Tis the finest house in all the Burgh!"

"It's well enough," Willie told her modestly, with the pride

shining out of him. "Or it will be, when I've built the cross wall inside.

"Two rooms!" said Grizel. And from her voice she might have been saying twenty!

"Aye. And when I've built the hearth, I'll make you a dresser to hold the dishes. But that must wait till I've built the byre."

For of course no house is complete until it has its byre for a cow out at the back, even if there's no cow to put in it! Ah well, they'd have a cow soon enough, for sure.

I mind standing and listening to them and the plans they had, and hearing behind their voices the sounds of the first fairground booths being set up around the tolbooth.

At first light next morning the Provost proclaimed the Midsummer Wool Fair from the steps of the Market Cross. And after that, well, you know how it is with the big fairs—by day it's serious business, with most of the year's buying and selling going on; but at night, folks take their ease in the taverns, with old friends and new ones, while the youngsters mostly take their fun and their drink in the streets. And it's then that accidents are most like to happen.

I was sitting in The Fighting Cocks, with a few merchants I'd done business with that day (for there's other things beside wool bought and sold at a wool fair), when a great noise and shouting started outside, and a laddie came running in, shouting, "Fire! Willie Anderson's house is afire! Come on, and we'll maybe save it . . ."

We ran out after him, Half Drumfyvie was running, it seemed; and I'd not stretched my old legs like that for many a long day. But the fire, starting somewhere in the roof, had got too good a hold, and there was not much we could do about saving Willie's house, not much at all.

Next morning I was in the workshop, and Willie and Grizel with me, white-faced as if the end of their world had come, when Rabbie Bell appeared in the doorway, looking a wee bit the worse for wear. I wasn't surprised at that, for I'd seen him by the flame-light, the night before, and there's no denying Rabbie is fond of a drop on Fair nights.

Willie gave him a stool, and he sat down thankfully. "It's my

71

head!" he groaned. "If it hadn't been for my head, I'd have remembered last night."

"Remembered what?" I demanded, not even giving him time to get his breath back.

"Thomas! As I was going home last night, I ran slap into Thomas, or he ran slap into me. And him looking as if he'd been pulled through a furze-bush backwards, and his eyes fair standing out of his head. He said he was away to his sick auntie, and then he was off down the street like a bolting horse."

Willie said slowly, "But Thomas's auntie died last week."

I stared from one of them to the other, scarcely believing what came into my mind. "Rabbie—It was after that you saw the fire? Think, man, *think*!"

"I've no need to think," Rabbie said. "I'd had a sup of ale, I know, but now that I remember, I remember clear enough. 'Twas after that I saw the fire. Aye, and there's another thing— I mind he smelled of burning, did Thomas!"

"That's an awful thing to say! Man, are you sure?" I minded the ale. But he was sober enough, now.

"Aye, I'm sure. I'd swear it before the Provost and Bailies."

There was a little sharp silence.

"And now, Thomas can't be found," I heard myself saying. "But that's daft. What would he gain by it?"

Rabbie shook his head. "Maybe he just thought to get his own back for the sight of Willie's roof-top tree and all it meant. Or maybe with the Fair to cover his tracks, he took his chance to stop the house being ready in time—seeing there's fires and such-like easy enough at Fair time. And then when he saw what he'd done he took fright and ran."

"Aye," I said, looking round at the three of them. "That could be the way of it. For if Thomas didn't do it, he'd no cause to run off. But if he did, then I hope he's got clear away."

Rabbie took my point. "Setting all the town at risk of fire— if he was caught and brought before the Burgh Court, he'd hang. So the further away the better, I'm thinking."

"I would like fine to see him hang for what he's done to Willie," said Grizel, in a small, dead voice.

"Whisht, lassie!" I told her, and turned myself to the lad, for there was another thing I had in mind. "Willie Anderson, it wasn't

to talk of Thomas that I asked your master for the loan of you this morning."

"No?" said Willie, dull-like.

"I hear the house is not altogether gone. Is that so?"

"The walls are standing. Most of the roof's gone. I'd need to come by another roofbeam."

"Well now, you'll mind Rabbie Bell and I stood pledge for you in that matter; so 'tis for us to see the house is finished in the proper time. I'm not exactly what you'd call a rich man, but I can find the price of a roofbeam, and—"

"No!" said Willie. "The bargain was that I should make my own way as *you* made yours. And I'll find my own roof-tree, thank you all the same."

I stared at him. "You're the stiff-necked one, Willie Anderson!"

"I'm not stiff-necked. I said 'Thank you'. And now, Master Scott will maybe need me, so I'll be on my way. Good-day to you, Master Meikle."

And he made for the door. But Grizel was there before him. "Willie," said she, "Willie, I've a silver shilling in my clothes-chest that I was keeping to buy pots and pans and coverlets, and I've a silver pin that was my mother's. You can have them—"

"We'll still need pots and pans and coverlets," Willie told her, "and you must keep the pin to wear at your wedding." And with that, he was out of the door and away.

He was in the right of it, though I wondered just how he *would* get another roof-tree! But seemingly, on his way back to Master Scott's, he minded that Sir Roger Maitland, the Sheriff, was having some new stables built. Maybe 'twas the sound of hammering and sawing from beyond the wall of the Castle bailey that gave him the idea as he went by; and there's long been a bond of friendship between Drumfyvie and its Sheriffs. At all events, as Willie told me later, he got the idea, and it fair took a grip on him.

So next day, up he goes to the Castle, taking with him, folded in a bit of clean cloth, the pair of doeskin gloves with the bonnie green tassels that he'd made for his Journeyman's Piece. In the usual way of things, of course, he'd have kept and treasured them, to show his sons and grandsons just what good workman-

ship should be. But now, he'd a better use for them, by his way of thinking.

Well, so up he goes, and asks can he see the Sheriff. And there *is* the Sheriff, taking a look at the work on his new stables, amid all the hammering and sawing and the shouting and whistling. And putting on a bold face over the desperate feeling inside him, Willie makes his way through the workmen and the Castle folk and the stacked timber and such, until he gets to the Sheriff himself. And once there, shouting a bit to get above the din, he told Sir Roger who he was and about his house that he must have ready by Michaelmas and about Grizel, and about the fire.

The Sheriff, watching now Willie and now the workmen, asked, a bit absent-minded, what Willie would have him do about it.

And Willie took a deep breath and got out, "You have some fine timber here for your new stables, my Lord Sheriff. I was thinking—that maybe there was a good stout beam you'd not be—exactly—needing?"

"Oh?" said the Sheriff, with a twitch at one side of his mouth. "And you were thinking that maybe I would make you a handsome gift of a new roof-tree?"

"I wasn't talking of a gift," said Willie. (Setting the Sheriff down much as he'd set me!)

"Then what do you offer in exchange?" said the Sheriff, a mite surprised.

"These," said Willie, whisking his precious gloves out of their cloth.

"I see. A pair of riding gloves—and good ones, too. But you'd not suggest that a pair of gloves, however well made, is fair exchange for a beam of seasoned oak—what—twenty, twenty-five feet long?"

"Not the one pair, no," Willie said, "but if you'll give me the beam now, so that I can have the house ready before my year's up, I'll make you a pair of riding gloves as good as these, and maybe better, every year, so long as you live—or so long as I do."

The Sheriff stood looking at young Willie in silence. And then on a sudden, he began to laugh.

"What—of all the cock-crow impudence!—You're the bold lad, Willie Anderson, and I like you for it! So—it's a bargain."

And he shouts for the steward to take Willie to choose his own roof-tree.

That's the story, as Willie told it to me later. Me, I wouldn't have dared, supposing I never got a roof-tree. But Willie's more determined than me.

So once again, the lad set to work. And his toft rang with building noises nearly as loud as up at the Castle. I seemed to have a lot of business down that way in the long light summer evenings, and I generally looked in on Willie in passing. There was no time before Michaelmas to build the byre, and the house had only the one long room, meanwhile, where Willie had thought to make two; but all that could come later, along with the dresser for Grizel's pots and pans. And just three days before Michaelmas, the last bit of heather thatch was finished, and Willie fixed the wee fir-tree to the gable end of his house for the second time. Grizel and I were there to see it done, and Rabbie and Mirren, too.

"Oh Willie, I'm so proud of you!" said Grizel, and put her arms round his neck and reached up to give him a kiss.

"I reckon we can both be proud of him," said I, "seeing he's coming into the business *and* the family, and him with the impudence to beard the Sheriff himself for a new roof-tree, to say nothing of his skill at the glove-making!"

Three days later, Willie paid over his five pence rent, that he'd kept aside carefully all that year, and started his first real year as a burgess of Drumfyvie. And Grizel set about gathering up her pots and pans and coverlets, and all her wedding gear.

Thomas? He's never been seen or heard of again in the Burgh. Which is just as well for Thomas, maybe.

The Pest Comes to Drumfyvie 6
A.D. 1450

Wattie Aiken, that's my name. Born and bred in Leith, close by Edinburgh town. Edinburgh was—still is, they tell me—the biggest and most thriving burgh in the whole land; and its port of Leith, on the Firth of Forth, a bustling and thriving place accordingly.

As much of my time as I could have to myself, I used to spend down at the harbour, watching the tall ships come and go. The sea was in my blood, as it was in my father's, and his father's before him, and I could scarce wait for the time when I'd be aboard one of those ships myself, outward bound for places half the world away.

But in the late summer of 1440, when I was rising fourteen, my father's ship went down with all hands. And that was the end of my seafaring. I could have run away, of course; but truly, I think that would have killed my mother—and her with the three young ones. At all events, I listened to her, and to my Uncle Andrew, who was the apothecary here in Drumfyvie and offered to take me as his apprentice, for my father's sake. And before the leaves were well turned from green to gold, and before the last of the swallows had flown south, here I was in the apothecary's shop, midway between the tolbooth and the turning into Fighting Cocks Lane, bound apprentice to my uncle, to run his errands and keep the shop and its back room clean and tidy in return for my board and lodging and for my training in the apothecary's craft.

I mind now, how dark and crowded and strange the place seemed on that first day of all. Strange looking, and strange smelling, too, with its shelves crowded with jars and boxes and bundles of spices and herbs that he used to make his medicines and salves, the pestles and mortars and measuring glasses, and even the skin of a snake hanging from the ceiling, which I learned later was just for the look of the thing. Aye, and I mind following him from one thing to another, trying to under-

stand what he told me—for my training began that first evening
—but making poor work of it, for I was tired and hungry and
sick at heart for home and the sea and the gulls crying, and my
own folk about me.

In the days that followed, it seemed to me the shop was never
empty, and scarce a customer came and went without sparing
time to tell me how good it was of my uncle to take me as his
apprentice, lacking even a penny piece for my training, and how
grateful I should be. I *was* grateful, though I still longed for the
sea. And after a few months, I began to feel less strange with
my new life.

My Uncle Andrew was a barber as well as an apothecary—
the two things often go together. And 'twas his favourite joke,
in fact I think it was his only one, that should he chance to
cut off a customer's head while shaving him, he could stitch it
back on again, and make up a syrup of honey and myrrh that
would cure the poor man's sore throat as well! He was all the
physician and surgeon Drumfyvie had—or needed, come to that.
Even Sir Robert Maitland, the Sheriff himself, had my Uncle
Andrew to bleed him every spring, instead of sending for a man
from Stirling. Aye, he was skilled in his craft, sure enough.
Wise, too, which is another matter.

I could have wished he'd had as much wisdom in understanding that a laddie needs a wee holiday once in a while. He never
wanted time off from work himself, and so he didn't think that
anyone else might; and maybe he'd forgotten his own young days
and the way a laddie gets to itching in his bones with the longing
to run free. So it's little enough time to myself I got in those
years.

I mind a day when I'd been with him the best part of three
years. Just after Blackthorn Fair, it was, the kind of day when
the wind smells of summer ahead of its time, and I got such an
itching in my bones that I was like to break out in green buds
as the briar bush in our yard was doing. I was alone in the shop,
for my uncle had gone away out to see a customer, and there
wasn't much for me to do—just a few mixtures to be made up
and the floor in need of a sweeping. Nought that couldn't wait
a while, I thought. So off I went to see did my friend, Christie
Fleming, the weaver's son, feel like a wee bit fishing. Christie

was forever ready for the fishing, and so the pair of us got our gear out from the place where we kept it hidden, and headed for the river. Christie had the forethought to gather up a handful of oatcakes from his mother's kitchen in the by-going. Aye, he'd his wits about him, that one!

There was sunshine, and a light wind chasing puffs of white cloud across a pale blue sky, and the water, with a couple of moorhens on it, lapping gently against the stones below the river-bank. We'd a good long, lazy afternoon, Christie and me; nothing spectacular, you'll understand, but we caught a couple of trout apiece, and were fair pleased with ourselves. And then we turned home to meet the trouble that would be waiting for both of us!

"Is that you, Wattie?" called my uncle, as soon as I opened the door.

"Aye, Uncle Andra'."

He came through from the inner room, looking as grim as ever I'd seen him. "And where have you been, my mannie?"

"I—er—went fishing, just for a wee while," I said. There was no lie would serve me any better than the truth, and me with the fish in my hand.

"So I see," said he. "You and young Christie Fleming, that would be? And I suppose you reckoned that while you were at the fishing, the salve for old Marget's sore leg and the worming-mixture for Bailie Wishart's bairns would get themselves made up by divine agency?"

"I'm—I'm sorry, Uncle Andra', I'll make them up now, before I take my supper."

"You'll do just that," my uncle agreed. "*And* sweep the floor and chop the kindling. And you may think yourself lucky if I give you any supper at all . . . If I did my duty by you, I'd give you a skelping you'd remember the rest of your days—only that you've shot up taller than I am myself, this past year."

"I've *said* I'm sorry."

" 'Sorry' doesn't set the world to rights; and a good apprentice doesn't go running off with his work half done. There's times I wonder if I'm wasting all my labour, trying to turn you into a good apothecary—there's times I wonder if you'll ever reach even to be a bad one!"

Oh aye, he could scold like a hen-wife when he'd a mind for it, could my Uncle Andrew.

Well, I did my work, and had my supper, and managed to make my peace with the wee man, and so the evening passed. I mind it well, for it was the last peaceful evening we were to know for a long while . . .

Next morning we heard that the Plague—the Pest, folks called it—had broken out in Edinburgh !

At noon, with the Town Drummer at his elbow, Bailie Wishart read the Sheriff's orders from the steps of the tolbooth. I mind his voice in the silence, and the terrible, desolate words.

". . . No one coming from Edinburgh nor from the Port of Leith shall be allowed within the gates of Drumfyvie, and no man, woman, nor child, of this Burgh shall take such a one into his house to shelter him, upon pain of losing his right hand. No goods nor cattle from Edinburgh or Leith shall enter this town, neither hides, iron, wool nor flax. And may God have mercy upon all that dwell herein."

So we cut ourselves off from Edinburgh, in the hope of cutting ourselves off from the Pest. I was stricken with fear for my mother and the young ones, and would have gone straight home. But Uncle Andrew said there was nothing I could do by going; and if I went, there'd be no coming back for dear knows how long, and if the worst happened, he'd need me, here in Drumfyvie. He was in the right of it—I knew that—so I stayed.

It must have been close on two weeks later that I woke from sleep one night, where I lay snug in my box-bed by the back-room hearth, and heard low voices in the shop. One of the speakers was Uncle Andrew, but the other was a woman, and for all that I could not make out what she was saying, the sound of it fair made the hair lift on the back of my neck. Grief, there was in it, and a kind of secret terror. Then the shop door closed quietly, and I knew that I was alone in the house, with just Solomon the old ginger tom for company.

The fear was on me still, which was a strange thing, for it wasn't the first time I'd known my uncle called out in the night hours; and I couldn't just lie there with the weight of it cold on my chest. So up I got, and re-made the fire with fresh kindling, and got out the ale jug, for my uncle often took a sup of

warm ale before getting back into his bed when he was called out in the dark of the night. Solomon seemed uneasy too, and kept weaving and winding himself about my legs, mewing piteously the while. They are strange beasties, are cats . . . When all was done, I pulled a creepy stool to the fire and sat myself down to wait, Solomon still wandering restlessly round and about.

It was well on towards dawn when I heard the shop door open and my uncle came in. I took one look at his face and got to my feet, knowing that I had been right to be afraid.

"Uncle Andra', what—what is it?"

But I think I knew.

"It's the Pest."

"The Pest?—Here in Drumfyvie? But—it can't be!" I said, as though by denying it I could thrust it away. "There's been no one come in from Edinburgh way this two weeks and more."

My uncle set himself down and took a wee sup of ale. It helped him some, I think. At least it got him speaking clear.

"Och, but there has! It seems the bailies of Edinburgh, the De'il take them, turned out all their beggars and vagabonds and fairground tumblers and the like, bidding them each away back to where they came from. And among them Tom Seton, him that went to see the world, dancing on his hands at street corners, rather than turn to an honest trade. So back he comes here to his mother. Where else would the likes of him go?"

"But they'd not let him through the gates," I said. "Nobody from Edinburgh or Leith's to be let in—the Sheriff's man said so."

"It seems he got in with the country folks last market day. Nobody recognized him, and there was no knowing he was from Edinburgh way. He must have had the Pest on him even then . . . His mother came for me a while since."

"I heard her," I said, stirring the fire to get a last flicker from the logs. "D'you mean she kept him hidden for nigh on a week?"

"What else would she do? He was her son. The only one she had."

"Had?" I echoed him, and there was a great coldness in me. "Then he's—"

"Dead," said Uncle Andrew. "He was dying when I got there. I've just been getting the Provost out of his bed with the news. And he didn't thank me for it."

"What—will they do to her?"

"Nought, I think, if she does as I bade her, and swears she didn't know he was from Edinburgh. I've already sworn as much to the Provost." He got up like one that is very weary. "I'm away into the yard to clean myself up at the well, then it's both of us for our beds, for it's little enough sleep we'll get in the time ahead."

Ill news spreads fast, and next day at noon all Drumfyvie turned out, white-faced, some of the women weeping quiet-like, to crowd the market place, and press close round the steps of the tolbooth and hear what the Provost had to say. And him standing there above us with his bonnet in his hand.

"Good people of Drumfyvie, pray God for His Mercy! The Pest is in our midst. Hear now and obey the orders of the Officers of this Burgh . . . Until it be declared clean again, the town gates shall be shut, and none allowed to pass out or in without leave. There shall be no public gatherings, save for Sunday worship in the Kirk. The weekly markets shall not be held. Any child under the age of fifteen found roaming the streets may be beaten or set in the stocks. Dogs and swine must be kept in house and hand, and any found loose in the streets are to be instantly slaughtered. The streets and alleys are to be cleansed of garbage, and all people shall keep indoors as much as may be, with the windows closed, that if the Pest be outside it may not come into them, and if it be within, it may not fly out upon the next house or the passers-by. The head of any household in which the Pest appears shall report it within twelve hours to one of the Bailies. . . . May God have mercy on us all, and deliver us out of this peril and affliction."

My Uncle Andrew was right—we'd little enough sleep in the time that followed; and we went about bleary-eyed by day and by night. For all that folks did as the Provost had bidden them, the Pest spread from house to house. It seemed never-ending. Soon there was scarce a door down the length of Fighting Cocks Lane that had not the Plague cross on it. Friend passed friend in the streets with their eyes turned away from each other,

and never a word spoken. Trade stopped, and all over the town hung the smell of fear, the smell of death. Men who were well at sun-rise sickened at noon, and the nights were broken by the clang of the Death Bell in the streets and the shuffling footsteps of men carrying yet another body to the Plague pit outside the gates.

But there would have been yet more taking that one-way journey, I'm thinking, if it had not been for my uncle, and for Master Simon, the friar that was our parish priest. Aye, and myself, come to that, young as I was.

In one way we were luckier than many other towns and villages where the Pest struck, for in some places, such as Haddington, the Lairds and the Sheriffs and the rich folks fled into the countryside away from danger—if they didn't take it with them—so few enough were left to care for the poorer folks. The traders with their customers gone, the crippled beggars no longer allowed to beg—these were left, with never a thought, to fend for themselves. I heard after, that in some places many of the oldest and poorest folk died, not from the Pest, but from hunger. We were better off than that, at least. Our Sheriff didn't desert us. For all Sir Robert Maitland was a hard man, he was one to stand with his own folk in time of trouble. And he stayed fast in his castle above the town, and his household with him.

But it's Master Simon I'll never forget. He went about by day and night, tending the sick and comforting the dying, and scolding folks into cleaning up their houses as if he were priest and apothecary and Leith fishwife rolled into one! He would storm into a house crying, "Och! This place is more like a midden than a decent home! Come on now, Mistress, stir yourself! Get yon filthy rat-ridden pile of rags out of doors! Young Geordie'll help you . . . Na! Na! *Not* into the street, you daft laddie! Do you want to spread the Pest? Into the back-yard and burn them! And give yon floor a good swill over with a pail of water and a good stout broom—and you with the soup pot not even on the fire yet?"

Aye well, between the three of us, we mebbe did something to check the spread of the Pest; and we saved quite a few of them that sickened. Quite a few. For the most part, my uncle

kept me busy in the shop, making up sulphur draughts to drive the poison out of the chest and lungs, and all kinds of soothing mixtures he hoped might ease the blood-vomit that was always a sure sign of death. At first that was all that he could do for them that sickened. But after a while, he noticed something. He was a great man in his way, was my Uncle Andrew.

"It seems," I mind him rubbing away at his red-rimmed eyes, and thinking as he spoke, "it seems that if these black ulcers on the skin swell up and burst, the poison of the disease drains out, and the man has some chance of life. But if the ulcers bide closed, the poison spreads all through him, and he has no chance at all. Now if we could *make* them burst . . . Wattie, make up a plaster with honey and soda such as we use for drawing a carbuncle to bursting point, and we'll try. It can do no harm, that's for sure."

It seemed we saved more after that—a few, anyway. But the bright days of summer went by, with scarce a day that some poor soul didn't sicken, sometimes three or four. As he grew more hard-pressed, my uncle took me with him more and more into the plague-stricken houses. Both of us with cloths wrung out in vinegar bound over our mouths and noses. To this day, the smell of vinegar is the smell of the Pest to me—the smell of death in a man's body while he yet lives.

It was slow to reach the Castle, mebbe because it stood higher than the town and the air was fresher. But 'twas among the men-at-arms by midsummer. Harvest-time came and went, though there was little enough to harvest, and few enough left standing to gather it. Then about Michaelmas—at first we scarce dared to believe it—the sickness began to abate. There would be a day without a new visitation, then two, then three . . . Only once after Michaelmas did two sicken on the same day. Sir Robert Maitland's ten-year-old son was one, and Christie Fleming was the other.

Yon's a queer thing about the Pest—there's times it will take the strong and spare the weak. It took big strong Christie in but three days . . . I was with him, and after all was done, I went back to the shop, not feeling much at all, just cold and empty. Uncle Andrew was there, gathering things he needed for another visit.

"Christie's gone," I said.

"Aye," said my uncle, cool and dry. "But Sir Robert's bairn isn't—yet. Take these things and carry them up to the Castle for me."

It's the hard man, I thought him! But he was no fool, my uncle, and knew more about folks and their needs than how to shave and physic them.

I took up the bundle without a word, and followed him as a good apprentice should, up to the Castle.

I'd never been inside the Sheriff's own private apartments before, though of course I knew the Great Hall, as all Drumfyvie did, and I'd been in and out of the guardrooms and servants' quarters often enough these past months.

The Sheriff's Great Chamber was very grand and rich, I mind. It's odd, the things a man notices at such unlikely times—there was a bonnie embroidered hanging on one wall. It was a picture of a lady and a unicorn, and every inch of the ground beneath their feet covered with wee bright flowers, pinks and periwinkles and harebells and heart's-ease pansies.

The boy's truckle bed was pulled out into the middle of the room beyond the foot of Sir Robert's own great curtained one, and Sir Robert and the Chaplain were beside him. I could smell the Pest even through the vinegar cloth across my face. The lad was tossing about, moaning with each breath he drew, and the priest knelt praying beside the bed. My uncle turned back the coverlet. "Now, let me look."

"I should not have kept him here," Sir Robert said, "I was a fool.—May God forgive me—"

"Doubtless He will, if there is need, Sir Robert," said my uncle, bending over the lad. "Aye . . . aye . . . He's weak, very weak, no doubt of that, but the fever has mounted no higher, and that's something . . . These ulcers, now—well, we can but try. Wattie, give me the pot of soda plaster, and boiling water—somebody get me boiling water—put a crock over the fire yonder."

So we set to work the best we could.

The first light was showing pale behind the narrow windows before all was done. I mind looking up at it and thinking 'twas going to be a fine day. My uncle straightened up and wiped

the sweat from his forehead. The laddie had fallen into a quiet sleep.

"Will he live?" said Sir Robert, as grey as the dawn-light.

"That's as God wills. But the fever is dropping. It is in my mind that he will live."

But he swayed a wee thing on his feet, and I saw his eyes wide above the vinegar cloth, and fear stirred in me.

We went down from the Castle and down the early morning street, my uncle leading, myself following with the gear. He never staggered once, all the way, but once back in the living-room behind the shop, he pitched down across the bed, all a-sprawl, like a man dead drunk. And when I got him on his back and stripped his clothes off him, there were the beginnings of the tell-tale swellings in the pits of his arms. The Pest!

"Aye," he croaked, answering as though I had spoken the words. "It's on me at last . . ."

"Bide still, I'll fetch Master Simon."

"That can wait. First—listen to me, and listen well, for there's no knowing how long I'll keep the wits to speak plain to you." He struggled up on to one elbow, in the urgency of what he had to say. "It's all in your hands now, Wattie Aiken. You've worked with me, and you know what to do, and how to do it. I'm— depending on you. So are—the folk of Drumfyvie."

I did what I could for him. I'd done it so often by then it seemed quite natural. Only somehow it didn't seem like me doing it but like somebody else, while I stood by watching. Then I went to find Master Simon. I came up with him at last, leaving Christie Fleming's home.

He said, "There's no good you can do here, Wattie lad, it's all by with."

I shook my head, "It's you I came looking for. It's my Uncle Andra'—the Pest is on him."

Just for an instant his face went stiff. Then he said, "Come, then," and set off down the street with a stride that had me running to keep up with him.

"It's for you now, Wattie," he said, much as my uncle had done. "You can do it."

"I'm afraid," I gasped.

"Of the Pest? Of your uncle's death?"

"Both. But most, of having people's lives in my hands, without him to tell me what to do. I've not learned enough yet, and I'm afraid."

"Put your trust in God," said Master Simon, never looking round. "And you'll find you've learned more than you think—and doubtless so shall I. Save your breath now, to speed your legs."

Just as Master Simon said, it seemed we'd both learned more than we'd thought. But still I'm not sure how we'd have done, in the early days at least, without the Widow Seton's help. She'd had the Pest in years gone by, and them that live through it seldom take it again. So when she came chapping on the door, I let her in. Without her, there must have been many a time when my uncle was left alone, while I was out about his business, and him mostly out of his wits after the first day and night. So if any one saved Uncle Andrew, I'm thinking 'twas the Widow Seton.

Aye, I'd my hands full, surely, for 'twas close on Christmas before the last house was fumigated with sulphur and burning heather, and the Burgh declared clean, with the folk free to come and go as before.

My uncle was long enough getting back his strength, but as soon as he could drag himself from his bed, he would be out in the shop, watching and listening to all that went on, questioning me, when I returned from being out, as to what sick folk I'd seen and what treatments I'd given. He gave me advice when I asked for it, but never a word of praise or blame, until the day when the Burgh was declared free.

That evening, as we were supping our broth at the fireside, he said, "Do you mind my telling you once I doubted you'd ever make even a bad apothecary, let alone a good one?"

He spoke of it as something that had happened long and long ago; and indeed it seemed as though it had been in another world.

"Aye," I said, "I mind it."

He took another mouthful of broth, and looked at me consideringly. "I was mistaken," he said, "I was mistaken, Wattie."

And that was all.

My mother and the young ones? The Pest raged in Leith even more fiercely than here at Drumfyvie—I've heard folk say it was carried by the rats from the shipping. My mother and the young ones? God rest their souls . . . It was all a long time ago . . .

The Man-at-Arms 7
A.D. 1513

It's me, Eckie Brock, that's telling my tale this grey autumn evening. One of Sir David's men-at-arms from Drumfyvie Castle. One of the few that, yesterday, won home from Flodden. And it's wearied I am! And Donal Dhu's not with me.

But I must start at the beginning, on the night I first happened on Donal Dhu.

I'd been to take a New Year's gift to a lassie I'd a liking for, down Watergate Lane, and I was on my way back to the Castle, meaning to look in at the Unicorn for a pot of ale in passing. It was almost dark, and maybe my head was too full of the merry-making of Old Year's Night, to look properly where I was going. But however it was, I never saw a respectable burgess sleeping all across the road, as peaceful as a babe unborn, with an empty flagon in his hand. So I fell headlong over his legs, and up he woke yelling, "Robbers!" and "Murder!"

"Help!" he roared, rolling about and trying to get to his feet and pull me off mine at the same time. "I'm robbed! I'm murdered, so I am!"

"Whisht!" said I. "You're not robbed nor yet murdered; will you stop trying to strangle me, you silly wee man . . .! It's your own fault then—take that!" And I hit him on the chin, to make him let go, seeing he wouldn't listen to decent Christian reason!

Of course the next thing was folks popping out of their houses like rabbits out of their burrows, to see what was wrong. Then down the lane came a couple of prentice lads that had begun seeing in the New Year with more ale than they could rightly carry. One of them had a lighted torch that lit up the scene finely and, well, townsfolk are never over fond of the men-at-arms from the Castle, except when there's an enemy hammering at the Burgh gates. So townsfolk and prentices joined forces and set about me with a will.

I mind one of the prentices giving tongue like a hound puppy,

" 'Tis one of those plaguey men-at-arms robbing a decent burgess! Come on all of you, and we'll show him!"

"I'm not then!" I yelled back. "He was lying drunk across the causeway, and I fell over his legs in the dark!"

They only jeered. "A likely tale! Never heed the rascal—come on!"

Well, I got my back against the high wall of somebody's yard, and felt to make sure my sword was loose in its sheath. I'd no wish to use it, so long as we didn't get beyond fists; but I caught the flicker of a knife-blade in the torchlight, and I wasn't for having my throat slit if I could help it. And then, just as things were starting to look really ugly, I heard a voice from somewhere above my head.

"Here! Over the wall!—I'll cover you."

I snatched a glance upward, and there, astride the wall, was a man with a quarter-staff in his hands, and him grinning from ear to ear. I'd no time to wonder if I could trust him. I just whipped round and reached for the top of the wall—it's not for nothing I've the longest reach of any man in Drumfyvie guard-room!—and swung myself up, kicking out backwards as I went. I felt my heel crash into somebody's face, and heard the quarter-staff crack on somebody's head. I heard their howls, too!

Next thing, I was over the wall and safe on the far side. A moment later, my helpful friend dropped beside me, and all the rest of the crowd were left baying like a hound pack in the lane.

"Run!" said my laddie. "Run, before they think to climb the wall on each other's shoulders!"

So we ran, the pair of us, doubling and twisting among the maze of back yards and kale plots, through hedges and over walls, down lanes and side alleys, till the sound of the hunt on our tails was lost in the ordinary garboil of Drumfyvie making merry for Hogmanay, and we dropped over the last wall on to the corner of Mill Lane, where it comes up to join the High Street. I mind a party of revellers passed us, singing at the tops of their voices, but they were over-busy trying to hold themselves and each other upright, to notice the likes of us. So we stopped a minute or so to catch our breath—we needed it!

"Thanks, friend, whatever—name you bear," I managed at

last. "I don't know why you'd be—putting yourself out for a man-at-arms, but—thanks, just the same!"

"Donal Dhu is the name I bear," said he, and I could hear the honest enjoyment in his voice. "I heard the fight starting up, you see, and I thought—maybe 'twould be worth joining in.—So I made that way, to see. And six or seven to one isn't fair odds, not fair odds at all. Besides, I enjoy a good fight.—It warms you up on a night that's like to bring snow any minute."

"There's some I know, would have kept clear of such odds, all the same," I told him. "But why are we standing here on a draughty street corner, when we could be sitting snug in The Fighting Cocks? Come on, and I'll buy you a pot of ale."

So we crossed the street to The Fighting Cocks tavern. There was a good handful of men-at-arms there already, and one pot leads to another; and Donal and I ended the evening swearing eternal brotherhood. And when at last we were for weaving our way back to the Castle, what should the old lad do but get on his feet to come along with us. He was not quite steady in his standing, and not all that clear in his speech, but his mind was clear made up.

"Ockie Breck, my shworn brother," said he, flinging an arm about my shoulders, "I've never known until this night, what—what I would be doing with my life. But now I am thinking that I will be coming up to the Castle with you and your frien's here, and offering myself to—to the Sheriff for a man-at-arms, for I was never so at home in any company before thish night!"

There was a roar of laughter from the rest of the lads, and they came crowding round to thump hi mon the back, crying, "Aye, Donal Dhu, you do that!" and—"Fine and glad we'll be to have you!"—" 'Tis a great life, a great life if you don't die of it!"

So away we went, the lot of us. Mind you, we'd never have got Donal through with us into the Castle, if it hadn't been the Season of Misrule, and everybody a wee thing off their heads. But as it was, we got him past the gate guard with no trouble. 'Twas beginning to snow thick and fast by that time, too, and that helped. And once through to the outer bailey, who should we come upon but the Sheriff himself, and some of his guests,

with squires carrying torches, all heading for the kennels. The Sheriff had been given a fine pair of Irish wolfhounds as a New Year gift, and I suppose he and his friends were off to take a look at them before bedtime, snowstorm and all. I mind thinking 'twas a bonnie picture they made in their gay clothes and furred cloaks, and the yellow flames of the torches under the dark of the night, and the snowflakes whirling down.

Well, so what should Donal do but step forward and plant himself full in Sir David's path, and doff his battered bonnet with a flourish you'd not have seen bettered in Holyrood Palace!

"My Lord Sheriff," said he, "you're the very man I was wanting to meet!"

The Sheriff stopped in his tracks, looking a mite surprised, but he answered Donal with all civility. "Am I so? And why would that be, friend?"

"I am wishful," Donal told him obligingly, "to join your men-at-arms."

"Well now," said Sir David, "you choose an unlikely time to come wishing it, surely? Rolf, bring that torch here . . . Uh-ha! Donal Dhu, if I'm not much mistaken! I've heard some wild tales of you, my mannie."

Donal beamed at him, "Your pardon, my Lord Sheriff—your men-at-arms are not just as peaceful as sucking doves, if all tales be true."

I broke in fast, "He's a bonnie fighting man, Sir David, and saved me from a broken head and maybe worse, this night."

The Sheriff nodded. "Well, that sounds a promising start! And we may be needing bonnie fighting men again before so long, if some of us read the signs aright . . . So now, Donal Dhu, if you are of the same mind by the sober light of tomorrow morning, we'll hand you over to the Captain, to see if he can make a man-at-arms of you. You, Eckie Brock, stow him somewhere for the night—he's your responsibility."

And with that, Sir David and his guests moved off towards the kennels again.

Donal was my responsibility all right! And next day, because he lacked the courage for it, so he said, it was I that had to go and tell his Aunt Leezy who'd brought him up, that he'd joined the

Castle men-at-arms! Down I went to her cottage in Thread-needle Wynd—he told me I'd know it by the thorn tree growing against the wall—and knocked on the door and introduced myself and gave her Donal's message. And when I'd done, she had that much to say about it, I thought she'd never get to the end; and I didn't wonder Donal had shirked coming himself! Aye well, she'd let me in, and the fire was warm.

But my she was a bleak-faced body!

"Well!" said she, with her arms folded tight across her chest. "I'm thankful his mother, my poor sister, didn't live to see it, that's all I can say!" (If only it had been!) "Wild blood there is in him—I've said it often enough to Mistress Anderson up the street yonder. I knew how it would be when my poor sister took up with that travelling Highland man. And when he got himself killed in some daft cattle raid, back she came in the end, with the bairn under her cloak! Donal Dhu . . . With his father's black eyes and hair even then, though he was but a few weeks old! She didn't live the year out, and there was I left with the bairn to rear! I treated him like he was my own. I brought him up on good food and the fear of God, and found him work with a respectable tradesman when he was of an age to earn his bread. But he lost it within the month. He never keeps any job, he goes missing that often . . ."

"I'm sure it does you credit, Mistress," I said, "but it's time I wasn't here. I've to be back on watch up at the Castle, come sundown."

"Any wild ploy," bewailed Aunt Leezy, "any mischief in the town, he'd be mixed up in it. The only skills that laddie has are with the quarter-staff and the bow. And God save us, where did he get his bow-skill but out in the forest after the King's deer! All Drumfyvie knows him for the wicked laddie he is—born to come to a bad end! I've told him so, time and time again. But it makes no difference, no difference at all . . ."

"It's me that'll come to a bad end if I'm late on watch," I tried again.

"And what can you *do* with a laddie like that?" demanded Aunt Leezy.

"I'd not be knowing," I said. I'd got as far as the door by that time. "But one thing I know fine—I wouldn't go talking

to Sir David's men-at-arms about Donal and the King's deer!"

But I doubt she even heard me; and her voice was still going on as I headed up the Wynd, "And now what must he do but join that roistering, godless crew up at the Castle. I've said it before, and I'll say it again, I'm thankful my poor sister didn't live to . . ."

I got back to the Castle just in time to snatch a hunk of bread and cheese before I went on watch. It felt like I'd been gone a long while!

Well, with a bit of training, Donal made a man-at-arms as good as any other. And Sir David was right, the day was coming when we'd need all the fighting men we could get.

By that time, England's Henry the Seventh was dead—him that had been married to our own Princess Margaret. Their son was King of England now—Henry the Eighth. The old King had been the kind that gets what he wants but does it by quiet means; but his son was a horse of a different colour, a hot-head like our King James. And he'd scarcely got his crown on before trouble started grumbling between us and England, like thunder along the Border Hills. It was all mixed up with wars across the Narrow Seas, in Europe. Being just a fighting man, there wasn't much I understood about that. Nobody expects the likes of us to know what we're fighting for—we just follow our leaders and draw sword when they tell us!

But I do know that the summer after Donal joined us, the old treaty of friendship between us and France was made good again. And our James told English Henry that if he wanted war with France, he could have war with Scotland, too, at one and the same time. There was arguing and parleying and goodness knows what-all, but by the next summer, the whole of Scotland knew fine that it was to be war with England again.

King James sent a messenger to Sir David, and messengers all across the land, for the lords and barons to muster their fighting men—and many of the Highland chiefs, too, for he had a great following in the Highlands. For the English Army was into France, and the English King with it.

"War!" said Donal, his black eyes dancing just as they must have done when he was off after the King's deer. "We're away to see life over the Border."

"Or death," I said. "War's a killing matter. Come down to The Fighting Cocks and have a drink."

So we went down to The Fighting Cocks, and all along the way we passed folks standing in knots and talking. The news was all abroad; and I mind the old men had gathered thick about the Market Cross, grave-faced, and telling any young ones who would listen, what war was like in *their* day; and there were women with their bairns at the house doors, and lassies wide-eyed with trouble for their lads. And everywhere we heard the one word—"War!" Even the light summer wind seemed to catch it up and carry it to and fro. "War—war . . ." And I mind thinking 'twas as if the voices of men long since dead in other wars were mingled with it in some way, and I shivered in the warm sunlight, and crossed myself, though I'm not the fanciful kind.

But that was a strange time, a strange time altogether. And there were all kinds of strange stories whispering around in the days that followed. Tales of signs and warnings. It was said that in Linlithgow when the King and his nobles were at mass, there came in an old man in a blue gown, begging the King not to set forth against the English; and when he'd given his warning, he disappeared in a puff of smoke. And it was said there'd been a voice heard from Edinburgh tolbooth, calling the names of all the nobles—the King's amongst them—that would be dead within forty days. Just the voice, and no man there at all.

Up at the Castle, the weird whisperings came and went, but we had little time to take account of them. The King's summons had come, and we were making ready. There were weapons to be furbished and horses to be shod, and supply carts to be loaded with spare arms and meal and salt beef and all else that an army needs to carry with it on the march. And then on the very day before we were due to set out, the Sheriff was thrown by a young horse he was trying, and laid by in his bed with a broken ankle. The news came to us in the guardroom, and ill news it was. "Who'll lead, then?" someone asked.

"His two sons, of course," said Willie Anstruther.

"And that's a fine look-out for us," said I. "The laddies have no more experience of battle than two babes unborn—and young Alan was only knighted three weeks ago."

"I'm not saying they're fit for it," said Willie. "I'm saying they're all we've got."

So, next morning, we saddled up, and with the pikemen marching behind us, we rode away down High Street and out through the East Port, to join the King's Army mustering in the Lammermuirs. The two laddies were happy enough to be taking over their father's command, and made their horses dance as though they were going to a tournament, for the benefit of the folks that had thronged down to see us on our way.

'Twas a fine army that the King led over the Border at summer's end—all the fighting men of Scotland from laddies of sixteen to greybeards of sixty, from the Highlands and the Lowlands and the farmost Western Isles. A great war-host, and all seemingly with their hearts high within them. But I don't think any of us had forgotten the voice calling from the Edinburgh tolbooth, for all that.

We spent the first couple of weeks taking the castles that lay across our path south from the Border. And Donal did a deal of grumbling about it. "It's a sorry waste of time, so it is! We should be pushing on, down into England. This way, the English will have the choosing of the battleground."

"And how many wars have you fought through, Donal?" said I. "Only a fool goes into battle leaving enemy-held castles behind him to cut off the way home if he needs it in a hurry!"

But looking back on it, I'm not so sure, for those two weeks gave the Earl of Surrey, him that was the English Commander, time to gather his levies from all across the North, aye, and bring up his big guns, too . . .

I mind the last night. We were camped all along Flodden Edge, above a river they call the Till. We could hear it sounding after the day's rain, below us in the dark. But the rain had stopped about sunset, only the ground was still slippery underfoot, and it was hard to find thorn and heather dry enough to feed the campfires. Donal had managed to knock over a hare, and was trying to cook it on the point of his sword over the smoky flames.

"You've not lost your skill then, Donal Dhu," said young Sandy, passing by.

Donal turned his sword like a spit. "It's not a fine fat buck, but 'twill serve to give a bit of savour to the bannock. Bide you, and join us."

"I'll do that, and gladly," said Sandy, "for there'll be no time for catching hares in the morning, and the Devil knows which of us will be needing supper."

"That's an ill-omened thing to say," I told him. "If you must have such thoughts, the least you can do is keep them under your own bonnet!"

But Donal grinned, examining the scorched but still-raw hare. "Sandy has the right of it. Food never tastes so good, nor the sun feels so warm on the back of your neck, nor the forest smells so fresh in the night-time, as when you have a good chance of losing it all next minute to an arrow between your ribs." He glanced up at me, "That's what my Aunt Leezy can never rightly understand, poor soul."

Well, so we ate our half-raw hare; and next day we fought our battle. Not that it was a battle—it was just a bloody massacre.

Right at the beginning, the English managed to outflank us, making for Branxton Hill in our rear, and after that 'twas which of us could gain the Hill first. The ground was so slippery with all the rain, that most of us kicked off our boots and ran barefoot, for a better grip on the miry slopes. Then the English guns opened up on us, before our own could be brought to bear. They tore great holes in our ranks as we charged—our battle-line was torn to rags before ever we reached Surrey's troops. I mind the men falling, and the blood, and the screaming of the horses . . .

That was when the Sheriff's younger laddie died.

But it was the English bills that finished us. The eight-foot, spear-tipped, axe-bladed bills. They hacked our long Scottish pikes to pieces, and when we had nothing left but our swords, they had the reach of us by four good feet. Sir Rolf got his left arm near hacked from his shoulder, though we brought him back with the breath still in him, thank the Lord!

But we didn't bring back the King, and we didn't bring back Donal Dhu . . .

So, we were defeated and driven from the field, and there's

96

few enough of us will ever come to our own homes again. Me and the handful of Sir David's men that are left, got back to Drumfyvie yesterday, as I told you in the beginning. But I'm not just sure how we did it. We carried Sir Rolf up here to the Castle, and gave him into his father's hands. And the news of young Alan's death, and all the rest. And after I'd got some food in my belly and a clean rag to tie up a scratch that I had on my arm, and a few hours sleep, I got leave from the Captain to go down into the town on business of my own. Weary business, but it must be tended to.

I went down to the wee house in Threadneedle Wynd, and knocked on the door. Aunt Leezy opened to me almost as if she'd been waiting, and she must have read the news in my face, for she said in a voice that was dry as a breaking stick, "He's dead, then?"

"Aye," I said. "He's dead. Will you let me in, Aunt Leezy?"

She drew me in and set me down by the fire. I was chilled to the heart's core, though the morning was warm enough for this time of year, and I couldn't stop my teeth chattering. She sat down across the hearth, her old hands gripped together in her lap, and waited for me to speak. But I couldn't speak about Donal, just at once. To gain time I said, "Ye'll have heard the news of the fighting, Aunt Leezy"

"Aye, we heard," she said, "after weeks of waiting. Every time a horseman came in through the East Port, we'd all come running to our doors, hoping 'twas word of a victory, and growing more afraid every time. And in between whiles the streets were that quiet, if a dog barked you could hear it from one end of Drumfyvie to the other. And then the word came . . . The man who brought it had a bloody clout round his head, and his horse was near to foundering. Folks ran out crying for news, but he only shouted to them to make way, his news was to the Castle. Then Davy Donaldson ran out and caught his horse's bridle, and shouted 'What news, man? Tell us, for the love of God!' And at that the man cried out, 'The blackest news that ever Scotland heard! The King is dead and the Army cut to pieces! Stand back now and let me through.' And he wrenched his bridle free and was away up to the Castle Wynd like a madman!"

I think Aunt Leezy had begun talking because, daft old besom

though she is, she saw that I needed time. But having got started, she kept on because she was afraid of what I'd tell her when she stopped. "Folks went running after him, calling and crying for word of their sons and brothers and husbands—as though he could know what had become of every man in the King's Army. I just went back to my baking. There seemed nothing else to do."

She stopped then, and we looked at each other across the hearth. Then she said slowly, "So now—tell me about Donal."

"The ground was slippery after all the rain," I said. "After we'd been fighting over it for a while it was like butter—red butter. And I slipped and went down, and Donal side-strode over me—getting to be a habit with Donal, 'twas, covering me from the enemy—and so he took the thrust that was meant for me. After that I'm not sure what happened. I must have got to my feet again, and Donal was still on his, just about, and we pulled back together. We were in a part of the line that fell back in reasonable order. We were well clear when he started coughing blood, and—I caught him as he fell. But there was nothing I could do, nothing anyone could do."

"I know that fine, or ye'd have done it," Aunt Leezy said.

But there was one thing more I still had to tell her. "Donal gave me a message for you. He said, 'Aunt Leezy always told me I'd come to a bad end. If you get out of this, tell her she had the right of it.' And he tried to laugh, but the blood got in the way."

"He was a great one for laughing," said Aunt Leezy after a moment. "God be good to him, the wild, wicked laddie that he was. Maybe, after all, the world would be a duller place without a few of his kind to set it hopping."

"That's the truth, Aunt Leezy," I said, and sat quiet a bit, feeling somehow better, as though I'd had a boil lanced and the poison drawn away. Then I gathered myself together to go. "Will I come back, Aunt Leezy?"

She looked down at her hands and then up at me, quiet-like. And I thought, she'd never managed to change Donal, but he'd changed her, sure enough. "Come you back whenever you've a mind to Eckie Brock. I'll be lonely, lacking Donal, for the rest of my days, and maybe, deep down, so will you. So come, and

welcome, but only if you come for your own sake, not just for Donal's, nor yet for mine."

Proud old besom!

I got to my feet; it was time I was away. "I'll be back," I said, "I'll be back, Aunt Leezy."

And so I will.

A House with Glass Windows
A.D. 1563

8

It must be close on thirty years ago, the day I got the message from Bailie Alan Ferguson, the wine merchant, to ask would I wait on him at his house on a matter of business. I knew, of course, what kind of business 'twas like to be, for I'm a Master Mason, by trade. Forsyth's the name—William Forsyth.

Bailie Ferguson, like most of the Drumfyvie merchants, lived in one of the tall old merchant houses in the High Street, with the shop and store-rooms and counting-house below, and the living-rooms above. Fine and handy, especially in the thick of winter when no man wants to be out and about more than he need. But lately, there'd been a rumour going round that the Bailie had bought himself a piece of land out beyond the old town walls, where some other of the merchants, feeling themselves too rich and grand nowadays to live over their businesses, had already built themselves fine new houses in which to become gentry. To be sure, he was considered to be one of the foremost merchants of the town—indeed there was talk that, come the next Michaelmas Head Court, he'd be elected Provost, no less.

So when I got the message, I combed my hair and beard and put on my Sunday jerkin, and went off looking more fit for Kirk than for a job of work, for I'd a sense of great occasion upon me.

"Good day to ye, Master Forsyth," said the Bailie, when I came into his counting-house. "Sit ye down, man, sit ye down . . . Now—ye'll maybe have some idea of the business that I'm minded to discuss with you?"

"Why now, Bailie, as to that, there's a wee bit talk in the town, I'll not deny," said I, "but I'd as lief wait for you to tell me, all the same."

"Well then, I'll come straight to the point. Ye'll have heard, no doubt, that I've bought me a bit of land on the Headrow. And a man only buys himself a bit of Headrow land for one reason, that I know of."

"To build a house on it," says I, for he still seemed to want an answer.

"Aye, well, I do feel that the time has come when I may be needing a house worthy of my—ehem—my position. I feel I owe it to myself, and to my family after me. Do you follow me, Master Forsyth?"

"Aye," I said, I knew well enough how his thoughts were running toward the time when he'd be Provost.

"Now, you're a fine craftsman, Master Forsyth, none better. I've seen the work you did for Bailie Anderson. Good, sound work. I was greatly impressed, I was indeed."

"Ye'll find none better in Stirling or St. Andrews," I told him.

"Just so—just so, Master Forsyth, which is why I am wishful that you should handle the building of this new house of mine," said he, coming out with it at last.

I never moved a muscle to let the man see I was pleased.—A Master Mason has his dignity to keep up, after all. "And what like of house would you have in mind, Bailie? And how large, about?" said I.

"Stone-built, Master Forsyth," he said, "stone-built—none of your timber-frame buildings for me. As to size—not over large, yet big enough to have a proper dignity . . . Wait, I've made a few sketches, just to give ye an idea . . ."

And he shuffled a couple of sheets from among the ledgers and business papers on the table, and spread them out for me to see. They were clear enough, and I could see 'twas a bonnie place he had in mind. The ground floor to be raised a few steps in the usual way over the cellars and store-rooms; and he'd sketched in a parlour, and a buttery, and a wee winter-parlour to keep in the warmth of the fire. Kitchens out back, of course. And on the floor above, a gallery for entertaining and dancing and the like, and all the bedchambers; and over all, an attic floor for the servants and the bairns.

"Aye," I said, "a bonnie house, and the sketches are fine and clear, Bailie."

"As ye see, the main chamber is to be here, on the first floor. My wife expressly wishes it so."

"That's according to the modern fashion," I took a closer look.

"Er—where would the stairs come in? I can't just see them marked."

There was a wee blank silence, then he said hurriedly, "I felt *you* should advise me as to that—tricky things, staircases, and I've more experience of wine. How would it be to have it coming up—*here* maybe, sheltered from the north and east?" And he put his finger on a spot that would have ruined the whole look of the house.

"And outside stair?" I said, "we-ell . . . I know it's been the usual way in the past, but if 'twas me, I'd consider an enclosed turnpike, here on the corner. No going out into the wind and weather at all."

He was fairly taken with the notion. "Aye, indeed it's an idea well worth considering. Well worth considering . . . The more I think of it, the more I like it . . . Now, as to the windows—a lantern-window, here at the west end, I was thinking—"

The door opened as he was speaking, and in sailed Mistress Ferguson—in a fine silk gown, and it no more than half-way through the morning—"Ah, I've come at the right moment," said she, sitting herself down. "Master Forsyth, the windows must be all of glass!"

"Glass?" said I, a wee thing taken by surprise. "Glass, Mistress? . . . 'Twill mean bringing in glaziers from Stirling and put the price up a goodish deal. If I might make so bold as to suggest—oiled silk with a lattice over it makes bonnie windows. —'Tis the usual, hereabouts—"

"As ye may see by looking at any one of a dozen new houses in Drumfyvie," said Mistress Ferguson, a mite waspish. "No, no, we must have *glass* windows. My husband owes it to his position as the new Pro—"

"Whisht! Isobel!" Master Ferguson put in hurriedly, "Have ye taken leave of your senses? That's not for speaking of as yet!" He turned back to me. "But certainly, glass windows, at least in the principal rooms. If need be, we must try to save the cost in other ways."

We were at it most of the morning, before at last I took my leave, and went home with a fistful of notes and sketches, to tell the news to Jeannie my wife, and work out my costings.

'Twould take a round £250, I reckoned, when I'd worked it

all out, to build the house Bailie Ferguson had in mind, glass windows included. So I made out a total of £275, to allow for bargaining,—the Bailie being a merchant-man, and therefore not one to pay the asked price for anything without a wee bit of a haggle.

Sure enough, when I went back with the costings, he threw up his hands in horror and offered me £230. So we ha dour spell of bargaining, and eventually came to agreement at £250, both of us well pleased with ourselves. Then we drew up the contract, listing all the usual matters that have to be agreed upon —the price, and how it's to be paid and when, and the finishing date and all. So there it was at last, all written down plain and fair on a crackling sheet of parchment.

"Contract between Alan Ferguson, Wine Merchant, of the Royal Burgh of Drumfyvie, and William Forsyth, Master Mason, of the same Burgh, for the building of a house . . . All stone and other materials and all workmanship throughout to be the best of their respective kinds . . . The agreed sum of £250, £20 to be paid at the start of the work, and a further £20 on the same date of every month until the total sum be reached, save for the final £10, which shall not be paid until the work be completed to the satisfaction of both Alan Ferguson and William Forsyth . . ."

And then the completion date, Midsummer's Eve, *Anno Domini* 1563.

That gave me a year, with a couple of months over for mishaps and winter weather.

The pair of us signed, and then the Bailie brought out a bottle of wine and two fine Venetian goblets to drink to the occasion.

"The new house!" said Master Ferguson and we clinked glasses.

"Good fortune and happiness upon it!" said I.

So all was settled, and we started work. And soon the plot of land on the Headrow was thrumming with activity, and you had to shout to make yourself heard above the noise of chisels on stone, and adze on timber and the trundling of cartwheels, and the shouts of the workmen. We ran into a bit of trouble almost at the start, for when we came to levelling and pegging

out the site, we had to change the course of the wee burn that runs through the Headrow. It was just a matter of turning it northward for a few feet, in a loop, to clear the stables and out-houses. Nothing to give anyone a sore head, as you might say. But the trouble was that this burn breaks out of the ground close under the curtain-wall of the Castle, and there's an old story that it has its beginning in an underground spring below the Castle mound, and another old story that before ever the Castle stood there, the mound belonged to the Fairy Kind. Me, I'm not paying much heed to fairies and such, and I reckon 'tis nought but an old wives' tale, but there's plenty folk believe it. Long Jock did, for one.

Long Jock was the best woodwright I ever had, but his head was as full of old unchancy stories as an egg is full of meat. "Yon's no old wives' tale," said he. "You should know that well enough, Master, you living all your days in Drumfyvie, and your father and grandfather before ye. And 'tis no old wives' tale that the first Sheriff was killed by his own falcon when he angered the Fairy Kind by building his Hall a'top their mound. That's solid history! Tamper with what belongs to Themselves, and Themselves will have a life in payment, so they will!"

Some of the lads just laughed at him, but there were others crossed their fingers and whispered among themselves that he was in the right of it. But the course of the burn had to be changed, old wives' tale or no', so changed it was, and I mind I kept a sharp eye out for accidents in the days that followed—just in case, you'll understand. But as time passed, and the building went on without mishap, the workmen's uneasiness grew less, and at last was seemingly forgotten.

But I'm getting a wee thing ahead of myself, for I must tell you that Long Jock had a niece—Nannie, they called her—whose father farmed Eldonrigg, a mile or so outside the town. She used to come in to the weekly market with eggs and cheese and the like—herbs, too, for she was a skilled herb-woman—and folks often went to her with their boils and belly-aches instead of to the local apothecary.

Well, so 'twas that on market days Nannie would come up to visit Jock as he worked, bringing him a bite of food in a napkin, and often a bit over for the other lads as well—so she was always

sure of a welcome. Och, but she'd have been as sure of a welcome empty-handed, that one, any place, any time.

It so happened that Nannie was there one day—it would be when we'd got the house walls two, three feet high—when Master Ferguson came by to see how the work was going forward. Mistress Ferguson was with him, towing wee Ritchie, the youngest bairn, by the hand. 'Twas like a royal visit, Mistress Ferguson in particular that gracious and condescending, with her "Excellent, Master Forsyth!" "How fast the work grows, Master Forsyth!" Then on a sudden she lets out a screech. "Ritchie! He's gone! He's lost! . . . Ritchie, my lambkin, where are you?"

"I thought you had him by the hand, Isobel," said the Bailie, just a mite impatient.

"I only let go of him for an instant—the merest instant!" wailed his lady.

Master Ferguson snorted. "An instant's all that limb of Satan needs. Master Forsyth, did you see him go?"

"Not me."

"Oh, Master Forsyth," fluttered the lady, "pray send some of your men to look for him. There are so many holes and rough places—find my baby before he comes to harm!"

So I set a couple of the lads to hunting around for him, but barely had they set off, calling his name, when Nannie came up the path from the burn, leading Ritchie by the hand, and both of them as gay as linties!

"See, here he is," said she, fine and calm. "He was helping me down by the burn, weren't you, Ritchie?"

Mistress Ferguson snatched him to her bosom. "Oh, my bairn! My wicked lamb!"

But Ritchie wriggled out of her grasp, and grabbed at Nannie's hand again. "I'm not wicked!" said he. "I was helping Nannie to mend the wee tree, so I was!"

Mistress Ferguson looked from one to the other, all confused. "Nannie? Who is Nannie? And what wee tree, my heart's love?"

Nannie smiled, she'd the bonniest smile. "I am Nannie, Mistress Ferguson, niece to Long Jock, the woodwright yonder. I came up to bring him a bannock after I'd sold my butter and cheese and herbs at the market. And as to the tree, that's a wee birch seedling that had its roots hurt when the lads were digging

back the bank of the burn. But I'm thinking 'twill do well enough now, and grow to be a bonnie tree in time."

"Aye," said Ritchie solemnly, "Nannie did things to its roots, and tied it up to a stick till it grows strong—I helped her."

"My lamb, of course you did," said Mistress Ferguson, fair doting, "such a clever boy!" And then she turned to Nannie, speaking to her kind enough, but maybe a bit as though she thought the lass were simple. "I should scold you for keeping him away from me, but I will not, for I am sure you meant no harm . . . And Nannie, I have been thinking that now I shall at last have some space for a garden—a herb plot and a rose border and the like; and since it seems that you have some skill with growing things, I dare say I may be glad of your help from time to time."

"To make a new garden?" I mind Nannie's voice was soft with delight. "My! That would be fine—I'll help you all I can, Mistress, and gladly."

So it happened, after that, that Nannie appeared at other times beside market days. And often, I'd see her and Mistress Ferguson with their heads together, planning to put an apple tree here and a border of lavender or rosemary there, and grow a white burnet rose up a south wall that wasn't built yet, nor wouldn't be for months to come. Most times, young Ritchie would be with them. Coming so long after the others, he was his mother's pet, but in truth, 'twas Nannie he trailed after—She had a way with bairns, as indeed she had with all living and growing things. And I mind her making him wee dollies out of poppy heads at harvest time, and showing him how to sail boats made from wild iris leaves when the next spring came round. But there I go, getting ahead of myself again . . .

Come the Head Court at Michaelmas, Bailie Ferguson was elected Provost, right enough, just as we'd all expected. And a wee while after that, we got the roof timbers up. I mind well the day when the last rafter was pegged into place, and we hoisted up the topping-out fir-tree—like a feather in the house's cap, ye might say—and celebrated with a keg of good ale provided by the new Provost. The man himself, and his lady, came out to see the tree go up. Though 'twas a day of wind and driving rain, and Mistress Ferguson's gown got fair ruined at the hem, with

all the mud there was about, I don't think she even noticed, she was that taken up with her fancies as she teetered around, clinging to the Provost's arm.

"It will be the grand house! The grandest in all Drumfyvie! I can see it now, with the sun shining back from its glass windows. . . . Mistress Kerr and Mistress Anderson will be fit to fly to pieces with envy!" And she gives a little shriek. "Oh my, I have *such* an idea, my love! Let us give a ball—a Midsummer Ball, and ask *everyone* of consequence! . . . Why, we can even invite the Sheriff and his Lady, now that we have a house fine enough to entertain them in!"

"Isobel, Isobel, not so fast!" begged the Provost. "*When* we have a house fit to entertain them in, maybe! In any case, I hardly think this one will be fit to hold a Ball in, the very day Master Forsyth and his men move out!"

But Mistress Ferguson overrode him. "Nonsense, husband. Midsummer's Eve is completion date for outbuildings and all. Now if the outbuildings were left till last—" She turned on me with her best smile. "Master Forsyth, *dear* Master Forsyth, you could have the house itself finished in time?—To pleasure me?"

"I think it could be done, Mistress," said I. (Remembering that I'd arranged for a bit of time in hand, but taking care not to make it sound too easy, all the same.)

She was fair delighted, and showed it with another of her little shrieks. "Oh, I can see it all! The moon and the candles, and the bonnie new French dances!"

One of the lads sniggered behind her back, but she didn't hear him. I think the Provost did—there's whiles, I was sorry for the Provost.

Howsoever, we got the roof of the main house shingled over before the winter was upon us, and after that, of course, we could get on with the inside work whenever the weather was too bad to be at the stables and outbuildings. Indeed, if Mistress Ferguson had had her way, we'd have been all the time at work on the gallery and the Great Chamber—the one with the lantern window—leaving the kitchens and stables to build themselves, seemingly.

Well, so the winter passed, and the spring, and the Provost's fine new house was all but finished, even to the green and blue

paint on the wainscoting, even to the glass in the windows. Aye, and the windows were bonnie, I'll say that.

"Bonnie," agreed Nannie, "like water shining in the sunlight, and grey and ripple-streaked on a rainy day. They seem to make the house and the burn kin to each other." She was always a fanciful lass, that one . . .

I reckon we'd have been finished and cleared away well before Midsummer, if Mistress Ferguson hadn't come up with another of her outlandish ideas! Dear save us—she suddenly took the notion for a garden-house—a thing I'd never heard of in all my born days! But seemingly she'd seen such a thing once, in the garden of some great English house.

"A wee garden-house in the loop of the burn, with two steps up to the door, and seats inside, and a flat roof with pots of growing things on it, and steps at the back to get up to the roof. 'Twill give the bonniest view westward. And there's no other garden in Drumfyvie has aught like it."

So there was I, away back to my drawing-board yet again! but even so, when Midsummer came round, the garden-house was finished but for a stretch of the balustrade round the flat roof.

The Provost and his folk had been in the house a good few days, by then, the servants polishing and scouring from top to bottom, and arranging and re-arranging the fine furniture according to Mistress Ferguson's orders. Even the horses were safe in their new stables and the groom and stable-boy pressed into service along with everybody else, to make ready for the Midsummer Ball. Oh aye, Mistress Ferguson got her Ball. She wasn't one to let go of an idea once she'd grasped it, not that one!

Jeannie and I weren't asked, of course—'twas for the gentry —but it being a fine night, I strolled up to take a look, after I'd had my supper.

There was a great round moon almost as yellow as the candle-light shining from the windows, and I could hear the music of lutes and viols and virginals, floating out from the Great Chamber into the warm, sweet-smelling summer-night. It all seemed to make a kind of magic that was new and strange to me.

I wasn't the only one to have thought of quietly "visiting" that night, and when I found myself—one thing leading to another—in the big new kitchen, there were some of my workmen there already. Long Jock was among them, and a good few others, friends and kinsfolk of the servants, come to see the fun—Nannie, too. She'd come up earlier with fresh herbs to season the supper dishes, and stayed on to tend to wee Ritchie, who had a touch of the colic.

"Aye," she was saying, "there's nought better than a poultice of boiled violet leaves to soothe away a bairn's colic."

We made a merry evening of it, I can tell you! With a bite to eat, and a sup or two of good ale, and now and then a trip up the turnpike stair for a peek at the dancing. Bonnie, it was, the ladies in their swinging bell-shaped skirts; the men in their silken doublets and hose, in all the colours of a summer garden; and the lace ruffs about their necks as fine as frost, and here and there a jewel blinking in the candlelight. And all pacing and circling and swanning to and fro in time to the music . . .

Close on midnight, one of the serving maids slipped upstairs to see was all well with Ritchie—someone had been doing that, odd times, all night—and came back with a face as white as a clout. "He's gone!" says she. "His bed's empty and not a sign of him!"

"He'll have walked off in his sleep—'twouldn't be the first time," said the cook.

Nannie was on her feet in a flash. "Sleepwalking, is it? And him wi' the colic on him, and in a strange house with all this to-ing and fro-ing? Hurry!—we must find him before he catches cold . . ."

So we set off this way and that, searching for the bairn indoors and out, for he could have been anywhere by that time.

'Twas Long Jock who spotted him first—all alone in the moonlight, up on the flat roof of the garden-house!

How he'd got past us all, I'll never know, unless the Fairy Folk had a hand in it. But maybe they did. Aye, maybe they did . . . At all events, there he was, and drifting straight across the roof towards the gap where the balustrade was not yet finished, on the side towards the burn!

We ran—all of us—ran as we'd never run before, across the

turf and up the narrow stair, me ahead of them all, with Long Jock at my heels. But by the time I gained the top, the bairn was standing on the far side, right in the gap; and then—it's hard to explain—a long trail of mist from the burn seemed to rise and curl round the wee one so he was all but lost in it! I'd my hand outstretched to grab him; and he took one more step, and went straight over the edge of the roof. I all but went after him, but I flung sideways and fetched up against the end of the balustrade that checked me, all a-sprawl.

Then it was as though the mist curled back, and all things took on the slowness of a dream, and I saw Nannie on the bank below me, her arms held out to catch the bairn, and by the Grace of God, wee Ritchie fell straight into them! But in catching him, she slipped on the burn-side grass, wet with the mist. She went down, with the bairn in her arms, and I heard the sickening crack as her head struck one of the stone blocks lying ready on the turf for use on the balustrade.

The next thing I mind, I was down there beside her, and a whole crowd with me. Someone took Ritchie from Nannie's arms, and he began howling fit to wake the dead; but 'twas only fear, there wasn't a scratch on him. Nannie lay there, never moving, and Jock bent over her, then looked round at us as though he was accusing us, one and all. "I warned you! I said if aught that had to do with the Fairy Folk was tampered with, Themselves would have a life in payment—one life or another . . . They've missed the bairn, but they've took Nannie, so they have!"

A kind of cold shiver passed through us all, like a whisper of wind through standing barley. But I saw that the lassie's eyelids were beginning to flutter. "Hold your croaking!" I said, "They've not taken Nannie—see now, her eyes are opening. She's coming back to herself."

Nannie turned her head slowly, her eyes open and wandering. "Ritchie? Is he safe?"

"Did ye ever hear a bairn bawl like that, who wasn't safe?" said I. "You broke his fall, and all's well with him save that he's a mite scared. Here, Mary, don't stand there gawping, dip your kerchief in the burn and give it me—she's a gash on her forehead needs bathing."

"No matter," Nannie whispered, as if she were half-asleep,

with a wee smile flickering in her face. "They didn't—take the bairn."

I carried her up to the house, and when I left she was sleeping, quiet as a bairn herself, curled up in the chimney corner, with her hair pushed back from the cut, and a good thick wad of cobwebs on it to stop the bleeding and make all well. And upstairs in the Great Chamber, the grand folks knew nothing of what had happened—not even the Provost and Mistress Ferguson until after. We could hear the music playing away as bonnie as ever.

But if Long Jock had the right of it, the Fairy Kind had begun to collect payment, that Midsummer's Eve. And as I made my way home, I wondered would they be satisfied, or come again for the full price. Ritchie? Or Nannie? Or whom?

Witch Hunt! 9
A.D. 1589

I went back to Drumfyvie last summer.—Me, Tam Webster, second son of Luke Webster the bonnet-maker, and myself Master of the *Mary Lindsay*. I'd always sworn I wouldn't. But when the *Mary Lindsay* docked at the port of Leith last June, there was word waiting for me that my father was dead—my mother died at my birth—and my elder brother needed to see me about my share of the bonnet-making business. So back I went for a few days, leaving my Mate in charge of the ship.

We settled the family business, and on the last evening, I walked over to see was anything left of Old Nannie's bothy on the edge of High Riggs Wood.

The end wall was still standing, and you could see where the doorway had been, though 'twas choked up with nettles, and the bracken grew as tall inside as out. And a white burnet rose—a seedling from the one that used to grow beside the gate—was flourishing where I mind the hearth-stone used to be. I picked a creamy, half-open bud and stuck it in my buttonhole. The scent of it seemed to come from a long way back, when I was a bairn . . . And I sat myself down on the broken remains of the front wall, and fell to thinking about the old days—about my own bairn-days, and about Nannie, who was so much a part of them.

Folks called her "Old Nannie" as far back as ever I can remember, but she couldn't have been as old as all that, for I mind her hair was still dark, save for one white streak over a scar on her forehead where she'd taken some hurt when she was a lassie.

'Twas said that before she got that dunt she was just like anybody else, and only afterwards that she kind of hid away within herself, and took to living by her lone in the old abandoned bothy on the edge of the woods, as though she were happier with the wild things than among her own kind.

But if she didn't go among folks, folks in plenty came to her.

Anyone with sore eyes, or the colic, or a cut that wouldn't heal; and she'd treat them with the herbs she grew in the wee plot behind the bothy or gathered on the moors and along the burnside. Coltsfoot or cockleburr to shift a cough, holyshorn and Grace-of-God for the kidneys, water pimpernel and clover for boils and such like . . . Master Donaldson, the surgeon-apothecary in Market Street, said she was like to put him clean out of business with her meddling. But Old Nannie was no meddler—she was a born healer! She had "The Gift" as some folks have "The Sight".

The first time I went to Old Nannie, I was no more than six or seven. I'd disturbed a wild bees' nest in the woods and got well and truly stung. I was awful scared, but I was near the bothy and a long way from home, and my left eye closing fast. So I gathered up what little courage I had and went to find Nannie.

She drew out the stings, and pressed cool green leaves over the places to soothe away the smart. And when all was done, I was filled with shame, for I'd nought to give her. Folks mostly paid for her skills with a couple of eggs or a fresh-baked bannock or the like. But when I told her that I'd nought she just took my face between her hands and looked into it, deep and deep down into it. Then she said, "No matter for that now. You shall pay me in gold, when you are a fine sea captain."

And the strange thing was that I was not startled or surprised. Somehow it seemed quite natural that she should know the thing that I had not told to a living soul.

Back in the early days of that spring, Mistress Morrison who lived next door to us had had a few days' visit from her sailor brother. I'd got hanging round him and he'd got telling me the tales that sailors do tell to bairns—not just the ones about mermaids and monsters, but about ships and the ways of ships, and storms and trade winds and foreign lands. And after that there was nothing in the world I wanted to be but a sailor, when I grew up. But as I say, I'd never told a living soul . . .

Just the once, a few years after I first went to Old Nannie with my bee stings, I did try telling my father. But all he said, when I'd done, was "Is the bonnet-making not good enough for you, then?"

"It's not that, Father," I protested, "it's just that I'm wanting to do something else with my life. You've got Willie for the bonnets—you'll not need the both of us, surely."

"There's room enough for the both of you in the business," said my father. "I didn't build it up for the pair of you after me, to have either one of you stravaiging off to a godless life at sea!"

And he banged his fist on the table in a way he had, that I knew all too well. So I never spoke to him about it again.

But I didn't forget. The thing stayed in my mind, and in my heart; though as time went by it got to be more like a dream —the kind that's bonnie and bright and you know fine will never be anything more than a dream in all its days.

I mind saying something of that to Old Nannie one evening— I was sixteen, by then, and 'twas St. Ninian's Day, so I'd a holiday from the bonnet-making, and was free to go where I would. Most often, at those kind of times, I went to Old Nannie for a while, in an odd kind of way like going home.

"So you see, I'll never get away from Drumfyvie and the bonnets."

"You will, when the time comes," she said, looking up from the herbs that she was making into bundles for drying.

"I'll never," I said, miserably. "I've not the courage to stand up to my father, and I've not even the courage to run away. The world outside of Drumfyvie's awful big and strange."

Nannie was still looking at me, that strange, deep look, the bundles of herbs lying on her lap. "You'll find the courage," she said, scarce above her breath. "All the courage you need, when the time comes, Tam, my Tam."

That evening as I was starting back for home, I caught sight of a sudden glint of red among the autumn-gold bracken by the gate that led to the herb plot. A fine dog-fox checked for an instant looking towards the bothy, before he slunk away.

"A fox!" I said. "Did you see it, Nannie?"

"Aye, surely. That's Rory. I found him with his foot in a trap, and brought him home till it healed. Now he's my friend, and comes to see me often."

"Like me."

She laughed and laid her hand on my shoulder. "More often

than you do. But then, I'm thinking he has more free time than you."

I went home feeling fine and brave, and meaning to tell my father that very night, that I was going for a seaman come what might. But as I got nearer to our house, the courage began to run out of my heels as usual. And when I came in at the door, and heard the voices of three of my father's cronies in the room behind the shop, there was a shameful upsurge of relief in me, because I'd have no chance to tell him tonight, after all!

My brother Willie was still away at St Ninian's Fair, and so I took my supper bowl and a creepy stool to the darkest corner of the room. The lantern on the table made a flickering orange glow on the faces of my father and his friends, and cast great crouching shadows on to the walls behind them, so that they looked for all the world like conspirators hatching some plot. And indeed it was of plots and matters of the dark that they were talking. "Francis Bothwell, is it?" my father was saying, as he filled up the ale jacks. "Francis Bothwell? 'Tis well known, that one's a warlock, in league with the Devil—aye, a Master of the Black Arts."

Rolf Fleming nodded, "And with some sort of claim to the Scottish throne, so they say."

"Only King James stands in his way," said my father.

Nat Hawthorn looked fine and shocked – and enjoying every shiver of it. "Mercy on us! Would he seek the King's death, think you?—I cannot believe it!"

"There's no doubt of it," said Rolf. "You'll mind when the King sailed to Denmark to fetch home his new Queen—and was close on wrecked by yon great storm at sea—"

"Everyone knows 'twas raised by yon Bothwell," put in Rob Henderson, "him and a great gathering of witches at North Berwick, weaving hideous spells and—and baptizing a cat with Christian rites and throwing it out to sea—"

"That's surely a fearful tale!" said my father, and took comfort in his ale pot.

Nat Hawthorn wagged his head. "O'course the evidence at Bothwell's trial *was* got under torture . . . A man—or a woman —is like to admit to anything, given a wee bit help with the thumbscrews."

"Maybe," sniffed Rolf. He'd his usual cold in his head. Nannie could have cured it. "Maybe. But there *was* the storm, and it came near enough to sinking the King's ship."

"We're none of us safe in our beds—or out of them, come to that," nodded my father.

"'Tis a fearful thing! The Devil loose in the land, and no saying who's taken service with him—even here in Drumfyvie."

Rob looked behind him into the shadows. "Not here in Drumfyvie, surely?"

"And whyfore no? I tell ye 'tis everywhere—even here in Drumfyvie, who's to say there's neither witch nor warlock in our very midst?"

There was a long silence, and then Rolf said slowly, "I've wondered, whiles, about Old Nannie, away in yon wee bothy in the woods . . . A week or two since, when I chanced to pass that way late—which is a thing I never do, let me tell you, without I carry a bit of St. John's-wort or a sprig of rowan in my pocket—she was out in her herb-plot, singing low to herself and walking round and round something that I couldn't see."

Rob was doubtful as to that. "There's many a goodwife uses a wee bit charm now and then, when she's planting out in her garden at the full of the moon."

"True," said Rolf, "and many a witch, too. But that's not all, for there was a shadow slunk out of the bracken by the gate as I came near—like a fox, 'twas, but larger than any mortal fox—and it walking lame on one paw."

I was cold and shaking, and suddenly I heard my own voice speaking up, like as it might have been somebody else's. "Yon's an ordinary fox that she brought home and cared for after it had had its foot caught in a trap. I've seen it plain, and she told me about it."

My father turned on me sharply, "And what would you be doing out that way, young Tam?"

I took a deep breath. "What would Master Fleming be doing out that way, come to that?"

Well, my father bade me hold my tongue, and the others joined in, exclaiming that young folks had no manners any more —speaking up like that in the face of their elders—and that their own fathers would have skelped them for such behaviour.

Then they turned back to Old Nannie. They hadn't finished with her yet.

"Och now," said Rolf, "and what would any *respectable* kind of a body be doing with a fox for company? That's no ordinary fox, I tell you, 'tis her devilkin, her familiar. Aye, she's a witch, sure enough."

I didn't wait to finish my supper—I felt sick!

It was not long after that, that the ill thing happened.—Nick Drummond, son of Bailie Drummond the silk merchant, had a fine, new-fangled fowling-piece as a present from his father, to welcome him home, with his studies finished, from St. Andrew's University. And after that there was no furred or feathered creature safe from him for a good five miles around the Burgh.

For once, I was in agreement with my father's cronies, when I heard them discussing the matter. "The likes of Nick Drummond should be kept to the good old-fashioned crossbow! By the time you've wound up one of *those*, you think twice as to what you loose off at."

"It makes little difference what he looses off at, that one—no aim, if his life depended on it."

"But you can't loose off so often, which may be the saving of some creature's life here and there. A gun's just that bit quicker —though, mind you, I hear it has a kick like a mule, fit to put your shoulder out, if you're not careful."

I wish it had put Nick's shoulder out before the day he blazed away at the red glint of a fox's pelt on the edge of High Riggs Wood! For when he and his friends went to pick up the poor beast, they found it lacked three toes on its left forefoot!

They hadn't the sense to keep silent, either, and by that time half Drumfyvie knew for sure that the lame fox was Old Nannie's devilkin . . .

So the mischief was done; and soon after, when a late autumn gale blew up out of nowhere and stripped half the roof from Bailie Drummond's warehouse so that his best silks and Florentine velvets were ruined by the rain, folks began to look at each other and whisper Old Nannie's name, with their fingers crossed.

" 'Twas Nick Drummond that shot Old Nannie's devilkin—and the storm didn't do much harm anywhere else . . ."

"Och away! Everyone knows you can't kill such things except with a silver bullet. 'Twas nought but a tame fox, by my reckoning."

"Be that as it may, 'twas Nannie's, and she's—well—she's not just like other people."

"They do say witches have power over wind and weather . . ."

That was when I began to be afraid for Nannie. Sore afraid.

All that winter, it seemed that nought could go well in Drumfyvie. Grannie Dunlop's cow went dry, and the Provost's wife lost a gold ring. Davey the Smith was kicked by a horse he was shoeing, and laid by for a couple of months with something broke inside him. And the winter itself was the worst that anyone could mind for snow and rain, and dragged on long after it should have turned to spring. So come lambing-time, the ground was cold and sodden, and the ewes sickened and many of the lambs were born dead. Then, worst of all, when the spring did come, it brought with it the Sweating Sickness. It comes to most towns nowadays from time to time, but that was the first spring ever it struck Drumfyvie. 'Tis not so bad as the Plague, but for all that, there wasn't a street in the Burgh that hadn't a death in it before 'twas over.

And folks whispered together more and more fearfully.

" 'Tis all since yon fox was shot . . . Nannies's fox!"

" 'Tis devilry and witchcraft!—Witchcraft!"

"Aye, she's cast her evil eye over all the town, since Nick Drummond shot her devilkin."

One evening, a bit past Easter, when the sweating sickness was at its height, my father sent me on an errand across the town, and when 'twas done, I came back along the Headrow, where some of the richest merchants have their grand private houses. There was a busy, snarling crowd, some with torches, gathered outside the house of Andrew Boyd, the Provost, and Master Boyd himself standing on the steps of his own front door, trying to make himself heard above the noise that they were making.

At first it was just noise, but as I drew nearer, it began to take on words, and then I grew cold afraid.

"The witch! Take out the witch and try her!"

"All our troubles are from her!"

"Make an end of the witch!"

Andrew Boyd made himself heard at last: "Hold your peace, good people! Such ills as we have suffered come to all towns from time to time. 'Tis the will of God, and we must suffer it with patience—"

"The will of the Devil, you mean, Andra' Boyd!" Rolf Fleming shouted.—I might have guessed he'd have been in it.

And a woman joined in, " 'Tis ever since the witch's fox was killed!"

"Aye, take Old Nannie and put her to the test!"

"We have no reason to think that our troubles have ought to do with Old Nannie—" the Provost began again.

But he was shouted down. "Prove it then! 'Tis easy to make sure!"

"Aye, swim the witch! Make sure!"

The Provost was as white as an Easter lily, in the ragged torch-light. "Good people, go home quietly and peaceably, and cool your heads. Let us have no more of this wicked talk!"

"Wicked, is it? Is the King wicked? He's a great one for testing witches! Are you above the King, then, Master Provost?"

And another woman cried out, her voice sharp with fear—indeed they were all afraid. Struck rigid on the fringe of the crowd, I could feel their fear; it was that that made them cruel and dangerous—" 'Thou shalt not suffer a witch to live!' It says so in the Good Book! What say you to *that* Andra' Boyd?"

And Rolf thrust in again, "If ye'll not follow the law and the Good Book, then we'll take the thing into our own hands!"

And the Provost was a weak man, like another in the Good Book, and ill-fitted to deal with such a crowd. He made a gesture as though he would have pushed them all away with his shaking hands, and cried out, "Do what you will, and may God forgive you! But remember, I have no part in it!"

And he stepped back through his open door and slammed it after him.

The crowd set up a kind of yowling, and someone cried, "Come on! Let's get the witch, and swim her in Piper's Pool!"

Behind me, I heard Rolf shouting something about fetching

some rope to bind the old hag. But I didn't wait for any more. I'd slipped away, and was already diving through the roots of somebody's garden hedge. I waded the burn that comes down the Headrow from its spring beneath the Castle walls, and ran as I'd never run before, towards High Riggs Wood. If only I could reach Nannie in time to warn her and get her away . . .

But the Devil was in that whole terrible night, and neither Nannie nor I were to win free, for in the dark, I put my foot in a rabbit hole, and came down, twisting my ankle under me, near to breaking the bone. For a few moments, I could do nought but crouch there, sick with pain; and when I hauled myself to my feet again, I could only hobble on at a snail's pace, fighting for every step of the way. I knew fine I'd no chance in the world now of reaching Nannie's bothy until long after the good Burgesses of Drumfyvie had got there and done what they came to do. So I turned downhill again, towards where the burn widened out into Piper's Pool.

I'd no idea of any good that I could do there, but 'twas sure I could do none anywhere else.—And there might be something —at all events, I had to be there. So I struggled on, making all the desperate speed I could . . .

When I came down to the edge of the pool, the moon was rising full and honey-coloured, with a drifting of thin cloud here and there in the dark of the sky. And by the moonlight and the light of the torches among the alder branches, I could see the crowd that were swarming there already—many more than there'd been before the Provost's door. They'd got Nannie on the ground in their midst, stripped to her white shift, and with her hands and feet bound together crosswise in front of her.

I heard myself shouting, "No! No! For the love of God, No!" as I struggled down towards them. I saw two men pick Nannie up, and heard her wailing cry and the splash as her thin body hit the water. And I fell, and floundered to my feet again. A woman grabbed at me, but I twisted out of her hold, and stumbled on. Then Rolf Fleming loomed up in front of me— and I couldn't break free of *his* grasp. It was all like some hideous nightmare. " 'Tis young Tam Webster come to join us! Use your eyes well, laddie, and ye'll see what comes to them that serves the Devil for their God. A sight to keep you in the path of

righteousness all the rest of—a-ah!" he ended on a yelp, as I ducked my head and bit with all my strength into his hand that was keeping me from Nannie. But he didn't let me go, and then someone else grabbed me from the other side, and Rab Henderson said, "Just bide quiet, will ye! If she's a witch, she'll float; and if she's not, and starts to sink, don't you see the rope round her middle, to pull her out?"

And almost in the same instant, there was a gasp from the crowd, and somebody cried out, "She's sinking!"

And someone else cried, "Quick! Haul her in!"

"Twice more," Rolf shouted. "It takes three times to make sure!"

But when she had been pulled in and laid on the bank, it was plain to all that there was no need to swim Old Nannie twice more. Maybe it was the shock of the cold water on top of the fear that she had suffered, and all the rough handling . . . She lay quite still, there on the bank among the alders and the water hemlock—and she looked awful small in the moonlight. The crowd had fallen suddenly quiet, and Rolf and his crony had let go of me, and I pushed my way through the people, and tumbled myself down beside Old Nannie. I felt, desperately, for her heart, under the criss-cross tangle where her hands and feet were lashed together—it wasn't beating. I looked up at the faces crowding in on me, looked round from one to another of them, not even hating them. I seemed too empty for hate.

"She's dead," I croaked. "You've killed Old Nannie, who never did you aught but good!"

There was a great silence. And then out of the midst of it, a man cleared his throat, and a woman said, "She can't be dead, not from a wee ducking the like of that."

They untied her hands and feet and straightened her out a bit on the bank, and tried slapping and shaking her. But Nannie had gone beyond all that. And in a while the crowd began to grow thin as folk melted away, making, I suppose, for their own homes, now that the evil was done and past undoing.

I must have got home myself, somehow, for I mind a long while later, the room behind the shop, and my father's face startled and unbelieving in the light of the lantern. He'd not been with the crowd before the Provost's house, nor yet at

Piper's Pool. That was something, but it wasn't enough, not for me.

If I'd had two good legs to walk on, I'd have been away from Drumfyvie that night. As it was, I had to wait more than a fortnight before my ankle would carry me properly. But as soon as it would, I just packed my clothes and few possessions into a bundle, while my father and Willie were out on business; and I took a bannock from the crock in the corner, and set out for the port of Leith.

It took me the best part of a week to get there, but I arrived at last, and got myself taken on by the Master of the *Dolphin*, bound for Amsterdam. And that was the beginning of my seafaring.

I worked hard—and 'twas work I loved, even at its hardest —and now, I'm the Master of the *Mary Lindsay*. And I always swore I'd never go back to Drumfyvie again; and I never did, till last June, as I was telling you . . .

Well, so there I was, sitting in the ruins of Old Nannie's bothy, with the bees booming among the burnet roses, and my mind going back to that first time of all, remembering how I'd gone to her with my bee-stings, and been ashamed because I had nothing to pay her with; and how she'd taken my face between her hands, and looked deep down into me, and I not yet seven years old, and said, "You shall pay me in gold, when you're a fine sea captain."

And, well, it sounds daft, maybe—I got up and went over to the cold broken hearth-stone, and scooped out a hollow there among the roots of the burnet rose; and I took from my ears the gold rings such as most seamen wear, and laid them in the wee hollow and smoothed the earth back over . . .

Next day I set out back to Leith and the *Mary Lindsay*. I'll not be going back Drumfyvie way—not ever again.

We Sign the Covenant
A.D. 1648

10

Hugh and Johnnie, Johnnie and Hugh—folks always spoke of us together, as though we were the two halves of a pair, as indeed we were, and had been since before either of us could remember; Hugh leading in all our ploys, and I following on behind.

On Hugh's ninth birthday, his father gave him a dirk, to prove he wasn't far off growing up. And the first use we put it to was to prick our thumbs with it, and mingle our blood on the blade. After that we reckoned that we were blood brothers, pledged to stand by each other in all things.

Hugh's father was Sir Robert Maitland, the Sheriff, and his home the big house with shining glass windows, inside the curtain-walls of Drumfyvie Castle.

My father was John Forsyth, the town's surgeon-apothecary, and my home was behind the apothecary's shop in the town below. But that wasn't the reason that Hugh led and I followed in all our ploys, nor was it that Hugh was five months older than me. 'Twas just that he was the kind that leads, whether they're born in a castle or in a hovel down Fighting Cocks Lane, while I—well, I've always been the kind that follows. What you might call a born follower, I am . . .

We were as wild as hawks, and there were times we all but made Drumfyvie too hot to hold us. Aye, and St. Andrew's University, for the matter of that. It seemed we were born to trouble, as the sparks fly upward; but we mostly got ourselves out of it with whole skins.

In our day, St. Andrew's was still fairly ringing with stories of James Graham, the young Earl of Montrose, who left the University a year or so before Hugh and I got there. I mind there was one tale of how he gave a great and glorious party to celebrate winning the silver medal for archery, and afterwards he and a few friends went strolling through the streets to cool their heads with a breath or two of night air, and James Graham loosed an arrow over the roof of St. Salvator's tower, for no

better reason than that it happened to be there, and it shot the Provost's hat clean off his head, he being on the other side of the kirk, in the next street—the decent man walking home late and thinking no evil.

"I wish we could have been at St. Andrew's a wee while earlier, or Jamie Graham a wee while later," Hugh said, once. "We would have done fine together, we three." And I reckon he was in the right of it.

When we were through with St. Andrew's, with letters after our names to prove us fairly educated, we came home again to Drumfyvie, each to follow his father's trade.

'Twas that summer that King Charles's new *Revised Prayer Book* was ordered to be used in all our Kirks.—Not that that was the start of the Troubles; they had begun back in the days of Charles's father, James the Sixth, him that ruled both Scotland and England after the English Queen, Elizabeth, was dead. He ruled both countries from London, so Charles was bred up in the south, and never understood a thing about the Scots—especially our ways of worshipping God. (There's times I doubt he understood much about the English, either, but that's another story.)

And from that came the Covenant, and all that followed after.

But I'd best explain : Neither Scotland nor England were Papist countries any more, not since the Reformation. But the Church in England—they call it the "Church", south of the Border—though it would have nought to do with the Pope and some of his ideas, still had bishops, and the bishops held on to many of the powers that their Papist fore-runners had had. There was *The Book of Common Prayer*, too, which was in some ways kin to the old Mass Books. And the English clergy still said a kind of Mass—only they called it "Holy Communion".

Up here in Scotland, we'd been taught by Master John Knox to have no truck at all with Papist ways. We didn't hold with bishops and such, and the Kirk was governed instead by a Representative Assembly. We had our simple forms of Service, and we'd our own Prayer Book, made for us by Master Knox, and called *Knox's Book of Common Order*.

But King Charles wanted English and Scots alike to worship in the same way—his way—and say our prayers from his new

Prayer Book. The Scots were not happy with this idea, not happy at all, and even when he came north to be crowned at Holyrood, in 1633, folks were whispering and shaking their heads; and we'd been uneasy ever since, seeing that the King was deep under the influence of William Laud, his Archbishop of Canterbury, a man no more one to live and let others live than he was himself. Four years later, they made up another new *Service Book* between them, and again, it was to be used in Scottish kirks alongside the English churches.

I mind my father and Master Beaton, the minister of St. Ninian's, discussing it one night while the minister was supping with us.

"And what," said my father, his temper clearly fraying at the edges, for he was an impatient man at the best of times, "and what will we be needing with this new *Service Book*, we that have already our own *Book of Common Order?*"

Master Beaton answered him gently. "If the King would have but a little patience; if he would explain his thoughts to us, and listen, in return, to ours, I think, given time and kindliness, we could maybe find a meeting-place, a point of agreement, even now. After all, it is the same God we worship, Scots and English both."

But my father would have none of such peaceable, middle-of-the-road talk. "That might be so, if the man Charles Stuart thought of himself *as* a man, and therefore fallible from time to time. But he thinks of himself only as a King, and above the need of listening to lesser folk; and 'tis there the whole trouble lies, that he will set himself between us and God, and tell us what God will have us do."

"There is truth in all that—" Master Beaton began, but my father had not yet finished his say.

"The Kirk can have no head but Almighty God Himself, neither King nor bishop. And the humblest man alive can speak direct from his heart to his Maker, without the need for his prayers written down for him in a printed book! Leave alone that the Scots clergy have not been consulted in the matter!"

"Aye," Master Beaton said, thoughtful. "There's none feels that more than one of the Scots clergy! But if the King would only wait a little . . ."

"If! If!" My father banged his fist on the supper table. "If pigs had wings, Andra' Beaton! And meanwhile we must even say our written-down prayers out of an *English* book!"

Master Beaton sighed. "*The New Prayer Book.* Aye, it's to be used in all the Edinburgh kirks from the twenty-third of the month, I hear. There'll be trouble . . . I greatly fear there'll be trouble!"

"It's to be hoped there will! I'm fair ashamed to think of good Scots folks tamely bowing their necks and following where a half Papist King and a wee English Archbishop lead them! And you, my mannie, should be out in front of them, with God's Holy Word in one hand, and a sword in the other! Not talking soft about waiting a little, and finding a meeting point!"

Master Beaton laughed, a wee thing wryly. "Alas! I was never much of a one with a sword. I'd rather keep my own small flock in peace, than war with the world and its princes."

And listening, I thought him a poor sort of Minister, and a poor sort of man altogether; and I wished I could be in one of the Edinburgh kirks when the new prayers were read, and maybe break a head or two myself, if heads were to be broken. I mind talking about it to Hugh next day, while we lay up on Grims Rigg, watching the wee white clouds sailing across the blue of the sky, and listening to a lark singing its heart out, so high up we couldn't see it at all.

". . . So there'll be trouble in Edinburgh, Sunday after next. I wish we could be there!"

"Like enough 'twill come to us before long," said Hugh, unusually sober, just for the moment. He took out the grass stem he'd been chewing, and squinted at it. "Master Beaton's in the right of it, I'm thinking. Go to meet a man half-way, and like enough he'll come the other half in his own good time. But threaten him with hell-fire or hanging if he doesn't come to your way of thinking, and he'll fight till he drops, or *you* do, before he'll give way an inch." He threw the grass stem away, and sat up. "There's another thing—this forcing of English forms of worship on us Scots that have good enough ways of our own— it's a threat to our rights and our freedom in other ways, too—"

"What my father calls 'our national liberty'?" I said.

"Just that. If it comes to fighting, I'll tell you this, Johnnie Forsyth—we'll be fighting for Scotland as well as our faith!"

Well, so, on the Sunday after next, the King's new prayers were read in all the kirks in Edinburgh. Most everybody knows the story of the riot that came of it, and how, in the High Kirk of St. Giles, Jenny Geddes, the cabbage woman, was so roused to fury that she got up off her creepy stool and flung it at the Dean's head! Hugh and I laughed ourselves almost sick when we heard the tale, and so did a deal of other folks up and down Scotland.

But the events that followed were no matter for laughter.

That autumn, a great gathering of nobles, lairds, burgesses and ministers met in the Parliament House in Edinburgh; and they stayed there most of the winter, drawing up what they called *The National Covenant*. It took them that long because it had to do two things: it must speak loud and clear against the King's intent to force all Scotland to worship in the English way; and at the same time, it had to make plain to the King that Scotland was loyal to himself. And it couldn't have been easy to do both of two things that seemed so completely to contradict each other. 'Twas done at last, though, and by February the finished Covenant lay in the Kirk of the Grey Friars in Edinburgh, open for all to see and sign their names to. And within a few days, copies were being carried by swift riders the length and breadth of Scotland, that every man, woman and bairn, in every town and village in the land, should have their chance to sign likewise.

I mind well, the day our copy of *The National Covenant* came to Drumfyvie. A fine, cold February day, and the thin sunshine seeming like an omen of success, to all of us gathered in the market-place to greet it. The great parchment was spread on a trestle table before the tolbooth, where there was space a'plenty for folks to come up for the signing, without getting tight-packed and in each other's way. And indeed there was need of space, for I'm thinking every soul in Drumfyvie was there—the biggest crowd that ever I saw there except on Fair days. But save that here and there a dog barked or a lost bairn bawled for its mother, 'twas a crowd that made surprising little noise; solemn almost, you might say, as though we felt that we in Drumfyvie

127

—as I suppose folks felt in every town and village—held the future of Scotland in our hands that day.

Certainly, Jamie Drummond the cobbler felt that way, addressing all and sundry, as they stood by waiting their turn to sign. "Och! 'Tis the great days we're living in!—The great days! We'll show the King sitting high on his throne in London town, that Drumfyvie folks are not bending their necks to worship God according to his orders!"

"I was hearing that, in Edinburgh, there's some has signed the Covenant in their own blood, to show him that the more clearly!" cried a woman's voice out of the crowd.

And then quite close beside me, someone said quietly over his shoulder to a friend, "Look behind the table—him with the blue ribbons in his bonnet . . . Yon's Montrose himself!" And those standing nearest him heard and took up his words, so that the name spread out through the crowd like the ripple-rings when a stone is dropped into a pool.

"Montrose!"—" 'Tis Montrose!"—"Montrose, God bless him!"

Hugh and I, waiting together to sign after our families had taken their turn, couldn't get much more than a glimpse of a blue ribbon, however we craned our necks, but that was enough for the moment, to set our hearts dancing. Then our bit of the line moved on a pace or two; and I mind how stern Sir Robert Maitland looked as he took one of the pens set ready, and stooped to put his name to the great parchment.

"Now," said Hugh, when our familes had signed, "Our turn, Johnnie."

And we pushed forward, to the table. There were three men standing behind it, and one of them pointed to the inkhorn. But we didn't have a use for the inkhorn. I'm not sure which of us first had the thought, but as usual, Hugh was the first to act on it.

"We can't have Drumfyvie less generous with it's blood than Edinburgh!" said he, and himself busy turning back the fine linen of his wristband as he spoke. And then he drew his dirk . . .

Aye, we signed the Covenant in our own blood, the both of us, Hugh's great careless signature sprawling all across the sheet, and my smaller, neater one beneath. I mind how we glanced at

each other as the dirk passed from his hand to mine, half-smiling but grave under it, just as we had done the day we pricked our thumbs and swore the blood brotherhood behind the pigsty wall.

But when I looked up from my signing, I met the gaze of the man with the blue ribbons in his bonnet. His eyes were cool and grave, but his mouth had a wee quirk to it. You could see the leader in him, the man who'd been riding the country to north, south, east and west, gathering men to the cause and the Covenant; but still maybe a trace of the wild lad who'd set St. Andrew's by the ears, and shot the Provost's hat off his head across St. Salvator's tower. And for just the one heartbeat of time, we looked at each other as though the market-place was empty and the two of us alone before the tolbooth steps.—I reckon it was the same for Hugh, the same for any man whom Montrose looked at . . . He wasn't just like other folk . . .

Nothing unusual happened for a couple of months. Folks talked about the Covenant, and what effect it would have, all the way down there in London town; but for a while it was just talk and guessing, with no news at all.

And then, on a quiet April evening, when I was putting the shutters up, a horseman came clattering through Drumfyvie, and reined up at the door of the manse, which you could just see from our shop. "Some poor body in need of the Minister," thought I. And I finished the shutters and went in to my supper.

'Twasn't until next day that Master Beaton looked in to tell my father what had happened. He had received some kind of letter (he and all the rest of the Scots ministers) bidding him swear to obey the King's wishes in all that had to do with the Kirk—to use the English *Prayer Book*; and have an altar set up in place of our plain communion table; and make folk come forward and kneel at it to receive the Sacrament, instead of being given it sitting in their seats.

My father listened, his face darkening every moment. "So," he said at the last, "and what did you say to that?"

It was then I learned the mistake I'd made in thinking Master Beaton a poor sort of minister and a poor sort of man.

"What could I do but answer the letter, as mannerly as might be, explaining that I could never swear an oath that would set the King between our congregation and the God we worship?" he said slowly.

My father sat up straight. "You've written the letter?"

"While the messenger waited."

"Man, they'll have you out of the manse for that."

"I know," said Master Beaton.

"But Andra', what will you do? You've spent half your life as our Minister, and you're not a young man. You're not trained to any other work!"

Master Beaton sat considering. "Well—I could maybe turn tutor. Or I could keep a merchant's account books, I think, and write out his bills for him . . . I'll just need to find what work I can, and starve if I can find none. God will show me what he wills for me."

In every town and village, the ministers were receiving the same orders; and soon all Scotland was seething like a pan of yeast at the fire to rise. And before Christmas there was a General Assembly at Glasgow, to consider what best to do. Aye, and having decided, they went ahead and did it without wasting time.

I mind the day the news reached Drumfyvie; all the excitement and rejoicing; and Jamie Drummond half-way up the Market Cross, shouting that the Assembly had thrown out all the Kirk changes that the King had forced on us; and Matt Spicer down below, flinging his cap in the air and shouting, "What did I tell ye? There's good-bye to the *Book of Common Prayer*!"

And we told ourselves that all was well.

But it was not! It was not indeed! The King was an angry man, and not one to give up his own will. Had he not turned out his own English Parliament a while back, for refusing to do as he wished? Now it seemed that he must either yield to us in Scotland, or make war on us—and yielding was not in the man. Yet how could he get the money to send troops against us, him being without a Parliament? Aye well, he scraped together an army somehow, and came marching north against us. But when he saw *our* army, the army of the Covenant waiting for him on the Borders—he turned back. For a while,

that is. 'Twas a breathing-space at all events, and Montrose made good use of it . . .

Hugh came into the shop one morning, and said, "Montrose is mustering troops, Johnnie."

As if I didn't know!

"Aye," I said, and waited.

"Last year when the King came north, I promised my father I wouldn't go—him being a sick man, these days, and Brother Robin still at St. Andrew's. But this year . . ."

I nodded. "This year Robin's through with Greek and Latin and can take your place."

"Aye, so I'm free to go."

"When do we start, then?"

"We?" Hugh said.

"You didn't think I'd let you go stravaigling off without me?"

He grinned. "I did not then. We'll ride tomorrow."

So we joined the Muster and rode south, following Montrose, each of us with a knot of blue ribbons in our bonnets, and the hearts high within us. And all along the way our numbers grew, as folks came in to join us from towns and villages and farmsteads in the bonnie Border countryside.

On a dark night with the silver slip of the new moon coming and going among the clouds, we reached the Tweed crossing, and found the water coming down in spate from a storm in the hills. Some of the lads hung back a bit, for the water looked awful dark and swift; but there was Montrose, out ahead, urging his roan down into the racing foam-streaked flood.

Someone shouted. "Look! He's out of his depth already! 'Tis madness!"

"He can't win across, it's not possible!"

"He's swimming his horse upstream against the current!"

"Sooner him than me," Alan Ferguson said. "I've no taste for drowning—nor for drowning my horse, come to that!"

And then those nearest the bank set up a ragged cheer. "He's over!" someone said. "My, but he's the great lad!"

Aye, he was the great lad! For the moment he was over, didn't he turn his horse and head straight back towards us!

A great torn-off tree branch riding the spate all but caught him, and a warning shout went up from the bank. I heard

Hugh's breath hiss through his teeth. "Safely past, thank God!"

"But why in Heaven's name is he coming back?" I demanded of the world in general. "He's not a fool—"

And an old soldier beside me laughed, "He's not, then—he's showing us how easy 'tis. That's all."

"A man to be hanged, maybe, but not drowned," said Geordie Hamilton. "Come on lads!—If Montrose can do it two or three times, we can get across the once, I'm thinking!"

And Montrose was at the near bank and turning his horse yet again—and we urged our horses after him. I mind the splash and the swirl of the icy water, and my old Swallow snorting and trying to fling sideways. "Easy!" I said. "Easy, boy!" And then there was the slipping scramble up the far bank, and the first of us were over, and more following every moment.

And so we crossed the Tweed without a horse or a man lost. And after that, the march into England was plain dull. We sat down in the Northern counties for a while, with never a blow struck; and by and by the King sent us his promise that we should keep our own ways of worship, and that there should be a proper Parliament again, and even sent us our soldiers' pay for the months we'd spent sitting in the North of England. And we just got up and marched away back to our homes again. It was all too easy, and somehow all wrong. You could smell the wrongness of it like thunder fouling the air before a storm . . .

When things had quietened down again, the King himself came to Edinburgh, seemingly bent on making better friends with his Scottish people. There was a lot of talk that if Montrose had beeen able to meet with the King at that time, he might have been able to make all things well. But during the whole time that the King was in Scotland, Montrose was in gaol on a trumped-up treason charge!—A charge that was dropped as soon as the King had gone south again! It seemed that someone had no wish for the King and Montrose to meet each other—and the common belief was that it was Archie Campbell, the Earl of Argyll.

There's seldom been any really dirty work done in Scotland that hasn't had the Argyll of the day somewhere at the back of it, and I make no doubt 'twill be the same in the future as it has in the past.

There'd been bad blood between Montrose and this particular Argyll since their time at St. Andrew's. The story had been still common knowledge when Hugh and I were there.—Archie Campbell was a lame man, and proud, and the only sport in which he could do well was archery. He had won the silver medal in his day, and then Montrose had won it. It made no difference that Argyll had left St. Andrew's by then—he would have hated any man who won the archery medal after him. And 'twas well known that where Argyll hated, he stabbed in the back if he got the chance.

But indeed the roots of the matter were deeper and darker than that, and were mingled with politics and religion . . .

There were many strange things happening these days in Presbyterian Scotland. "Presbyterian" was what we called ourselves now; it had to do with the way the Kirk was governed. But the Kirk, with all the King's new prayers and ceremonies thrown out, was still far different from the way Master Knox had made it. It had got into the hands of the wrong people, and grown to be a grim place, lacking all warmth and even kindness, and full of nonsensical new rules, and threats of hell-fire for any that disobeyed them. Even the dead couldn't get Christian burial if they hadn't signed the Covenant, and poor old Grannie Baird sat three hours in the stocks for picking her gooseberries when she should have been in kirk listening to the sermon. Everything was a sin, and no one knew where he stood, save for a few, who believed themselves God's chosen. Worst of all, or so it seemed to me, no books were allowed that did not say just what the Presbyterians wanted them to say.

"Wherever Master Beaton is, this lot will seem as ill to him as ever the King's *New Prayer Book* did," I mind saying to my father.

But my father had changed, along with so many other things and people in those drear days. "The Lords of Convention will have good reason for their rulings," he told me sternly. "Master Beaton must learn a humble spirit, to accept them."

I stared at him, feeling as if I was looking at a stranger. "Father! You're putting the Lords of Convention in the very same place where, none so long since, you would not have the King—between the Kirk and God!"

"Hold your tongue!" My father let out a roar. "I'll have no such wicked talk in this house! The Lords of Convention are busy about God's work, and you cannot root out the Devil with a gentle hand!"

And he had me on my knees for a solid hour, while he wrestled in prayer for the saving of my soul.

I think it was that night I realized to the full, for the first time, what our new Reformed Kirk could do to folks—turning the like of my father from a good-hearted though stern man, into a kind of huntsman, out after sin, and wrathful if he didn't find it.

By that time, King Charles was openly at war with his Parliament in England. And folk were joining themselves together to fight for the one or the other. Here in Scotland our leaders were mustering the Army of the Covenant again, to fight with the English Parliament against the King. But this time the heart was different within it, and this time 'twas to be led by grim old Alexander Leslie. And Montrose, our Montrose, sickened by what the cause of the Covenant had become, was away across the Border to fight for the King!

Hugh and I hadn't seen much of each other for months past. That was another thing that was changed. But he came seeking me before he rode out to join Leslie's army. I was in the shop, mixing Grannie Jessop's cough physic, and I looked up, and he was standing in the doorway, just as he had been that other time.

We looked at each other in silence a moment, and then he said, "I'm away in the morning."

"So I was hearing. There's a good few going from Drumfyvie, they tell me."

"I thought," he said, in a careful, dead-level kind of voice, "I thought maybe we could ride together, as we did before."

But he didn't really think it, I could see that in his face. There was a kind of glimmer of half-hope, but no more.

"That was when we followed Montrose."

"Montrose is a turncoat!"

"No," I said, "Montrose is no turncoat, nor ever could be. It's not him that's changed, it's the cause."

Hugh shook his head. "The *times* have changed, Johnnie.

Times always do, and the cause must change with them, if 'tis to stay alive."

"Then maybe it had better die," I said. I mind noticing that I was still stirring away at Grannie Jessop's physic, and I put it down on the counter, very carefully, as if the stoneware jar was made of eggshell. "Hugh, do you mind the day we signed *The National Covenant*, for the sake of freedom to worship God in our own way, and not the King's? Now it's become *The Solemn League and Covenant*, and would force all England to worship God in the Presbyterian way, in return for Scotland's help against the King. It's—you couldn't call it freedom of worship, now, could you?"

"I told you—the times have changed—"

"You mind what you said once about threatening another man with hell-fire or hanging if he didn't accept your belief? You said, then, that if you do that he'll fight till he drops, or *you* do, before he gives way an inch."

Hugh flushed. "That was boy's talk, Johnnie. Och, no—they would have done it to us, and we must do it to them. There's no half-way—you must see that."

"I'm not sure," I said, "I'm not sure of anything, any more, except that I don't believe we should join the English Parliament to fight against our rightful King."

You could have heard the silence ring between us. A long, long silence. And then Hugh said, "So you'll not ride south with us, Johnnie?"

"If Montrose comes back to gather troops, then I'll ride south again," I said, "but I'll ride no more with the Army of the Covenant."

"Then here's the parting of our ways; and I can't even say 'God be with you,' Johnnie."

"We can't say that to each other, ever again."

And he turned and went, without a backward glance.

But there was one more time—just one more—long after . . . I'll tell you, by and by.

"God Be with You" 11
A.D. 1650

After Hugh Maitland rode south with the Army of the Covenant, I bided on in Drumfyvie, helping in the shop, and learning to be a surgeon-apothecary, like my father. But always, I think, in the back of my mind, was the thought that one day Montrose would come gathering troops again . . .

It was a long wait, I had, for it seemed the King set more trust in Archie Campbell, yon cold-hearted Earl of Argyll—and him already a power behind the Covenanters, for dark reasons of his own, if the whispered stories were true!

But at last the waiting time came to an end, and word was running wild through Scotland—Argyll was openly head of the Covenanters and Montrose was back over the Border!

I mind listening with a racing heart to Davy Anderson the cordwainer and Ian Murray from the Unicorn inn discussing the news in my father's shop.

"Back over the Border, and naught but a handful of followers," Davy was big with importance. "But they're saying in Perth that he's to meet up with Alasdair MacDonald and the Antrim men!"

Ian gave a soundless whistle. "The Antrim men! Those will be the MacDonalds that were hounded west into Ireland by the Campbells. Yon should set the heather alight! Aye, and there's no bonnier fighting man in the world than a MacDonald with a grievance!"

But Tam Gillespie, who had just come in, shook his head in doubt. "He's a year too late, is Montrose, by my way of thinking. The Covenanters have got their claws too deep into the land, by now."

"Argyll has, ye mean," Davy retorted.

And then Ian said, "Whisht!" and glanced toward the street door as my father came in from his rounds. And the shame rose in my throat.

A few days later, we heard that Montrose was mustering Lowland troops. And on the day *that* news came, I left the drug

jars and the pill-board, and rode off to join the muster . . . What my father said, I'll not trouble you with, save that he swore I was no longer a son of his.

There was a good few of us rode out from Drumfyvie that day, and all of us with knots of blue ribbons in our bonnets to show ourselves Montrose's men. In time we came to be known as The Blue Bonnets, and the name stuck. There was even a song about us: "All the Blue Bonnets are over the Border . . ." That stuck, too. I heard an errand laddie whistling it in the street only the other day . . .

When we joined the muster, the MacDonalds had still not arrived, but there could be no more waiting for them, not with things going the way they were in England. So as soon as the muster was complete, Montrose gave the order, and we marched south.

But we arrived too late! There'd been a great battle at a place called Marston Moor, and the armies of Parliament and the Covenant between them had had the victory. They had won the whole of the North of England from King Charles; and near four thousand of his men were left dead on the Moor, with the whaups crying in the wind above them. Most of the Royalist guns had been captured, too; York had surrendered to the Parliament men, and some fifteen hundred men taken prisoner. 'Twas Leslie and his Covenanters that tipped the scale that day. If we'd got there in time, we could maybe have tipped it the other way. But we didn't get there in time.

Montrose went off to see the King. And in the bits of skirmishing that were still going on, I got a wound in my shoulder—and since a wounded man is naught but a burden to his fellows, I was sent off, with a good few more, in a supply waggon going empty back to the north.

My father was not glad to see me, and I doubt he'd have let me over the threshold but for my wound. And for my part, I doubt I'd have gone back to the shop, only I was too sick in heart and body to care where I laid my head. But be that as it may, home I went, and he took me in.

And when he was cleaning up the hole in my shoulder, he said, "You'll have heard that Hugh Maitland was at Marston Moor?"

I mind I started a bit, and then held myself very still, lest he should think I was flinching from the pain. "I guessed he would be. Leslie and his Covenanters were there."

"Aye, and Hugh rode with the Covenanting Army. I was hearing he got a scratch there."

"How bad?" I said quickly.

"Hold still, will you," said my father. "Do you expect me to deal with this, and you twitching about like a restive horse? Not bad, I think, but how would I be knowing?"

"He's not at home, then?"

"No, still in the south with the Army of the Lord." He set aside the bowl of filthy, blood-stained water and began to spread salve on a piece of linen. "A proud man, Sir Robert Maitland must be!"

It was like that all the while I was home, my father seldom missing a chance to let me see what he thought of me. So I did not bide home long. Barely until my shoulder was healed. But I'd have gone then anyway, for Montrose, now made a Marquis and the King's Lieutenant, was back in Scotland and raising troops yet again. He'd met up at last with Alasdair MacDonald, so 'twas said, and together, him and that red-headed giant of a man with a two-handed sword so heavy that none but he could use it, they'd taken Perth!

So off I set for Perth. But when I got there, the army was away already, and I caught up with them at last, camped for the night, on the road for Aberdeen. Whenever I mind that night, I see the glow of camp-fires on faces alight with victory, and hear the rattle of a drum played as I've not heard it played before or since.—For they'd a drummer boy with them, by the name of Watt, son to one of Montrose's captains who'd been his friend since St. Andrew's days. The laddie's father had been killed, so I heard—not in battle but in his sleep, by one of his own followers, before the man fled to join Argyll—and Montrose had taken young Watt as though he were his own. Not much above twelve years old, he wasn't, and there he squatted, in the firelight before the opening of Montrose's tent, rattling away at his drum, rataplan, rataplan, like a grown man that had been at it all his life, and a grin on his face that split it from one pricked ear to the other. He could play light and soft so you'd

think 'twas the feet of the Fairy Folk; or strong and menacing, so that a man must needs look behind him for fear of an enemy at his back; or quick and urgent to set a man's blood leaping in the face of death. And wherever Montrose walked, young Watt followed like his shadow or his dog.

And if you think I'm wandering from the story, I am not, for it was for the sake of Watt that we sacked Aberdeen!

There had been no sacking of Perth, by Montrose's orders, and there was to be none in Aberdeen either—indeed I never knew him to allow the sacking of any town, except that once . . . We halted before the gates, the townsfolk opened to us, and Montrose sent in Lord Graham as his envoy, with a handful of others, and ahead of them a drummer, as the custom is. Aye, young Watt.

We heard the sound of his drum dying away within the city. And outside the gates we waited, in a silence broken only by the creak of saddle leather or the jink of a bridle bit as a horse fidgeted where it stood. Time seemed to stretch out long and thin.

"They're surely an awful long time coming to terms," someone muttered, behind me.

And almost in the same instant, a single shot cracked through the waiting air.

Someone cried out, "In God's name, what's happened?"

And then from beyond the gate came a flurry of voices and movement, and we could make out our own men coming back to us, through a crowd fallen suddenly silent. But there was no drummer going before them; and as the crowd parted, we could see that Lord Graham was carrying young Watt. The laddie hung limp in his arms. And I think we knew; in that first moment I think we knew, even before Lord Graham checked at Montrose's stirrup, and the word spread back from those nearest, to the rearmost ranks. "He's dead—trouble as they were leaving.— There was trouble of some kind and they've shot the laddie, under the flag to truce!"

I was near enough to Montrose to hear, when he raised his hand for quiet, and gave his orders. "No more talk of terms! Trumpeter—sound the Attack!"

So we sacked Aberdeen. There was red between the cobbles, and half the town went up in flames at that day's end. I'm not

exactly proud of my part in it. But then, I'd not be proud to have shot down a twelve-year-old boy in cold blood, either.

That autumn, Alasdair MacDonald was away raising Highland troops, for with one thing and another, we'd not much above five hundred men left. We couldn't come to open battle with so few as that, but we did not lie idle while he was away. Aye, we led the Army of the Covenant a fine dance up and down and round about the Lowland hills, so that Argyll had his hands too full to turn south to aid General Leslie, which was something gained, anyway.

In November, Alasdair came back with his raw recruits behind him, spoiling for a fight, and then we might have marched south to join the King. But to do that straight away would have left Argyll, the King's chiefest enemy, all-powerful in Scotland. So we went Argyll-hunting, Campbell-hunting. And rare sport we made for ourselves in the doing of it. We drove him from his own castle of Inveraray, and then from Inverallochy—though mind you, Argyll wasn't the only man with troubles, as the chill winter months went by—we had plenty ourselves, with the King promising us our soldiers' pay and never sending it, and men trickling away back to their own crofts or the fishing. I mind hearing Montrose and Red Alasdair talking about it one night when I was on watch before the General's tent. And I mind also that there was something near to hopelessness in Montrose's voice —the first time I'd ever heard it there—and it shook me!

"Oh but I'm tired, Alasdair—tired and sick at heart . . . It's the same after every victory; when the first glow of it cools down, the men start to melt away. Now we're down to six hundred, less than a quarter of what we were a month ago."

"You're too soft with them," Alasdair returned. "You should be treating them as the deserters they are. Hunt down a few and shoot them! That will be a useful lesson to the rest!"

"If only the King would keep his promises!" Montrose said bitterly. "If they had their pay to send home to their wives and bairns!—Then, make no mistake about it, my friend, I *would* treat them as deserters. But how can I hunt down and shoot men who know that their families will starve if they do not go home to work the crofts and the fishing?"

"So, then, what will ye do?" Alasdair said grimly.

"March on Dundee," Montrose said. "Before what heart the lads still have is lost to them."

I mind there was a short sharp pause, and then Alasdair laughed—but there was no mirth in the laughter. "You are losing men like midges in a summer's mist, and so you will be choosing to attack the strongest Covenanting town in all Angus!"

But Montrose was in the right of it. Demand the impossible of a few men, and they will work miracles, if you have their hearts.

So we took Dundee. And while Montrose with a few of his captains was receiving the town's surrender, we were swarming through the streets from house to house and shop to shop in search of food and drink—we'd had little enough of either in the past days. And we were dog-weary, with forced marching, and the drink went straight to the heads and legs of most of us, so that we just dropped in the streets and slept easy where we lay.

I wasn't drunk, myself, but I wasn't above taking a nap in a sheltered corner of the kirkyard wall. Seems like I'd scarce lain down when I was roused by the drum of horse's hooves within a few feet of my head, and I struggled up out of a pit of sleep as one of our outpost scouts went by at full gallop, shouting "Montrose! Where's Montrose? There's General Baillie and three thousand of the enemy within a mile of the West Port!"

Then the drums were beating to arms, and—like a kind of dark, confused dream, it was—we were up and running, from all corners of the town, those of us that were not too far gone in the drink and the weariness, that is, mustering on the market-place, where Montrose was already up on the steps of the cross, and Alasdair and others of the captains with him.

I mind thinking that we were wasting our time heading that way; that the only thing we could do was to make a stand at the West Port and pull as many of Baillie's men as we could manage down to Hell with us.

And Johnnie Fleming, a comrade of mine, had the same thought, but carried it a stage further, for he shouted out to Montrose, "Make for the East Port, my Lord! Get away and raise another army. We'll hold Baillie's lot in check till you get clear!"

And Montrose, above us, shouted back, "It's I that give the

orders here! And I've every intention of getting away—but not alone—Gordon, MacDonald, Sutherland—" And he called over his captains each by name, "Get each your men together and march them out by the East Port."

"And how will we be doing that?" demanded Alasdair Mac-Donald, "and half of them lying for dead in the streets, with the drink and the weariness on them?"

"With the point of your dirks, if need be," Montrose said.

And somehow, we did it. I mind the drums beating as I ran with a handful of others behind my own captain; I mind diving into dark alleys and kicking up men asleep on doorsteps, yelling in their ears that the Covenanters were at the gates. *How* we did it I'll never know, but we even got the horses—and Montrose and the remains of his army rode out through the East Port just as General Baillie and his Covenanters clattered into the far side of the town.

We—the cavalry—brought up the rear to cover the weary foot-soldiers from Baillie's troops that we knew would be after us the moment they found us gone. Aye, and they were—but by some miracle we beat off their attack and struggled on. I mind there began to be a soft heavy rain that soon turned the road to a quagmire under the horses' hooves and the weary feet of the men. Presently one of the scouts that had been sent on ahead loomed out of the rainy darkness with word there was cavalry ahead of us. We were in no state for cross-country marching, but nor were we in a state for meeting enemy troops, half-dead in our saddles, half-dead on our feet, as we were. Montrose was riding with us in the rearguard, and I heard him give his orders, "Alasdair, Gordon, get the lads off the road; the rough country westward should give us cover to get by."

And then there was sodden heather underfoot, and the rain-mist driving, and somehow we did get by, and gained the cover of our own familiar hills. Among the bogs and the steep rocky brae-sides, we knew that Baillie's heavily-armed troops could never come at us, and we dropped into the young rain-drenched heather to finish out the sleep we'd begun in the streets of Dundee.

There was no more deserting after that for a while, indeed men began coming in to join us again. I've often thought it

strange how the word of that forced march rang through Scotland louder than any victory. Strange, the things that will kindle the hearts of men. I suppose, in its way, it was the stuff that songs are made of.

We were like an army of the mist, that spring, leading General Baillie the fine dance up and down the Border hills. In May, we fought him at Aldearn, and scattered the Covenanters like autumn leaves over the countryside. In July, at Alford, we did it again, and came near to capturing Argyll himself. The pity is that we didn't quite—'twould have saved a deal of sorrow after! A month later we were at Kilsyth, with the heather swimming in the August heat. That was a battle to make songs about, too, and when 'twas over, there was scarce what you might call a Covenanting Army left north of the Border at all.

So—in spite of all that was against him, Montrose had won Scotland for the King. And now that 'twas done, the King called on him to march us south to meet him, joining up with two of the great Border Earls, Roxburgh and Hume, at Kelso on the way. We knew it, all over the camp, almost as soon as Montrose did, and oh, but our hearts were high when we marched for the Border!

But the King held back, and while he dallied, David Leslie, him that was kinsman to old Alexander Leslie, and a greater soldier by far, got word of our march, and brought up his troops to join Argyll at Newcastle.

By that time, what with delays and uneasiness about the King, and harvest-time calling each man back, at it always does, to his own croft, the desertions were starting again. And not only among the small folk, either. Alasdair MacDonald had joined Montrose for the Campbell-hunting, but he cared nought for fighting in England—so he took his men and melted westward again. And then our General Gordon had some sort of a quarrel with Montrose, and swept off, taking the most of his cavalry with him.

Aye, the bad days were with us again.

Still, given time, I reckon Montrose could have taken himself back to the hills and gathered another army. He could always whistle men to him, that one. But there *was* no time— not with Leslie already marching against us; and if there *had*

been time, I doubt he'd have turned back, not with the King's orders still standing. Anyway, there were still Hume and Roxburgh to join us. With the troops they brought, we'd soon be an army again. So the few of us that were left told each other hopefully at nights round the campfire. But when we marched into Kelso, we found neither hide nor hair of Roxburgh, nor yet of Hume! Misliking the idea of joining with an army that had dwindled away so small, our bonnie pair of Earls had surrendered themselves to Leslie, that being the easiest way out!

After that, whatever the King's orders, there was no choice but to turn back to the Highlands. And the sore pity was, as I heard later from men near to him, that in turning north again, Montrose was convinced that he had failed his King. Lord Erskine, one of the captains, told him 'twas the King who had failed *him*, but he would not accept that.—Maybe he could not, for it would have been harder even to bear than his own failure.

Well, so we started the long road north. We reached Selkirk on the evening of September 12th, and made camp on the level ground below the town, where the streams of Yarrow and Ettrick meet—Philliphaugh, the place was called. Our mounted patrols scoured the countryside for miles around, and reported it bare of the enemy. There's some say their guides were in Argyll's pay, but there was a mist that night, could have done Argyll's work for him without pay . . .

But howsoever it was, Leslie's men attacked the camp just as we were cooking our morning meal. Thousands of them, mainly cavalry, charging in on us out of the mist; and we were but a few hundred, and taken by surprise. The few Irish troops that we still had with us fought like heroes, and died where they fought, but most of the Lowland troops, raw recruits, ran like rabbits—not that that helped them any, poor devils, for the musket fire got them, and they went down like ripe barley before a hailstorm. I was with our handful of cavalry, following Montrose. We charged and charged again into the thick of the enemy, trying to hold them back from our scattered foot. That was when my old Swallow was shot under me. I'd no time for grieving, I just staggered clear as he rolled over, and pushed on blindly, following my comrades on foot. There were flying manes and tails and the drum of hooves and the flash of steel all around

me. And I'd not lurched many steps before I got in the way of a spent bullet. It didn't feel as you'd expect a bullet to feel, just as though someone had flicked across the side of my head with a whip; but I knew that I was hit, and I mind thinking, with a queer kind of detached interest, as if I were standing outside of myself, looking on, "Here's an end to Johnnie Forsyth."

And then the trampled ground fair rose up and hit me.

When I came back to myself—and dear knows how long or how short a time that took—everything was quiet round me, the terrible quiet of a spent battlefield. There was nought for me to do but get away, if I could. I didn't care much whether I did or no', but I suppose the feel for life is strong in a man's body, even when his mind and heart have little care for it. So I struggled to my feet, the world swimming and dipping around me, and staggered off towards a broken-down hedge that seemed as though it might give me some cover. I got there somehow, and straightway fell over a grey-coated Covenanter lying sprawled under the hedge-tangle. He gave a moan, and his arm that had been across his face, as though to shield it from the cavalry that had passed that way, fell wide. Something made me take a closer look at him as I hauled myself up to my knees again—and suddenly I felt that I was caught in some kind of dream.

"Hugh!" I said. "Hugh!"

He looked at me, puzzled, and slowly fumbled out a hand towards me. "Johnnie?"

"Surely," I said. "Who else? Bide still, now."

"No need to tell me—that." He spoke so low and breathless that I had to bend close to make him out. "It's—very quiet."

"The fight's over," I said. "I reckon those of us that aren't dead or rounded up are on the run—I doubt they'll not get far."

"Take my coat," Hugh mumbled. " 'Twill maybe help you get away, and—I'll not be needing it any more."

"I'm not leaving you," I said.

"Johnnie—don't be—a fool. I'll not—last the hour out."

"I'm not leaving you."

There was a small distant flurry of shouting, then a musket shot. The Covenanters would be still rounding up strays.

Hugh turned his head to listen, then looked up at me. "Thirsty . . . There's a pond just—through the hedge . . ."

"I'll get you some water," I said, and looked about me. His steel cap lay close by among the heather; I reached over for it, then got to my feet.

He was watching me with a kind of shadow of a smile. "God be with you, Johnnie."

"And with you," I said. "Bide, and I'll be back—"

I scrambled through the wreckage of the hedge and made for the little pond on the far side. But before I ever got there, I heard a pistol shot behind me.

I'd forgotten he still had his pistol.

"No!" I shouted stupidly. "No, Hugh!" And began to run back, diving through the hedge, and knowing all the while what I should find. I squatted on my heels beside him, and let the steel cap roll away into the heather. He'd not be wanting water now . . . He'd made sure I shouldn't bide with him till I fell into Leslie's hands—made sure that there was nothing left to bide for.

Well, we'd wished each other "God be with you", once more.

I struggled out of my jacket, and then, as gently as might be, eased off his grey coat. Like as he'd said, he'd not be needing it any more. I pulled it on, and then laid my own over him. I touched his shoulder in farewell; and then in Hugh's coat, with Hugh's blood on it, I went my way. I'd no notion what direction to take, but somehow I got clear off from Philliphaugh—one of the few that did.

As soon as I could, I sent word to my father, and to Sir Robert Maitland, telling him that Hugh was away, though not the full manner of his going. That was between Hugh and me. But I never went back to Drumfyvie. I'd have been a danger to my father, with the Covenant men in power, and an embarrassment in any case. Instead, I made my way to Aberdeen, when my days of hiding in barns and skulking in ditches were over. And I got work with an apothecary there, a decent soul, who didn't ask too many questions. He taught me well, and so I came at last to be a surgeon-apothecary, just as I should have done if I had never left my father's house to follow Montrose.

And Montrose?

He got away overseas after Philliphaugh, but being the man he was, he couldn't bear to bide in safety, while there was still

a cause to serve. So—the year after the Parliament men beheaded King Charles, back he came to raise the clans for the dead King's son; him that's Charles the Second now. He was betrayed, and carried captive to Argyll in Edinburgh. And Argyll—may his soul rot for it!—hanged him high on a gallows in Edinburgh Lawn Market, and had his bonnie head hacked from his shoulders and his body butchered as they butcher the bodies of traitors.

I felt like a lost dog, after I heard the news. For I've always been a born follower, as I told you at the outset of my tale; and with Hugh and Montrose both dead, I'd no one to follow any more.

Anderson Brothers
A.D. 1740 — 12

We lived in one of Drumfyvie's tall tenement houses down
Market Street, when I was a laddie. Even then, Market Street
was not the most genteel part of the town, but it was convenient
for my father's business. He was the elder partner in the firm of
Anderson Brothers—and at least our house was one of the best
in the street. To be sure, there was a corn-chandler's on the
ground floor, which annoyed my father because he said it bred
rats; but we lived three floors up, where there was plenty of
light and air, and if there were any rats we never saw them.

And on the floor above us lived a baronet's widow, no less! A
small, sharp-nosed body, always dressed in rustling black silks
that must have cost full half-a-guinea a yard. It gave great
pleasure to my mother that we lived alongside the "Quality"
even though we only met My Lady in the passing, to exchange the
time of day on the common stair!

There was just the four of us: my parents and myself—
Hugh by name—and Kirsty, our maidservant. It was a tight
fit, for the place was not large, and Kirsty had her fold-away
bed beneath the kitchen dresser—though indeed such an arrange-
ment is usual enough. And sometimes there was my Uncle John,
the other half of Anderson Brothers, the sea-going half, as you
might say. For he had no home of his own, except his ship,
and lived with us between voyages.

Somehow the house always seemed much more full when my
Uncle John was home. It wasn't just the extra bed and place
at table, it was something about the man himself—like a west
wind blowing through! He was much younger than my father,
his face burned by the sea winds and the suns of far-away places;
and when he laughed, his eyes would turn to dancing blue slits,
and he'd have us all laughing, too, over maybe just the silliest
trifle. And his fair hair and short strong beard always looked as
though he'd begun to comb them and then stopped half-way
because he'd thought of something more exciting to do.

He was Captain of the *North Star*, and he and my father owned a half share in the ship between them, while the other half was divided between two more Drumfyvie merchants. Most merchants would rather have a part share in several ships than own a whole ship to themselves. That way you can have different shipments coming and going all the time from different parts of the world. It's safer that way, too, with the risk of a heavy loss divided between four or five folk, in case of shipwreck or other mischance at sea.

We were—still are, for that matter—general merchants, not just sticking to the one commodity as some folks do. We bought wool from the Quaker dealers in Kelso, and sold it in Sweden; and linen in Perth for shipping to London; and woollen goods from Aberdeen, which always find a ready market in France. Then we took coal from Alloa to Rotterdam, and loaded corn from the Moray Firth for Norway. And the ships would come back laden with Swedish pig-iron, and timber from the dark Norwegian forests, and Polish flax to be turned into Paisley linens and shipped back overseas again. And of course, we brought in fine wines from Bordeaux and the Spanish ports—the Scottish gentry like a good wine as well as the next man! Needles and rye and sugar-candy and prunes, we brought them all in; and drugs for the apothecaries, and weavers' dye-stuffs, and even kirk bells! The new tenor bell for the Old Kirk here in Drumfyvie came in one of our ships. Sweet-sounding it is, too.

Many an evening, when I was a bairn, I spent sitting on my creepy-stool at the fireside, listening to the tales my Uncle John had to tell, or just to the talk of cargoes and far-off parts going to and fro between him and my father. For me, it had all a kind of magic, and I never tired of listening.

I mind one autumn night, hearing my Uncle John speaking seriously about the Bordeaux wine trade. "Give it a miss for next season," he was saying. "Most years you can catch the smell of the grape harvest before even you drop anchor. But this has been the worst autumn most of the wine-growers can remember. It will be scarce worth trying for a load there, unless we add Spanish leather goods or the like."

My father scratched thoughtfully at his ear. "Hmm . . . that's luxury trade, and luxury trade is over-chancy for my taste—

unless of course we've a definite order for the goods in advance."

"Maybe you're right at that," my uncle nodded, and the shadow of his big golden head nodded on the wall behind him. "You know, William, the thought's been growing in me for a while past, that it's time Anderson Brothers looked further afield, towards the trade that's opening up with the New World."

"Now, Johnnie! Are you thinking to be one of those new Tobacco Lords, flaunting their scarlet cloaks and silver-topped canes in the streets of Glasgow?" My father's voice was edged with alarm.

My uncle laughed. "There's other things beside tobacco to be fetched from the New World, William. Rum from the West Indies—coffee—molasses—all sorts of stuff . . . The days are coming for a man to look beyond his own backyard; and we merchants must keep our eyes open. There's a whole new trading-world opening up, ours for the taking, if we don't let the chance go whistling by!"

I never heard the end of the discussion, for I was away in foreign parts, making pictures in my head, the way a laddie will, just day dreaming . . .

I sometimes wonder, looking back, that I was never hankering to follow my Uncle John, with a ship to captain, and the seas of all the world open to me, and the strange and wonderful lands that the seas led to. But—oh, I don't know—his visits were like treats, to be looked forward to from one to the next, and enjoyed in the having. But they were not a part of ordinary life. They had a special magic to them, and when he'd gone, the magic went along with him. And when the magic and the laughter and the traveller's tales were gone, I was content enough with the plain bread-and-butter world again. Content enough to follow my father into the counting-house and the home-keeping half of the business, as he'd always meant I should.

So it was, that on my fifteenth birthday, I was apprenticed to my father, to learn the merchant's trade. Very official and solemn, it was, for all must be done as though I was a stranger coming into the business, and not my father's son at all. There was a crackling parchment document to be signed by the two of us, and a couple of my father's merchant friends standing by

to witness the signing. First of all, my father read the document to me—all of it, for he was a most meticulous man, even the part about agreeing to give me lodging, and feed and clothe me, and my promising to be honest and sober and keep myself clean.

But the part that followed was the part that interested me, and he gave a wee impressive cough when he came to it: "And I, William Anderson, do solemnly undertake to employ Hugh Anderson as my apprentice, and to train him in all matters, subjects and ways belonging to one who shall, at the end of his seven years' apprenticeship, be ready and able to become a full merchant of quality and repute . . . To send the aforesaid apprentice, Hugh Anderson, for the necessary time, to the Merchant School at Rotterdam, that he may learn in the Dutch language and in the practice of Arithmetic . . . To send him overseas with cargoes on at least three occasions during his apprenticeship, to learn at first hand the business of buying and selling in foreign parts . . . To instruct him in all the arts and skills necessary to the profession of a merchant . . . And to this I hereby set my name."

After that he dipped his quill into the big silver inkstand, and wrote his name in his clear, neat handwriting, with the wee curlicue at the end that was peculiarly his own, at the foot of the Indentures he'd just read. I mind the squeak of the pen as he did it.

"William—Anderson, General Merchant of the Free Burgh —of Drumfyvie . . . There! Now your signature, Hugh, here beneath mine. That's it! Now the witnesses. If you please, Master Baird—Master Jamieson . . . I thank you! And now, Gentlemen, we'll drink to that."

And so saying, my father set about opening a bottle of good Canary wine, and pouring it into our best glasses. Not that there was much in mine, just a drop in honour of the occasion. And as I tasted it, resolving to make it last as long as possible, my father took the floor again, addressing me somewhat as though I were a public meeting. "So, now you are a legal apprentice, my lad, and have agreed to be such, of your own free will. And an apprentice with a great deal to learn, at that! And you'll work hard, for I'll have no idle hands about the place—least of

all in my own son that's to take over the business after me. Mind that, now!"

So I minded . . . It was my place, and I was by nature biddable, maybe because I lacked the rough and tumble that comes with a tribe of brothers and sisters. But the work was interesting, and I'd a good head for figures, and for cargo lists and the like, and so I did none so badly. And life went on for another couple of years.

And then something happened—a thing we'd never expected nor dreamed of, somehow. We knew the *North Star* was on the high seas, homeward bound from Spain, and then we got the usual message that she'd docked at Leith, and there was nothing surprising in that. What took us fairly by storm was a private letter from my Uncle John, that came along with the message.

Mostly, he wasn't a writing man, and my father took hold of it as though he thought it might blow up in his face when opened. It did, too, in a manner of speaking.

In the first moments, he couldn't even get his words out straight. "Eh—well!" he spluttered, "Eh—well! I never thought to see this day! *Johnnie* of all men! Well I'll be—I don't know if I'm coming or going—I can hardly believe it!—*Johnnie*!"

"What's wrong?" I managed to get in at last. "What's Uncle John done, Father?"

But I might as well not have been there, for all the heed he paid. He just turned back to the beginning, and read the letter over again, shaking his head. "If ever there was a shipmaster who's ship was all the wife he ever wanted, I'd have said it was Johnnie! Eh, mercy me, if any man had told me this, I'd have . . ." he broke off short. "Your Mother! Whatever will your Mother say when she hears?"

By now I was really alarmed. "Hears *what*, Father? *What has Uncle John done?*"

He put down the letter at last, and stared at me like one in a dream. "Got himself married! That's what he's done! Brought a bride home with him—and a Spanish one at that. Eh, dear, what will your Mother say? And the pair of them on the doorstep in a day or so!"

My Mother had plenty to say, for she didn't care for changes. "*Married!*" She made it sound as if it were a fatal disease,

and catching at that. "Married? And coming *here*? The *pair* of them?"

"Well, it's hardly likely the man will come without his wife, and where else would they come but here?" By that time my father had got himself near back to normal. "It's his home, is it not? Take a hold of yourself, now."

"But—married! How in the world are we to find room for him and a lassie, in a house the size of this? It's a close fit with John himself, let alone his wife. And—dear heavens!" my mother shrieked. "She'll likely be a Papist, at that!"

She'd a rare horror of Papists, had my mother, never, so far as I know, having passed the time of day with one.

"Now, now, Elspeth," my father soothed her, "as to that, she'll take up no more room Papist than Presbyterian. Calm yourself, do, my love. No doubt John will be setting up an establishment of his own now he's wed; and meanwhile they must have Hugh's room, and Hugh must have a mattress on the parlour floor; and it will not be for long, you'll see."

So my mother, in a rare fluster, set about making arrangements, and then changing to other arrangements, and finally going back to the first arrangements. And three days later, my uncle and his bride arrived.

"Well now," he demanded, almost before he was into the house, "and what do you think of the *North Star*'s latest cargo? She's called Anita—isn't it a bonnie name?"

"That's no way to speak of your wife, John," said my mother, fussing round the lassie kindly enough, taking her cloak and making her welcome, and trying to look as if she wasn't taking in everything about her from head to heel at the same time.

But Anita was laughing at us all.

"Ah—he tease me," she told my mother. "But I am happy he tease me, and I do not mind he call me 'Cargo'."

My father smiled at her. "And we are happy to welcome you home, Anita."

"Though no doubt John will soon be finding you a home of your own," my mother said, just to make sure that my uncle understood his duty.

"Oh yes," Anita answered for him. "But my real home shall be the *North Star*. The wives of sea captains go with their

husbands, yes? I am Juan's wife; therefore, for me, the *North Star*."

I mind her, standing a little behind my uncle in our grey, respectable parlour, with her hand on his arm. And she was tiny and dark and bonnie—and something else that I couldn't put a name to at the time, though I can now . . . I've made a good few voyagers since then, in the course of trade, some of them to the New World, and I've seen the tiny bright birds they call humming-birds, no bigger than butterflies—like—like—feathered jewels that hover and dart among the great flowers of those parts. And I've never seen a humming-bird that it didn't call Anita to my mind. And yet, that day, she was wearing a dark stuff gown, and there were no flowers in our parlour.

The next few days must have been hard for her, with strangers all about her, while she tried to get used to our unfamiliar ways of living. For it was a different kind of life altogether, from anything she'd known before. Even the pattern of our days must have been strange to her. Here in Drumfyvie, the merchants' households rose at five in the morning, and the shops were open and busy before seven. We had our breakfast around eight o'clock—a good stout meal of mutton or fowl washed down with ale—and we were still fine and ready for our dinners, which in those days were around one o'clock (nowadays it's fashionable to dine at four in the afternoon), and after dinner the men used to go back to their warehouses or counting-houses, or meet customers in the coffee houses to talk business, while their ladies drank tea with each other at four of the clock.

My mother gave Anita less than a week to learn our ways, and then she invited two or three of her closest friends to drink tea and inspect the bride, while letting Anita have a first sight of a chosen few of the neighbours.

In the usual way of things, I'd have been at the counting-house all the afternoon; but my father had left at home some papers that he needed, and sent me back home for them. And from our lobby you could hear easy enough what went on in the parlour. I didn't eavesdrop, you understand, but I'd have had to plug my ears not to hear Mistress Gilchrist talking in the fine genteel head-voice that she had.

"You speak very good English, Mistress John. How would you

154

have come to learn it?—If you will excuse the question?"

"I will excuse the question," said Anita. "My father, he had many English merchants and sea captains at our house. So, you see, I have heard much English talking, and I listen, and I learn, and I do not mind to be laughed at."

Mistress Kerr's voice sounded shocked. "And your father allowed you to meet and talk with all-comers? I find that most surprising, I do indeed!"

"My mother, she die when I am so so small. It is for me, my father's daughter, to make the welcome for his guests, you understand," Anita explained.

"Eh me!" said Mistress Gilchrist. "I thought Spanish lassies were strictly brought up—close guarded, as you might say, and not allowed to talk with strangers."

Anita gave a bubble of laughter. "I think I am very badly brought up! Oh very! I had a *duenna*—how do you say?—a companion? A governess? An aunt of my mother's, but she was old and fat, and slept much in the sunshine. Me, I spend more time with our cook. She was half a gipsy, and she teach me to dance the gipsy way—exciting dancing! I like! It was the music, like this—"

But before Anita could disgrace the family for ever by bursting into a Spanish gipsy tune in the middle of a polite Scottish tea-drinking, my mother silenced her. "Anita, my love, our friends will think you are quite wild . . ! Another dish of tay, Mistress Gilchrist? Mistress Kerr?"

And while the ladies accepted, I slipped away, and went back to the counting-house with the papers I'd been sent for. In spite of not being allowed to sing, it was clear that Anita was managing fine!

I found my father and Uncle John discussing a piece of troublesome news that had just reached them. Alan Murray, the Captain of the *Black-Eyed Susan* had gone down with a fever.

"And what a time for it to happen!" said my father. "The ship due to sail in but four days!"

"Fever's a queer thing; it can go as quickly as it comes. Are you sure there's no chance Murray will be fit in time?" asked my uncle.

"None in the world, and dear knows where we'll find another captain at such short notice."

Uncle John sat thinking a while, his chin propped on his hand. Then his face cleared. "Well, there's one way out! Here's another captain under your nose, brother William—I'll take her myself."

"*You*, Johnnie? But the *North Star*?"

"Will not be through with the re-fit and ready to turn round for at least another fortnight," Uncle John told him. "That should give you plenty of time to find a reliable captain for her if Murray isn't on his feet again. And when I get the *Black-Eyed Susan* back to Leith, Murray can have her back and I'll take a spell ashore till the *Star* does likewise. How does that suit?"

"Well!" My father was fair astounded. "I never thought to see the day you'd as much as think of letting another man take the *North Star* to sea!"

"I wouldn't think of it now, if we'd any choice. But we can't afford to lose the whole trading run; and if we wait, the *Happy Dispatch* will reach Danzig ahead of us and get the best prices."

So it was agreed, and there was but one thing to mar the scheme. The *Black-Eyed Susan* was the smallest of our vessels, and her captain's quarters were that cramped and small, it was no ship to take a wife to sea in. So when my Uncle John took the coach for Edinburgh next day, Anita must bide with us.

She wept a bit at first; but she'd been brought up among merchants and sea-going men; she knew the kind of thing that was like to happen, and she soon gathered up her spirits again. I used to listen to her singing softly to herself about the house— mostly gipsy songs. There was one special tune—I could never get my tongue round the name, but I took a liking for it, and I mind trying to whistle it after her. I could whistle blithe as a blackbird when I was a laddie.—Anita would listen to my efforts, and laugh at me. "No, no—you have it not right. Listen—I teach you!"

And she did. She taught me until I had it perfect, and that tune has stuck in my head through all the years.—Maybe because of one special time that I whistled it for her. But that's quite a story—and this was the way of it—

In Drumfyvie, and I suppose it's the same in most towns, it's the custom for newcomers to be presented to Society by appearing at one of the monthly subscription dances in the Assembly Rooms. Young lassies just finished with their schooling make their first appearance in Society in the same way, with their mothers there to keep an eye on their behaviour, and see they don't cause Talk by dancing too often with the same young man! There's a Lady Directress, to arrange the dancers and watch out for any that forget their manners. Very strict is the Lady Directress, and you'd best be genteel in all you say and do, or when the next month comes round, you'll find there's no ticket available!

There was to be one such dance while my Uncle John was away; and my mother decided to present Anita at it. And as my father fairly hated all such gatherings, it was decided that I should go too, making my own entry into Society at the same time, to escort the ladies. I was only just past my seventeenth birthday, but tall and well built for my age, and I mind the pride I had in myself that night; and me in a new suit specially made for the occasion! My mother wasn't quite so happy, Anita being still a mite strange to her. But she meant to do her duty by the newcomer to the family, and so she started telling her just what and what not to do, well ahead of time.

"Now mind, my love, the eyes of all Drumfyvie Society will be upon you; and coming, as you do, from a foreign country, you will be of special interest, I do assure you. And Mistress Mac-Alisdair, the Directress of our dances for this year, is a great one for correct behaviour, and will not approve of strange Spanish ways. So keep your eyes on the rest of the ladies, I beg you. Do just as they do in all things, and you'll be following the pink of Scottish behaviour."

And Anita promised she'd do as she was bid.

My, but she looked bonnie when she came into the parlour that evening, dressed and ready! My mother and she had had what you might call a difference of opinion as to a suitable gown for the occasion. My mother favoured pale pink silk, and Anita was for scarlet damask, which my mother wouldn't hear of, saying that scarlet was no colour for a lady. But they had come to an agreement at last, on yellow muslin. And Anita dressed her

black silky hair high on her head in the Spanish way, with a tall tortoise-shell comb, and a piece of fine black lace they call a *mantilla* over it.

I heard the little gasp as she entered the Assembly Rooms! Drumfyvie had never seen anything quite like her, and you could *feel* the buzz of curiosity and comment under the music of the minuet that the fiddler was playing at the far end of the room. There were lassies enough there, in flower-coloured silks and satins, with the light of the candles in their eyes, but none to touch Anita. She drew all eyes in her direction, and the young men were fairly taken with her, one and all! I was proud to walk beside her, and I held my head high, I can tell you!

Once in the ballroom, it was the custom for the ladies to take their places at one end, and the gentlemen at the other, Mistress MacAlisdair calling out maybe four or six couples at a time, to pace their way through the minuet, while the rest of us stood looking on. Then things got a wee bit more lively, with Ben the fiddler playing country dances that all of us, even the youngest, could join in—in a sober and seemly fashion, you'll understand. Only Anita could not join in, for, of course, she knew nothing of our Scottish ways of dancing. But she tapped her foot in time to "The Flowers of Edinburgh", which is a lilting tune if ever there was one, and her eyes were busy taking in every movement of the dancers. And I thought it would not be long before she was up and dancing with the best of them.

After an hour or so, the older folk were beginning to drift towards the card-room, where tea and coffee were served. And then—I'm not quite sure even now, how it happened—there was more than one young man offering to show Anita the steps, so she didn't see, through the throng of them, my mother beckon to her from the card-room doorway. I started across the room, to tell her, but just as I reached her she was saying to Ian Hamilton, the Provost's son, "Sir, this dance I do not yet know, you see. But I thank you that you are wishing to help me. I think not now is the time to learn; but you are kind, and I dance for you all, from my old home in Spain.—You like?"

There was a chorus of approval and some quiet hand-clapping from the crowd that by now had gathered round about. Then another laddie—Tom Shaw it was, I think—asked her, "But the

music, Mistress? What will we do for music? I doubt old Ben knows any Spanish tunes."

Anita looked round and saw me standing near, and laughed. "We will not need to trouble Old Ben. My music come now, I think—Hugh? You will whistle for me, yes? The tune I taught you?"

For a moment I was so dumbfounded that I couldn't speak. But I nodded. And I did it! I took a good deep breath, and whistled away with never a false note. I knew I shouldn't. I knew there'd be the Devil to pay afterwards, when my mother got hold of me. But it was the one great and glorious moment of revolt that ever I had in all my life; and it warms me yet, when I look back on it.

Then, as I stood whistling, Old Ben cocked his head and began to pick up the tune from me, haltingly at first, then more and more sure. And there was Anita out on the ballroom floor, her feet flickering, her skirts twirling, her fingers snapping like castanets, as graceful as a flower in the wind, all to the music that Ben and I were making for her. And surely there was magic on all three of us! All the young folk stood round, their own feet tapping, full of delight . . . Until Mistress MacAlisdair came click-clacking on her high heels across the floor from the card-room, my mother with her. And then it all died away.

Mistress MacAlisdair let the silence thicken until you could feel it like a damp cloth; and then she spoke, cool and calm, fit to quench the candles.

"I am sure we are all most grateful to you, Mistress Anderson, for this display of the most *unusual* dancing of your native country!"

My mother put in her own word before Anita had time to answer—"You are looking tired, my love, and small wonder! I think perhaps we should be going home. Hugh, kindly go down and call us two sedan chairs."

So I went, my face as red as a holly berry. And when we got home, my mother was scarce upstairs and over the threshold before she spoke her mind to the pair of us.

"Anita! How could you do such a thing? And after all my warnings! Shaming us *all* before the *whole* town with your—your vulgar gipsy caperings! How can we ever show our *faces*

in the Assembly Rooms again? What will Mistress Kerr and Mistress Gilchrist think? You have disgraced the name of Anderson for ever, and—"

But Anita cut across her with gentle dignity. "If I disgrace anyone, then it is only *I* that I disgrace, not you. But others were dancing the dances of *your* country, and I am not knowing these. They ask to teach me, but I say 'No' for I will look foolish perhaps, and so you will not like. So I dance from *my* country, to make friendly to the kind people. Tell me, please, where is the shame in this?"

"She has a point there. Give it a thought, my love," said my father who had just joined us, and had only the vaguest idea of what the trouble was about. But my mother took no notice. She had yet to start on me for my part in the business; and I braced myself for what was coming.

"And Hugh! By rights you should be whipped, so you should, seventeen years or no'! For you've had a good Christian upbringing, and I've always taught you to be mannerly, so you're more to blame than she is! I'm fair mortified to think a son of mine should stand there in the Assembly Rooms, whistling away like a common errand-laddie in a back street! And on your first presentation to Society, too! I'll never lift my head in Drumfyvie again, and that's for sure!"

I'd no word to say for myself, but Anita—she was brave, that one! "He only did what I ask of him," she said, "because we are the friends—yes, Hugh?"

I swallowed. "Because we are the friends, Anita."

But my mother would have her say out, as well we knew— and it took her till well past bedtime to express her feelings to her own satisfaction.

And what happened after? Not much more. And if we were the nine-days shameful wonder my mother seemed to think, I never heard of it.

And then a while later, my Uncle John arrived home. I mind Anita running to greet him, calling joyfully, "Juan! Juan . . !" They bided with us two or three more weeks. And what I chiefly mind about those weeks is that the sun seemed to shine for every day of them . . .

And then the *North Star* docked at Leith once more, and

when she sailed again, with my uncle once more her Captain, Anita went too, as she'd always said she would. The house seemed very quiet, after that.

Two weeks later, there was a great storm off Finisterre. Folks said afterwards the *North Star*'s cargo must have shifted in the hold. But no one ever knew for sure, because there were no survivors. None at all, you see . . .

I can still see my father's face when the news came. All of a sudden he looked grey and old. He said, "God rest their souls." And then he said, "Thank God we were but half-owners, and we're fully insured."

At the time, I was so stunned by the news that I scarcely heard him. After, I remembered, and was as shocked and sickened as if he'd struck me across the face. But later still, I understood. Life has to go on; and there was Anderson Brothers to be considered.

We kept the old sign up over the counting-house door, and when the time comes for my sons to take over the business after me—aye, I've two fine sons, though I married something late in life, so they're little more than laddies as yet—'twill be Anderson Brothers again, in fact as well as in name.

But I'm fair sorry for those two, that when they go on their apprentice runs to the New World (we do most of our trade with the New World, nowadays), and see their first humming-birds, they'll not know any memory of Anita; and the humming-birds will be—just humming-birds, to them.

Drumfyvie Elects a Provost
A.D. 1785

13

It is I, Rory McKinnan—Rory the Dirk, men called me, for I was the swift one with the dirk in my soldiering days. I was a bonnie fighting man, being by birth a Highlander. But the luck was not with me, for I came home from the wars lacking an eye and two fingers of my left hand.

First, with my soldiering days behind me, I thought maybe to find myself work as a groom, for the Army had taught me skill in the ways of horses. But it seemed that nobody was wanting a groom with but one eye and lacking the half of a hand. And there was nothing else that I was skilled at, so in the end I had little choice but to turn beggar, like many another of my kind.

But even that was not so simple. Not so simple at all . . . As long as there have been laws in Scotland, there have been two kinds of beggars. To the one kind belong the Helpless Poor; the old, the sick, the maimed—them that are put away in almshouses, or given licences to beg, but only within the bounds of their own parish. And to the other kind belong the Sturdy Beggars—them that are strong enough to work, but prefer to beg—and these are flogged, and made to toil for their bread, when they are caught at their trade! Oh aye, I could have gone back to the Highlands, and got me a licence to beg in the village where I was born.—Beg from my own folk, and the men who were laddies with me!

I would rather die! And since I had no wish to die, I threw in my lot with the Sturdy Beggars, that are beyond the law, and took my chances as they came. I did none so badly, either, none so badly at all.

Until one day in Drumfyvie Market I was caught using a little friendly persuasion on a bright young popinjay—him carrying more money than seemed decent, and needing a lesson in charity towards poor lost souls such as myself.

So I was set in the stocks for a while and a while to be pelted with filth by the law-abiding Christians of the Burgh; and at the

last, flogged at the cart's tail through the streets to the East Port, and kicked out through it, and the rags of my soldier's plaid flung after me with vile abuse! Me, that has in my veins the blood of ancient Kings! But I have always been as able with my tongue as with my dirk, and I gave back as good as I got, I can promise ye!

It was well into the autumn, and frost in the air, and I could have been doing with my plaid wrapped about me, but my back was too sore. So I gathered the tattered folds under my arm, and went my way as best I could. I took the bridle-path leading down to the burn; and when the town was well behind me, settled down among a clump of alder bushes on the bank, to wash the blood from my back. It is none too easy to wash one's own back that has been flogged to the likeness of raw meat, and I was still at it when up the bridle-path came a man on a good roan horse.

Fine and prosperous he looked, with a good broadcloth coat on his back. "A pigeon ripe for the plucking," thought I to myself, peering through the tangled twigs of the alders. "The Lord hath provided. Thanks be to His same this day!" But just as he drew level with me, a blackbird rose, scolding, beneath his horse's nose. The beast reared up, snorting with fright, and off came my mannie, cursing the while, right under his own horse's hooves; and himself in sore danger of having his brains kicked out where he lay.

'Twas no concern of mine, but—och well, I'd no time to be thinking of that. I just dived out of cover and went for the horse's head. "Back now!" said I, swinging like a bell on his bridle as I tried to get him round and away. "Softly! Softly! No need for all this squealing and trampling . . .!" I got him clear with no more harm done, and dropped his bridle over an alder branch, and went back to his rider. He was just about coming to himself, sitting up slowly, and still cursing. A rare and beautiful flow of language he had. Aye, indeed.

I helped him to his feet, and he stood there, a wee thing shaky, but seemingly with no bones broke, trying to dust himself down. "Thanks, friend," said he. "Yon brute was near to braining me, plague take him!"

"The same thought was in my own mind," I told him, cursing

within myself, for you cannot turn to and rob a man who's life you have just saved. It is not seemly.

"Ye have a way with horses, that's for sure," said he. "Och, curse it—my head's running blood the way a mill-stream runs water!"

"Let you dip your neckerchief in the burn, and give it a douse with the cold water, and 'twill soon stop," I told him; and while he set about it, I turned to the roan, who was still fidgeting. He must have looked round while my back was to him, for when I came down the bank to see how he was getting on, "Man!" said he, between dabs with his dripping neckerchief, "That's some beating you've taken!"

"I was flogged out of Drumfyvie, so I was, for begging without a licence," I told him. "It is the poor job you are making of your head.—Here, let me be at it."

I took the kerchief from him and got to work on his skull where it had met the trackway, the pair of us sitting side by side on the bank like kin. After I'd got the dust out of it and the bleeding stopped, my mannie asked me, "Where did you lose your eye and your two fingers, then, friend beggar-with-no-licence?"

"In the same place where I learned to handle horses, and clean up a wound."

He nodded, looking at me with a pair of blue eyes as shrewd as ever I saw. "Ye have the look of an old soldier. Aye."

"A soldier I was, till they turned me loose to beg."

"Have ye ever thought to try honest work?" asked he, fine and interested.

"Until I found that there was none, for a man with one eye and a couple of fingers short."

"Well then, why no licence to beg? You could have got one easy enough, an old soldier the like of you."

"A licence to beg the length and breadth of my own parish— to beg my bread from the men I fought and laughed and poached the salmon with, when I was a laddie! That is not for Rory the Dirk!"

"Pride's an awful sinful thing," said he, but there was a glint in his eye. "But that's a proud name ye bear. It would be gained in your soldiering days, like all the rest?"

"Aye."

"And so ye joined the ranks of the lawless company. Well, maybe it's as well for me you did. For if you'd not been here washing the blood off your back, I'd like enough have been lying in the track with my brains kicked out, now."

"Ye could that," I agreed.

He looked at me consideringly. "I am thinking that you could have stood by and let it happen, and gone through my pockets comfortably at your leisure, afterwards."

"Surely—if I had but thought of it in time, Master Whatever-your-name-might-be!"

"Steenie Drummond," said he. "And 'tis my opinion that you think too slowly to make a success of the begging trade . . . Och well, my head's stopped bleeding, and I'll be getting on home." He seemed to make up his mind about something. "How are your legs for walking, Rory the Dirk? You can hang on to my stirrup if you've a mind to come my way."

"Up to Drumfyvie, that would be?" said I. "Myself that's just been flogged out of the place? 'Tis the fine welcome I'd be getting, surely."

"Why now," said he, grinning suddenly like a wicked laddie, "as Rory the Dirk, I'll grant you your welcome might not just be of the warmest. But as Steenie Drummond's new groom . . ?"

I mind staring at him a moment, not quite sure that I had his meaning right. "You would be offering me the work?"

"Aye," he said, "an eye and a couple of fingers you may lack, but you've a way with horses, as I've good cause to know, and I'm in need of a new groom. I reckon you'll do just fine, if you've a mind to it."

I looked him up and down, all the short, square-set length of him. And I was liking what I saw. "I've a mind to it," I said.

So 'twas that I, Rory the Dirk, became groom to Steenie Drummond, Wool Merchant, of Drumfyvie. And that was the best day's work ever I did for myself. He was not doing so badly, either, for I've served him well, all these years—with just the wee fall from grace now and then, me being fond of good ale.

It would be a year or so after, that Steenie Drummond got to be a Bailie. And after a few years more, he was standing for

Provost at the Michaelmas Head Court election. Mostly there is just the one man standing for the place, but this year there were the two, Steenie Drummond and a certain Nathaniel Wedderburn; and both of them fine and eager, the like of hounds straining at the leash.

In the main, the citizens of Drumfyvie had more of a liking for my Steenie, but then again, Nathaniel Wedderburn had behind him the full support of the Kirk. And this particular year the whole matter of choosing a Provost rested on what was to be done about the Helpless Poor of the Burgh, and where should the money for it come from. And both Nathaniel and Steenie had their own thoughts on the subject. Things were like to get lively as time went on, and I'd not much trust of the enemy, so I kept close to Steenie, from the first moment of the first meeting that he and Nathaniel Wedderburn held on the steps of the tolbooth.

I mind that when the crowd began to gather, 'twas Wedderburn that got first at the speaking.—And him bowing and smiling and waving his great red hands about the while. "My friends," says he, like to embrace us one and all, "we all know that there is a need, a most urgent need, for a proper and fitting almshouse in this Burgh. And my first care as Provost, should you elect me to that position, would be the setting up of a place of shelter for the aged and helpless poor, them that so sorely need our care and pity! Eh—not a very large place, maybe, at first— say, of a size to house eight or ten God-fearing men and women . . ."

"Aye, well—" Steenie put in his piece. "For a Burgh of some four thousand souls, I'll agree yon's not an over-large shelter for our aged and helpless poor. But since it seems Nathaniel Wedderburn is making this fine gift to the Burgh, we must thank him, surely, and see that the name of the generous founder is writ plain above the almshouse door, when 'tis built!"

The crowd laughed and cheered, and there was Master Wedderburn shouting and waving, trying to get silence, to make it clear that 'twas no gift he had in mind.

"Dear save us! Master Drummond must always have his wee joke! But no, no, folks do not appreciate what they have had no hand in the paying for . . . I was thinking more that the cost

might be met by a small—och, a very small—increase in the price of meal."

"Meal?" asked Steenie, his face all innocent as a sucking-babe. "Meal! There's just the one wee point—that 'tis the poor folk that live mostly on greens and bannock, while the rich can afford flesher's meat."

Wee Davy McCrae that was standing next myself muttered in my ear—as near up as he could come to it—"Trust Bailie Wedderburn to hit on a tax that will hit the like of you and me more than it will the like of himself!"

And Donald Grieve, that scratched a living holding horses and running errands and the like, joined in—"Aye, you're in the right of it. A tax on wine would raise the money just as well. But the grand folk drink the wine, and they're all alike, these rich merchants—'tis hands off their own pockets. I'm fair sickened with the whole lot of them! I am that!"

But Steenie was saying his say again, and the folk grew quiet to listen, for it wasn't any wee joke he was having now. "However the cost of Master Wedderburn's almshouse might be found, 'tis certain sure that such an almshouse could help but the smallest part of Drumfyvie's poor. What we need, friends, is not just shelter for a few, together with licences to beg for the rest." I mind how his voice swelled out, drowning Bailie Wedderburn's efforts to interrupt him. "Licences to beg in their own parishes and no other, so that whenever the charity of that parish wears thin, they must spill over into the next, and so become vagrants, with the law's hand against them! Och no, 'tis a proper Poor Rate we're needing. Not just a collection at the kirk door from time to time, and the income from a few wee plots of land here and there, all kept tight in the hands of the Kirk Sessions, and doled out by the minister to the godly poor!—Don't be taking me up wrong, now, I'm a great one for the godly poor—but the ungodly poor needs to feed their bellies too, for all they may be sinners!"

I fairly enjoyed that last bit! So by way of encouraging my Master, I lifted up my voice and shouted, "Here's to the ungodly poor!" The ungodly among the crowd was swift to take up the cry, and Nat Wedderburn was beside himself with trying to get in his next bit above the noise that they were making.

"We all know Bailie Drummond's fondness for the ungodly!" he shouted, as soon as he could make himself heard. "You have but to look at his choice of servants!—But leave that bye. Who's to do the paying of this 'proper Poor Rate'? Tell me that!"

Steenie told him, in words that every one among us could understand fine and plain. "You, me, every man that pays rates already, in the Burgh of Drumfyvie, whether he eats more of bannock or flesher's meat!"

There was a moment's silence while we took this in; and then someone in the crowd shouted out, "There's not half a dozen Burghs the length and breadth of Scotland pays a Poor Rate!"

"So far," said Steenie. "Let's add one more to the tally."

"Let's stick to the old ways!" someone else shouted.

And a third put in, " 'Twill come awful hard on us smaller men! It costs ye to live, these days, what with one thing and another!"

"It will not come hard on the smaller men," Steenie said, "for those that have little property pay the lowest rates, and their share will be the lightest. The heaviest burden—not that even that will be so very heavy—will be falling on the like of Bailie Wedderburn and myself, which is as it should be."

Och, ye should have seen Bailie Wedderburn's face. Yellow it was, greenish-yellow, fair beautiful to behold!

Well, so the days passed, and Michaelmas and the Head Court drew closer. My Steenie was doing well, so he was, with more people every day coming over to his way of thinking. Oh, I know fine 'tis the Burgh Council that elects the Provost, and not just the people; but there's not a Burgh Council in the land can afford to go against the will of its burgesses, for it's the burgesses that elect the Burgh Council!

But I was not forgetting that Bailie Wedderburn still had the Kirk behind him!

And then, just a few days before the election, Steenie Drummond and me were walking down Watergate Street, making for Lorimer's Wynd, to pick up a new saddle, myself walking a few paces behind, as was fitting. So what should we do but come up with a cart unloading barrels of salt herring, at the very moment that a rope broke, and the barrels began rolling themselves off the cart tail into the street—and a wee ragged bairn playing in

the gutter just behind! She'd have been killed for sure, but that Steenie—he being the nearest—dived in and snatched her clear, and in doing it, took one of the barrels himself on the point of his shoulder.

There was a great uproar from the by-standers and the crashing of barrels and the bairn screaming—and her mother screaming too, covering her eyes and not daring to look. And in the midst of it all, cool as a sprig of water-mint, Steenie handed the bairn over, saying, "Here she is, safe and sound. But take better care of her in future, Mistress, for you near enough lost her this day!"

And then he turned to me, and said under his breath, "Get me home, Rory. I think yon cursed barrel's broken my arm."

Well of course, that won him a deal more popularity, so it did; but there were some that held he had planned the whole thing to make himself a hero in the eyes of the Drumfyvie folk. There was a nasty, squint-eyed, blabbermouthed, journeyman cordwainer, Geordie Heriot by name, who I heard saying just that.

"And would you be saying also, that Bailie Drummond is not laid by with an arm that is near splintered to pieces?" I asked him.

"As to that," said he, "I'm no' so sure in my mind about it. He hasn't showed it to me, ye see."

"Then here's to clear your mind for ye," I said, and I hit him. If I'd had two good fists I could have given him all that he deserved, but as it was, well, I had the advantage of him in weight and reach, and the Lord was on my side. 'Twould be long enough, I reckoned, before his two black eyes were back to their usual, and his split lip mended. But after a while a crowd gathered, and some busy-body called the Watch—so I came away, leaving Geordie bubbling in the gutter. 'Twas the night before the election, you see, and I was not for spending next day in the gaol!

I went to ground for a while, among the outbuildings behind the Unicorn Inn, that being the nearest cover that I could think of. I was fine and familiar with the Unicorn, for it had become a gathering place for Steenie and his supporters through the past few weeks; while Nathaniel Wedderburn gathered to the Cross Keys in Castle Wynd.

I settled myself in a corner of the woodstack close to the kitchen door, fine and snug, and no one like to find me there in the dark. So 'twas as good a place as any to wait till I judged it safe to be strolling home. But hardly had I come to roost there, when the kitchen door opened, stealthy like, and there was the glim of a rushlight, and under-breath voices close at hand.

"Well—have you done it?" said one, that I didn't recognize.

And another, which I was sure enough was the innkeeper's, said uneasily, "Aye, I've put the stuff in their drink, and they're supping away, great style. But I'm not liking it! I'm not liking it at all, and that's the truth!"

"Ye'll like this well enough, though," I heard the chink of coins. "Five golden guineas, for the easiest bit of work you've ever had to do!"

"Aye, 'tis easy enough, but what may come of it, that's what I'm worried sick about," said the innkeeper.

The other gave a wee chuckle. I was sure I knew that chuckle, a thin kind of chuckle—Nat Wedderburn! "Och, man, no harm can come of it. 'Tis nought but a pinch of gunpowder in the wine. They'll but sleep the sooner and the sounder for it, aye, and the longer—and wake up with sorer heads, I grant you. No more . . . Now, ye've the place ready for storing them?"

"The spare hayloft, aye. And the ostlers all set to get them there. They'll lie snug till morning. But when they wake up—what then?"

"By the mercy of Providence, they're like to sleep till the election's over and done with. But for being on the safe side, see to it that the door's jambed on the outside—och, accidentally of course! With the heads those five will have on them, I reckon 'twill be a while before they can make theirselves heard!"

And with that the kitchen door shut, and I heard Nat Wedderburn's footsteps away into the night. Well "All things work together for Good", saith the good Book, and 'tis surely true, for if I hadn't blacked Geordie's eye and needed to keep clear of the Watch for a while, there'd have been none to hear Bailie Wedderburn at his dirty work!

It was too late to stop the thing, for 'twas already done; but I did some hurried thinking, and it came to my mind that there might yet be a way to set all things right. Now, though I had

turned respectable for myself, I had more friends than one in Drumfyvie among the beggars and the ungodly poor, and I knew where to find them, in the dark alleyways and the corners of empty buildings, with the stray cats of the Burgh for company. So I slipped out from the Unicorn yard, and set off on a round of visitings in the dark of the night, waking this one and that in their corners and crannies.

The first I came on, in the ruins of a barn close to the Watergate, was old Gabby, and him and Grizel his woman gnawing away at a couple of mouldy crusts. "Gabby," said I, "Up with you, my mannie, and Grizel too. There's work to do this night. There's five of Steenie Drummond's side made drunk and shut away in the spare hayloft behind the Unicorn. Get you a hold of Kenny and Long Luke and pass the word round among any that are able for it, to join me at the head of Market Lane at first light . . ."

Then I found Humpy—so named for that his back was as bent as the business end of a shepherd's crook—but he'd a good head on him for all that, so I took him with me to be my Lieutenant, and on we went.

We worked away, steady and sure. And at first light there was a sizeable crowd of us gathered at the head of Market Lane, our plans fixed and ready. We were leaving our five bonnie lads in the hayloft till the full grey of dawn was on us, to give them as long as might be for sleeping off Bailie Wedderburn's hell-brew, but no later than that, for we had to allow time for sobering them up before the Head Court started. So at what we judged was the right moment, we arrived in ones and twos, soft-footed, to the gate of the Unicorn's stableyard—a company of ragged grey shadows, but with a good stout purpose within us all.

We went over the gate—not through it, for the snib was rusty and like to creak—and there we were, inside the enemy stronghold, as ye might say, and none a wit the wiser. "Now the haystore—over yonder," I whispered, and we moved on. But this time we were not so lucky, for Grizel fell over a brick left lying, and measured her length on the ground—and her swearing the length of her tongue where she lay. She roused the whole place, and down upon us came the innkeeper and half-a-dozen sleepy ostlers at his heels.

Och, it was the good hot-blooded start to the day! Half my lads taking on the Unicorn people, while the other half dragged aside the cart that had accidentally got itself backed half across the door to the hayloft. I could a'most have felt sorry for the innfolk, for they were sore outnumbered, and the innkeeper with a broken head, calling for the Watch.

"I would not be doing that," said I, standing over him, "for you will not be finding it easy to explain just how it is you have five of the town's Bailies and them lying for dead and penned in your spare hayloft this day!"

After that he lost heart in calling for the Watch, and just sat on the mounting-block and watched us at our work, like one in a dream, and bleeding quietly to himself from the gash in his head, the while.

By now my lads had found the five Bailies and were busy trying to wake them to life; and them only wanting to be left to die in peace, with the sore heads they had on them.

"Up with ye, my bonnie man!" Kenny was saying to the one that he was tending to.

"Eh! My *head*!" the good man groaned, as well as he could for the shaking he was getting. " 'Twill burst! Leave me be, will ye!"

"It will feel better in the open air," I told him kindly. "Get him to the horse trough, Kenny, and see, will a dash of cold water help."

Gabby's man seemed to be altogether gone in the legs. " 'Tis useless," he told me. "As quick as ye haul him up, down he goes again—overmuch like hard work, so 'tis."

"Here, let me try," I said, and I bent down and roared in his ear, "Will you just be lying there and have a mealy-mouthed hypocrite the like of Nat Wedderburn for Provost? Black shame on ye—"

I was about to fair take him apart, so I was, when a dreary wee voice at my elbow said, "Coffee . . . I was hearing once that coffee is fine for helping them that has overmuch of the strong drink in them."

And I looked round to see Grizel, and she speaking more sense than I had heard from a living soul that morning.

"Coffee!" said I. "That's for sure!—Gabby, away with you

and rouse up Mistress Girvan next door. She sells coffee.—Ask her will she be selling us a handful or two."

"Who's to pay?" said Gabby. "She'll not let the likes of me have it on promise."

"Why, Master Peterson, our innkeeper here!" said I. "Out of five golden guineas that he has by him."

He wailed and protested to fair wring the heart, but he went and fetched the money at last from where he'd hidden it under the feather-bed, myself going along with him, in case he needed help.

So we got the coffee and set the potboy to brewing it up, hot and strong, and we got back to work in good earnest, so we did, to get our five sorry Bailies on their feet again.

It was a near thing, I'll not be denying, a very near thing, for all that the coffee helped . . . We poured it, black and smoking, down their throats. And in the end we got them all sobered up and in fair marching order, with the help of the horse trough. Then we headed them towards the tolbooth, me and the ungodly poor, having sent Humpy on with the good news ahead of us.

Humpy had spread the word as he went along, and there were a good few folk out along High Street and into the market-place to see us go by. 'Twas what ye might call a triumphal procession, with the folks cheering us on, and the bairns and stray dogs trotting alongside.

The Clerk of the Burgh Court was standing on the tolbooth steps, looking up and down, fine and worried lest the missing Bailies should stay missing, and peering at the big turnip watch in his hand. Some of the Council were out there too, as anxious as himself, and amongst them my Steenie with his arm in a sling. —And no sooner did he see us coming along than he fell to laughing till he must needs lean against the doorpost to keep from falling, and I was sure he must spring the broken bones apart and have to have his arm re-set!

"Rory!" cried he as we drew near. "Rory the Dirk! Man, but that's a bonnie band of cut-throats you have at your tail!"

And in the same moment, the Clerk put his watch back where it belonged, and proclaimed loud and clear, "Since the last of the

Bailies are now here, the proceedings of the Michaelmas Head Court may now commence!"

Nat Wedderburn was standing just behind him, and his face was worth looking at! Aye, it was so. I cheer myself up with remembering it to this very day, if I should chance to feel low!

Oh aye, Steenie got elected Provost. And 'tis an indisputed fact that 'twas myself, Rory the Dirk, together with the beggars of Drumfyvie on both sides of the law, that put him in the Provost's chair.

So the Poor Relief was added to the Burgh Laws. For he was always one to keep his word. Still is, for the matter of that, and well enough liked, though there's some say he's over-fond of ungodly company, the like of my own.

The Jubilee Wing
A.D. 1897

14

June 22nd, 1897. Our beloved Queen's Diamond Jubilee!

All safely over, and here in Drumfyvie, it has been a memorable occasion. Strange to think that most of us alive today—myself included, John Meikle, Minister of St. Ninian's Kirk beside the Market Cross—were not born when Her Majesty came to her crowning. She was just a lassie then, and now she's an old body with a widow's cap on her; and sixty years between the two great days! Sixty glorious years! And throughout her realms, in cities and towns and villages, her people have celebrated with her in great rejoicing. Bonfires on the hills, and kirk bells pealing, and Jubilee mugs for the schoolchildren . . .

And here in Drumfyvie, we've celebrated in a special kind of way, for we had the new Accident Wing of the General Hospital to open. "Gilead" folk generally call the hospital, for it has, carved over the main doorway, the words of the prophet Jeremiah, "Is there no balm in Gilead", the which I have always thought a comforting thing and a godly one. And when it seemed clear that the new wing would be ready to receive patients at about the time of the Jubilee, we thought to have the opening ceremony on the same day, and to call it "The Jubilee Wing". That way we could share our personal celebrations with Her Gracious Majesty, as 'twere.

So we formed a Diamond Jubilee Committee for our double purpose, with the Provost and Bailies of the Burgh, the headmaster of the Grammar School, the Town Clerk and other notable citizens

"Are you aware, Gentlemen," said Robert Patterson, the Town Clerk, at our very first meeting, "that this year, the sixtieth of Her Majesty's glorious reign, is also the seven *hundred* and sixtieth from the founding of this Burgh? One might almost say that for Drumfyvie itself, it is a kind of Jubilee, as well as for the Queen."

"Havers!" said Bailie Moffat, who is not one for such

fanciful notions. "I've never heard that Seven Hundred and Sixty years was any kind of a Jubilee. And if you've quite done with your wee sums, could we now get on with the business in hand, for there's plenty of it."

But most of us were more than a little taken with the coincidence. And so were the good folk of Drumfyvie, when word of it got around. It seemed to make Her Majesty's Jubilee ours also in a special kind of way; and everyone was set on making a twofold success of it.

The first thing, of course, was to decide upon some personage to open the new hospital wing. "We must, of course, ask the Sheriff's Lady first," said the Provost. "It would be most unmannerly to pass her over."

So we asked the Sheriff's Lady. But we were not sorry when she declined, being, as she said, "in too delicate a state of health" for so great a task. Nor were we surprised, that state of health being usual to her; for she and the Sheriff seem set on possessing the largest brood in the Burgh—which is a godly ambition and makes for a brave show when they all come to kirk on the Sabbath.

Ah well, as I say, we were not so very sorry, for though the Sheriff and his Lady are well liked, she can be seen any day, driving through the town in her carriage, or even, now and again, making purchases for the children from Mistress Dinwiddie who keeps the haberdasher's shop near the tolbooth. And in kirk, of course. And there's no denying we all felt that some notability from outside the Burgh would lend a greater air of Consequence to the occasion.

So in the end, it was decided that we should write to Her Grace, the Duchess of Strathardle, inviting her—accompanied, of course, by the Duke, her husband—to perform the opening ceremony. We reckoned it to be a particularly happy choice, for Drumfyvie's first Sheriff, the notorious Duncan the Red, was Thane of Strathardle before King David I gave him his new-made Burgh. That way, the wheel would come full circle, as you might say.

Her Grace accepted, with great condescension and amiability. So that was one less thing on our minds, and we thankfully turned to the rest of our plans for the Great Day.

It must begin, of course, with a service of thanksgiving in St. Ninian's, that being the original kirk of Drumfyvie amid all the other kirks and chapels and wee tin tabernacles of later years. Aye, it's an old kirk, St. Ninian's, grown old along with the Burgh, and sheltering the tombs of the Maitlands that were Sheriffs here for more than five hundred years, from the first Sir Robert lying in full armour in the chancel, his dog at his feet, to the last Sir Robert in a full-bottomed periwig on the marble wall tomb in the north aisle. But I'm running on a bit, I fear— it's a fault of mine when I'm on the subject of the Old Kirk.

So then—a service of thanksgiving; and an ox-roast in the Market Square for all comers; and a tea, with Jubilee mugs, for the schoolchildren. And of course, the grand opening ceremony of the Jubilee Wing, performed by Her Grace the Duchess. "And," said Bailie Morrison, "fireworks at night! Just to round the whole thing off, you know."

There was even some talk of a pageant, from William Scott, the Headmaster of the Grammar School.

"Seven hundred and sixty years of history, we've seen! There should be material for a fine pageant in that! And some of my older pupils have quite remarkable acting ability, I do assure you."

But when we examined the idea in detail, it was not so easy. Drumfyvie has seen its share of history, true enough. We signed the Covenant—and there's a tale that two of our laddies signed in their own blood; and we had a visitation of the Plague; and a good few sons of the Burgh must have gone to Flodden and the like. But these things happen in every Burgh. And if you take the few events that are peculiarly our own—well, it would be none so simple to enact the storming of the Castle by the towns-folk to rid it of its English garrison during the Wars of Independence. And as to the story of Red Duncan and his fearsome end—well, apart from the difficulty of finding anyone able to handle a falcon, supposing there was a trained falcon to be found either, it might be difficult to arrange for a thunderstorm at just the right moment, even allowing for the efficacy of prayer!

So at last, after much discussion, the idea of a pageant was laid aside. Willie Scott the Headmaster was somewhat affronted, but there was just no help for it.

A few days later, Geordie Breck came seeking me at the manse, one evening.

I have always had a fondness for Geordie Breck. Of course, a minister should have a fondness for all his flock, even while he battles with the Devil within them. But a bit extra for Geordie, since the day I first passed him at his work in the Ornamental Gardens, when I was taking a short-cut across them to visit a sick parishioner. He was tying up a rose bush that had taken a battering in the summer storm of the night before. A bonnie thing, the flowers almost the colour of our native amethysts. I've one like it in the manse garden, for I'm a great one for roses, myself. So I stopped to look, saying "Poor Cardinal Richelieu's taken a sore beating."

"Aye, but there's no real harm done," he said, his big red hands still at their work, as gentle as a woman's on a sick bairn. And then, "Why would they be calling it Cardinal Richelieu, Minister?"

"Flowers, especially roses, are often named after some personage," I told him.

"Whyfore roses more than other flowers? Why not a nice geranium?" His voice turned dreamy and far-off. "I like fine a red geranium. Whiles, when I'm taking the cuttings, or planting out, I think to myself could I breed one bigger and brighter than ever was seen before?" I could see the idea growing in his head, slow, but more dazzling every moment, He even left off work, and just stood, nursing the ball of twine in his hands. "Maybe if I did that, they'd call after me! And then I'd have my name in the paper. 'Geordie Breck', not just 'Daft Geordie', the way they call me now. And all Drumfyvie would read what I'd done, and be proud of me!"

Poor Geordie, just a trifle slow in his wits, and always so eager to win a name for himself, and make the Burgh proud of him, the way he was proud of the Burgh.

And now, here he stood in my study, his tall fiery head seeming to light up the rainy spring evening, and his bright blue eyes gazing down at me, full of hope as a laddie's, while he turned his Sabbath bonnet round and round in his hands.

"You wished to speak with me, Geordie?" I said.

He swallowed. "Aye, Master Meikle, Minister—Your Reverence. 'Tis the Jubilee celebrations—" And there he stuck.

"I am sure the Ornamental Gardens will do you credit," I said, wishing to get him started again.

"Aye. Me and the other lads—But it's not just the Ornamental Gardens I was wishful to speak with you about, Minister."

"What then, Geordie?"

"I hear tell there's like to be a pageant, setting forth the story of Drumfyvie from the beginning, and—"

It was like Geordie to be a little behindhand with the news.

"Why, you see, Geordie—" I began.

But having got himself started, he was now in full cry, and not to be stopped, "And I was thinking, Sir—Your Reverence—that you'll be needing someone to play the part of Red Duncan. And—and I know fine it's a bold thing to say, and I'm hoping you'll not take it for presumption, but it was in my mind—I'm about the tallest chield in Drumfyvie, and with the reddest hair—"

"But Geordie—" I began again. I might as well have tried to stop the Forth in spate!

"And if you're thinking about the falcon, I know fine you've a sore problem there, but my Auntie Grizel has a grey parrot. 'Tis a mite blasphemous in its talk, it having once belonged to a seafaring man, but maybe the folks wouldn't be close enough to hear, and—"

He ran himself down at last, and just stood looking at me, where I sat in silence at my desk. The bright hope in his face nearly broke my heart. To play Red Duncan must have seemed such a great and splendid chance to get his name in the paper and make all Drumfyvie proud of him. Even better than breeding a new geranium. And 'twas I that had to rob him of his hope.

"Geordie, man," I said, "haven't you heard? The Jubilee Committee have decided not to have a pageant after all. You see, it would be so difficult in many ways, beside the falcon."

And oh!—but I was thankful that it was so; for to have denied the part to Geordie, if the pageant had been going forward, was more than I would have cared to answer for at the Judgement Day!

As it was, I saw the light fade slowly from his face. He shook his head like one confused. "No pageant?"

"No pageant, Geordie."

"So you'll not be needing a Red Duncan?"

"No, Geordie. But I most deeply appreciate your offer, and so, I am sure, will the whole Committee, when I tell them of it. You would have made a splendid Duncan—of that I am convinced."

"Ah well," he said after a moment, "I'll not take up any more of your time, Minister. I'll away back to my geraniums while there's still some light left."

"To be sure. You'll need to have the Gardens looking their very best for the Firework Display in the evening," I told him. "And none of the other lads has just your hand with the roses or the geraniums, Geordie, not one."

Well, so, in the course of time, we arrived at the Great Day. Yesterday. A trifle misty in the early morning, but the sun breaking through before most folk had done with their breakfasts. By that time Davey the town-crier was ringing his way through the streets, proclaiming the Day's programme of events; and folk began to be out and about in their best holiday clothes. Margaret, my wife, had spent most of the day before in putting the finishing touches to new summer dresses for our own two lassies—blue for Meg, and pink for Jennie—and had then been up half the night, goffering the frills on her own best blouse. As for me, I had new Geneva bands—hem-stitched at that, though I told her plain ones would do just as well!

Punctually at noon, the Edinburgh train steamed into the station, where the Sheriff and his Lady, together with the Provost and Bailies, and indeed half the population of Drumfyvie, all waited to receive our illustrious guests. I, of course, was already at the Old Kirk, and therefore missed this almost Royal welcome, but I was later told on all sides that it was a truly magnificent spectacle. The Duchess stepped down from the train, followed by the Duke, as the town band struck up "See the Conquering Hero Comes". The Sheriff and the Provost with their ladies moved forward to greet them, thus, by great good fortune, screening from their august eyes wee Maisie Dundas,

who chose that moment to be sick with excitement, narrowly missing the red carpet laid down for the celebrities to walk upon.

There followed a triumphal drive in open carriages through the streets to the Market Square. The Duchess and the Sheriff led the way, Her Grace frequently inclining her head and gently waving her gloved hand to the cheering populace. Next came the Duke, with the Sheriff's Lady, the Provost and Bailies with their wives following on behind, and all the folk of Drum-fyvie who were not already in the kirk lining the streets or running alongside; and the horses titupping along as though well aware of the importance of the occasion, their manes and tails flying, and the brightwork on their harness and on the carriages jinking and glittering in the sunlight.

They drew up before the kirk, and the Duchess descended, clad—so I was later informed by Margaret, who has, I fear, a quicker eye for such worldly frivolities than is perhaps wholly proper in a minister's wife—in a gown of lilac silk, and a hat of fine leghorn trimmed with ostrich feathers, and carrying a lilac parasol. Her Grace was followed by the Duke, who made less impression than his wife, but seemed a nice enough little man, so far as one could tell behind his moustache and whiskers.

I greeted their Graces at the West Door, then gave them into the hands of my worthy Elders, who would show them to their seats while I withdrew to the vestry.

I had, of course, carefully prepared the service for such a unique occasion, and bearing in mind the many events of the Great Day still to take place within the Burgh, I had, after much thought and prayer for guidance, decided to keep it as short as possible. We were to begin by singing the metrical version of the Twenty-third Psalm, which would be followed by a prayer of thanksgiving for Her Majesty's life and works; and then, I had determined to preach for only forty-five minutes instead of the customary hour. But my sermon, based on part of the first verse of Pslam 127—"Except the Lord build the house, they labour in vain that build it"—should be full of godly meat, making plain how the Almighty Himself, using the frail hands of Our Gracious Queen, had, in His Goodness, and to His Glory, built for Britain a Mighty Empire, for which we must return our grateful thanks. Making plain also, how He had guided and empowered

us, in our lesser way, here in Drumfyvie, to build the new Accident Wing on to the Hospital, for the healing and comforting of the people of the Burgh and the surrounding countryside. Making plain how, in both great and small, the Lord had built the house, and that both were joined in being part of His Divine Plan . . .

My Elders, having settled the Duke and Duchess, came to escort me into the kirk, and after a short prayer, we left the vestry, preceded by the Beadle carrying the Holy Bible, and took our places before the assembled congregation.

The Lord was indeed with us, and all went well, the good folk of Drumfyvie sang their best, accompanied by Johnnie Gillespie at the fine organ which was installed some ten years since, and adds so greatly to the beauty of our services. And after the singing of the final psalm, followed by the Grace, the congregation departed in seemly fashion, to their homes, while the Sheriff and his Lady took Their Graces up to the Castle for a late luncheon. Returning myself to the manse, by way of the Market Square, I saw and smelled the ox-roast going forward most satisfactorily for the evening's feasting.

A little before three o'clock, I and my family rejoined the populace gathering at the hospital, where the red carpet had been brought up from the station, and re-laid across the drive to the main entrance. Their Graces were greeted by the Matron and Dr Gilchrist, and I was called upon to pronounce a brief prayer of consecration for the Jubilee Wing, and for the speedy relief from suffering of all who should come within its shelter. And after this, Her Grace was presented with a small pair of gold scissors, by the Sheriff's youngest but two, who overbalanced in trying to curtsy, so that the Duchess must pick her up and quieten her bellowing.

Out of the corner of my eye, meanwhile, I saw young Tam Drummond from the Drumfyvie Chronicle, scribbling for dear life in his notebook, my wife beside him, plainly giving him much the same information as she had given me. Indeed I distinctly heard her murmur, "Boots of dove-grey kid."

When all was quiet once more, Her Grace set the child down and performed the opening ceremony, by cutting the scarlet ribbon across the doorway with the golden scissors. And after

much applause, we all set forth, led by Matron, on a tour of the New Wing.

It did not take so very long. It had been intended the place should be already in use when the Great Day came; but there'd been a a bit of trouble getting things altogether finished in time, and so there were no patients in the neat beds, for the Duchess to have a few gracious words with in passing. Just the bare, empty wards and offices, looking, as I heard Tam Drummond whisper to someone behind me, as if they were sitting up and begging for an accident to happen!

Well, so the Jubilee Wing was fairly opened, and the Duchess, with her Duke, returned to the Sheriff's carriage, to drive to the station for the five o'clock train back to Strathardle. As the carriage drove off, Jamie Wedderburn and Nat Thornton rushed to roll up the red carpet, and set off, carrying it, at a smart trot, on its way down Threadneedle Wynd, and by a short-cut back to the station. It's a trifle awkward when there's just the one red carpet needing to be in two places at almost the same time!

The rest of the day went off splendidly, with the tea and the Jubilee mugs for the schoolchildren, and everybody eating their fill of hot roast beef in the market-place. And when all the beef was eaten, and the sky turning the colour you'll see sometimes in a fading harebell, folks began drifting off through the summer dusk to the Ornamental Gardens and the Grand Firework Display. I went that way myself—Margaret and the lassies were eager for the sight—and a minister should be with his flock in times of rejoicing as well as times of sorrow, to my way of thinking.

The Gardens were a charming sight, with lines of paper lanterns strung between the branches of the fine old trees—for part of the Ornamental Gardens covers what were once the grounds of rich merchants' houses along the Headrow, and there remains still the fine ilex or chestnut or copper beech, here and there.

Crimson and blue and pink and golden lanterns, their candles glimmering bravely within them, looking, said Jennie my youngest, "Like great big magic fruit growing in the Garden of Eden." That child is over-fanciful, I fear. I must speak to her about it some time.—Some time.

The town band was already playing its heart out under the largest of the chestnut trees, where the lanterns clustered thickest; and the place was beginning to fill with folk, as I shepherded my family towards the fountain in the middle of the Gardens, from which the best view of the fireworks would be obtained. A very fine fountain, of the best Italian marble, set up to commemorate our beloved Queen's Coronation, and making use of the stream which, issuing as a spring beneath the Castle mount used to wind along the Headrow.

A circle of flowerbeds surround the fountain-base, and this year Geordie, in a burst of patriotic fervour, has filled them with geraniums of a particularly blazing scarlet, edged with white alyssum and deep blue lobelia. For all that he is a stout Scot, Her Majesty has no more loyal subject than Geordie Breck!— And on this night of nights, Geordie himself sat perched on the rim of the fountain basin, with one or two friends, and Tam Drummond with his notebook where the glim of a lantern fell on its pages. My Jenny thought to join them, but mercifully her mother had a hand firmly twisted in the back gathers of her dress.

We had just comfortable time to find places and look about us, and then the fireworks began. From opposite sides of the Gardens, the rockets leapt up with a hiss and and a bang, arching and crossing and meeting each other high overhead, till at times we seemed to be under a dancing tracery of light—a kind of canopy of floating flowers and stars and streamers all of coloured fire that quite dimmed the soft light of the paper lanterns. And each time a rocket went up with a rush into the dark sky, every face was upturned, waiting for the bang and the burst of stars; and the "Oohs!" and "Ah-h-hs!" and cries of "Man, will ye look at yon!" fairly drowned the music of the band. Aye, and there were sparklers for the little ones to hold, making a silvery fire-fly dance all among the flowerbeds, and lighting up the small excited faces. It was the bonniest sight that ever a man might wish to see!

Then, towards the end of the display, when it was close on time for the great Set Piece, there was what you might call a slight mishap. One of the rockets did not take off properly, but rose a short way, spluttering and hissing, and shedding just the

odd spark here and there. Then it arched over and plunged down again, landing, as if it had been directly aimed, in the box over across the Gardens, where there were a few fireworks still left lying! I can hear it yet, the fizz and the cannonade of bangs, as all went sky-high together! All, that is, but one rocket, which set off by itself across the Gardens, darting and swerving close along the ground, hissing and spitting out showers of sparks as it went.

Folk shrieked and jostled to get out of its way; and by the mercy of Divine Providence it hit nobody. But it was too much for Willie Henderson's dog Sandy. A dog of wide interests and independent spirit is Sandy, and had sat watching the display like a Christian, throughout, but as that rocket came spitting towards him, he leapt up with a howl, and fled as though the Devil himself was on his tail—straight for the fountain and Geordie Breck's geraniums!

Into them and through them from one side to the other, before he swung round to dive back again!

Geordie let out a howl of pure anguish. "My geraniums! My bonnie flowers! Och away, ye fearsome brute!" And hurled himself from his perch on the rim of the fountain, to defend his precious blooms! What with the darkness and the flying sparks and the general confusion, I did not see precisely what happened, though I was standing close by. But he must have landed clumsily, or maybe stumbled on the marble curlicues of the fountain-base, for his shouts changed tone and grew sharper—surprised-sounding more than anything else. And suddenly there he was, all a-sprawl amid the geraniums, his right foot twisted under him, while Sandy howled his way into the distance, and the rocket, having done its mischief, lay spluttering in the grass near by.

Folk began to crowd in, peering down at Geordie, and asking, "What is it, man?" "Can ye not get up?" "Are you all right, Geordie lad?"

But 'twas plain enough that Geordie was *not* all right, and I pushed through the crowd to get to him.

"It's my ankle!" he groaned, "Och, I'm sore hurt, Minister, that's for sure—and my geraniums—my poor geraniums—"

Dr Gilchrist had also pushed through to Geordie's side, and

was stooping over him. Someone unhooked a paper lantern, and by its light, he examined the damage. "Yes, a broken ankle," he said, after a moment or so; and then, getting up from his knees, "Best take him along to the hospital, so I can get it set."

Geordie let out another howl. "I'm not wanting the hospital! Not me! Just get me to my bed, and I'll heal in a wee while!"

Then the Almighty put the right words into my mouth. "Geordie," I said, "think, man! You'll be the very first accident to get mended in the new Accident Wing! There's fame for you!"

"Aye," Dr Gilchrist told him, "the very first patient in the Jubilee! Why, I'd not be surprised if you were to have your name in the paper!"

A kind of flicker passed over Geordie's face, as if, even in that moment, the prospect of fame meant something to him, though I think he was near to fainting with the pain of his ankle. Seemingly Archie Armstrong, the town drunkard, was of the same opinion as to that, for he thrust a bottle between Geordie's lips, saying, "Here, take a sup of this, ol' lad. 'Twill put heart into you." And whatever the stuff was, it did indeed put a spark of life back into the poor soul.

In the meantime Dr Gilchrist was issuing orders to right and left; and as folk hurried to carry them out, Geordie lay among his geraniums, even managing to take half an interest in the Set Piece, with the aid of an occasional sup from Archie's bottle. And the Set Piece was indeed a sight worth the seeing, as it blossomed on the darkness into a great golden crown, with the letters V.R. beneath it, while the band excelled itself in its rendering of "God Save the Queen".

As this final splendour began to fade, willing helpers returned with the flat barrow in which tools and bedding-out plants and the like are wheeled about the garden; and Geordie was lifted on to it, under the Doctor's watchful eye, and made as comfortable as possible with a pile of empty sacks to lie on. After which, half a dozen of his special friends set themselves to push and pull him to the hospital.

A goodly number of the populace followed them with cries of encouragement; and the town-crier, thoughtful soul, went ahead, ringing his bell to clear the way. The rear of the procession

was brought up by Sandy, over his fright and barking his head off; and Tam Drummond with his notebook in one hand and a large bunch of geraniums which he must have snatched up from the wrecked flowerbed, in the other.

Standing to watch them go, I thought that in its way it was quite as much a triumphal procession as the one that had brought Their Graces from the station in the morning. Maybe more so.

Ah well, there was nothing I could do just then, but leave Geordie to the care of those who had the skills I lacked. So I rejoined my family and took them home. But this morning, first thing, I went to visit him in the hospital.

I found him, in a clean white nightshirt, sitting up in bed at the far end of the otherwise empty Men's Ward, looking a trifle wan, and still smelling of chloroform. But his smile stretched from ear to ear! He had a pretty young nurse fussing over him; and beside his bed, blazing like a joyful beacon, in all that clean white emptiness, stood a huge jug full of battered but still valiant scarlet geraniums! Clearly, either last night or this morning, Tam Drummond had been there before me!

I gave Geordie a blessing, and asked after his ankle.

"It's fine," he said, "just fine, Minister. A wee thing sore, but 'tis all mended and tied up tight—and they tell me 'twill soon be as good as new. And I never felt a thing! They gave me stuff to breathe—it smelled sweet and made me catch my breath; and I fell asleep, and next thing I knew, 'twas all over!"

"That makes good hearing," I said. "Fine hearing, Geordie; and you looking so grand with all those red geraniums beside you!"

He glanced at them proudly. "Tam Drummond brought me those, for he knew fine, I couldn't bear to think of them lying broken and unwanted when all was done. *And* he brought his wee notebook, and wrote things down in it—a whole lot of things, for there's to be a piece about me in the paper, naming me Geordie Breck, and not just Daft Geordie, because of me being the first accident to be mended in the Accident Wing! Tam says all Drumfyvie will be proud of me! Awful proud, Tam says!" And he heaved a sigh of pure bliss.

Aye well, I said the Diamond Jubilee Celebrations went off well, here in Drumfyvie. But I've a feeling that here—and I

suppose in all the other places that yesterday rejoiced with Our Gracious Queen—it seems like the end of something—an era— the end of an old world, maybe. Yet not sadly so, for it's the beginning of other things; and Drumfyvie has always been a sturdy place that looks to the future as well as to the past.

And one thing I'm very sure of—there's been few happier men in all the Burgh's seven hundred and sixty years, than Geordie Breck this fine summer morning!